Lexington County Public Library System
Cayce-West Columbia Branch Library
1500 Augusta Road
West Columbia, SC 29169

BLOOD AND BULLETS

BLOOD AND BULLETS

DEACON CHALK, OCCULT BOUNTY HUNTER

JAMES R. TUCK

Copyright ©2022 by James R. Tuck

Cover Design by Natania Barron

All rights reserved.

No part of this book may be reproduced in any form or by any electronic or mechanical means, including information storage and retrieval systems, without written permission from the author, except for the use of brief quotations in a book review.

Dedicated to Laurell K. Hamilton.

Without her, there would not be a genre called Urban Fantasy.

ONE

SOME NIGHTS ARE JUST DESTINED to go to hell.

Not literally, at least not usually, but from the start of them, you know they are going to turn on you like a rabid dog.

I was having one of those nights.

Which is why I found myself with a semiautomatic pistol aimed at a vampire who wore my daughter's face.

My eyes were fixed on the laser dot that screamed red against her forehead, marking where a bullet would part her skull like magick if I even twitched my finger, while my mind raced back through memories of my little girl. The pain was a surgical strike. It was inside before I could close my guard, so quick and clean that I didn't feel it until scalpel hit bone.

Memories of her, my wife, and my son, are acid etched in my mind. It's been five years since they were killed, stolen from me by a monster back when I didn't even know monsters were real. Their deaths started me on the road I'm on now: hunting monsters for money until the day I run up on one nasty enough to take me out so I can go be with them. Their deaths burn in the wound where my heart once was—ugly, venomous, and cruel.

I keep all of that locked tight just so I can function and move through each day. Now, this vampire girl looked like my daughter and all that pain rushed back through my mind like a flood of boiling water.

Everything I never told her.
Everything I never taught her.
Every time I was busy or self-absorbed.
Every.
Damned.
Moment.
I will NEVER.
Get.
Back.

Some small movement on her part clicked me back to the present.

I studied her through narrow eyes. She had the same thick blond hair as my daughter, although the vampire's hadn't seen the business end of a brush in a long time, maybe not even once since she had crawled out of whatever grave she'd been buried in. She had the same wide, blue–gray eyes and dash of freckles scattered across her nose. Different lips, although this vampire's lips still looked made for laughing, not drinking blood.

This-was-NOT-my-daughter.

She was similar, but not the same. Cut from the same cloth. She would look like a part of the family. A niece, a cousin maybe, but not my daughter's twin.

I blinked and stared to make sure, fighting through the haze of five years without seeing my daughter's face in person. The resemblance had triggered those deep buried memories, but that's all it was.

Fucking memories.

The breath I had been holding pushed out of my lungs and I willed my heart to slow its turbo-charged pounding. Sweat bathed my palm, making my skin oily and slick against the grip of my gun.

I had no way to measure how long I'd been lost in my own trauma. A moment. Maybe two.

It happens. More than I will admit.

I'll be fine for a while and then suddenly, from nowhere, a random thing will smash my world askew and I'll be back to the pain of losing them. I get a bit jumpy when that happens and do things like pull out my gun.

But now? Now, I was back on the clock.

Stepping back, I kept my gun pointed at the vampire. Her wide eyes were focused on the barrel, as they should have been. It's not an impressive gun to look at, not like a Desert Eagle or something similar, but it's still a gun.

A good gun. A daily driver. A workhorse.

CZ 75 in 9mm. It has black finish and holds fifteen silver-jacketed bullets, if you are willing to keep one in the chamber.

I always have one in the chamber.

Damn thing only weighs two and a half pounds fully loaded. However, with the right ammo, it'll put a baseball-size hole in even the toughest vampire, or almost any other bogeyman I run into in my line of work.

Vampires are monsters, even if their packaging looks like an innocent fifteen-year-old girl. You don't play games with them. You kill them or you leave them the hell alone.

The red laser dot stayed on her forehead as I took another step back, increasing the distance between us. I had just come out of Polecats, the club I own and use as a base of operations, to find this vampire leaning against my car.

I don't like humans leaning on my car, but a vampire?

Oh, hell no.

She's a fully restored 1966 Mercury Comet and she deserves better than that. Normally, I'd shoot first and ask questions never, but this vampire had called out my name.

Oh yeah, I'm Deacon Chalk, occult bounty hunter, sometimes vampire slayer.

This should be interesting.

"Stay right there," I said. "And tell me what you want."

She didn't move except to tilt her head sideways, regarding me like a snake does a wounded bird on the ground.

"I want you to protect me from the Nyteblade," she said.

Thin arms held out the flat package in her hands. It was a manila envelope. "I have information here to help you find him."

She looked earnestly at me in the sodium light. Small white teeth bit her bottom lip and she had the good grace to keep her fangs sheathed. The effect was scared little girl and it pulled to that non-logic-protect-children place inside me again.

"There is money in here. I know you get paid to protect people from monsters. I want to hire you."

What?

Wait.

The vampire wanted to *hire* me?

I've had vampires try to kill me, and I've had them run from me, but I have never, ever, ev-er had one try to hire me. The whole idea of it went against my one and only rule.

"I don't work for monsters. I kill them."

That thick mess of hair hung low around her face in what looked like shame.

Her voice became quiet. "You know I am a vampire? How?"

"It's my job to know."

And that is the truth.

Most normal people would have been fooled by her, think she was just a strange girl since she was barefoot and bare-armed in a summer dress when it was deep Georgia fall. It wasn't cold enough to think too much about it, but it was a pretty cool night. Jacket weather. So, her wearing just a sundress was weird, but not a reason to be alarmed.

Not a reason to suspect anything out of the normal.

I knew what she was because she was just *off*. Moving either just a bit too fast to be human or stopping a bit too still, like only the undead can.

But the thing that unmistakably marked her as a vampire was the *smell* of her.

Vampires smell like big snakes, all venom and shed skin. I don't know why, but they do.

And a little like roasted almonds.

Heat grew in the muscles of my neck and shoulders, signaling the buildup of lactic acid. Widening my stance, I shifted the angle I held the gun at. You can't hold any gun, much less mine, for very long in one position. You have to keep moving around or your muscles fatigue pretty quickly. The problem with moving around is it's not conducive to shooting your target.

A target like the vampire standing in front of you.

"So," I asked to distract her, "exactly what is a 'Nyteblade'?"

She swayed in the sullen, sodium lighting of the parking lot. Back and forth, back and forth, over and over and over again, just ever-so-slightly back and forth. The manila envelope slipped completely from thin fingers, spinning as it fell to her bare feet. Narrow shoulders hunched, drawing her chin down to her chest like an owl, and she wrapped both slender arms around herself. A fine tremble raised tendons to stand in stark relief beneath her skin like steel cables.

This vampire chick was starting to really freak me out.

I know vampires, and they don't act like that. They are usually either an oil-slick-smooth, diabolical predator or a bloodthirsty, slaughterous, vicious predator. What they did *not* act like were scared, little-girl, meth addicts.

I whistled and it made her skin jump.

She didn't look at me, but I had her attention.

"Again," I repeated. *"What is a Nyteblade?"*

The voice that answered was a strangled whisper from inside the tangled veil of her hair.

"He is a monster. A hunter of vampires." Her weak mewl faltered, the words coming in halts and stops. "He is an agent of destruction."

Her body was now shaking so bad it caused her teeth to rattle.

My grip tightened on the gun.

Whistling again, I tried to derail her breakdown.

"Please help me," she squeezed out. "I *have* to convince you." Her hands wrung together, bones *clickety-clacking* against each other.

Hair along my arms stood on end. A tiny move of my finger pulled the CZ's trigger to the break. Another twitch would plant a bullet in her skull.

Nappy blond hair whipped as her head turned in my direction

again. It was a jerky, too-fast-to-be-human movement. Those big eyes of hers had glazed over, chin waggling, her mouth hanging open.

She looked like someone listening to music no one else could hear. The air *snapped* as her attention came back to me. I felt the cold magick of her vampirism on my neck, making skin on the back of my scalp tightened like a fist.

In a breath of a moment, black pupils dilated impossibly big to cover her entire iris. Blood pooled from the corners of her eyes, turning the whites to crimson. Muscles in her cheeks and neck knotted, distending her jaw and allowing fangs to slide out of her gums wetly.

She stood still like that for the length of a thought.

Then she *moved*.

With a flash of yellow dress and chalk-white limbs, she leaped in the air toward me. My finger squeezed the trigger that last fraction of an inch and a silver bullet spat across her hip while she was in midair. Black gore burst out of her and hung in space for a moment before splattering like rain on the asphalt. The impact canted her sideways in mid-leap, so instead of hitting me with fangs and claws, she windmilled past, slamming into the pavement. Her bones rattled against the asphalt with a staccato beat.

Tracking the laser to the center of her chest, I squeezed the trigger twice. The recoil jolted up my arm and her chest exploded, more gore blossoming in inky wet flowers.

It took the fight right out of her.

First rule of killing vampires: Take the heart and take the head. You do that and they are dead. My bullets are modified silver hollowpoints, wax sealed with silver nitrate in the tips. Most things otherworldly have weakness to silver. Vampires certainly do. The bullets are manufactured by Orion Outfitters, a company that provides items specifically for what people like me do.

Looking down, I could see inside the gaping hole in her chest. The edges running black as the silver poisoning took effect.

Heart taken care of?

Check.

My left hand pulled the phone out of my pocket. If she was a recently turned vampire, then she was someone's missing daughter and maybe on a child watch list. If not, then maybe she would be in the database of vamps and I could find some information about her, although the database was strictly volunteer run and had no budget so it pretty much sucked. No pun intended.

Maybe I would even find out why she tried to hire me before freaking out and attacking me.

What a weird night, even for me.

The phone was silent as it snapped a picture of her face. Gore from the chest wound covered her collarbones and throat like a turtleneck, but left her face clean, calm, and smooth. The trauma of the bullet wounds had put her in a near-catatonic state. If I left her, and she could find cover from the sun in the morning, she would be able to heal even this much damage. Vampires are like that. Because they're undead, they are really, really hard to kill.

Should it be second kill?

Remurder?

You get the point.

It took almost no movement to bring the red dot to the bridge of her nose. Those big blue–gray eyes fluttered closed one last time just before I pulled the trigger.

Normally, finishing the job doesn't bother me, but this one…

I stamped my boots to shake dust off them. That is one good thing about bloodsuckers, they don't leave much behind to clean up. This one was fairly young, so she *crumbled* into dust instead of *exploding* into dust, but she was still just a pile of dust and a thin yellow sundress full of holes. Even her blood and viscera turned to dust when she did.

My conscience had a nasty little nag in it.

She was so young when she was turned. I knew she was a vampire. A monster. Hell, she had attacked me, but that non-logic place in me still twinged at killing a young girl.

Shake it off. Stay on task.

Scooping up the manila envelope and shaking the dust off it, I got in the Comet. Opening the envelope, I found a file folder with what looked to be a series of hand-scrawled notes and grainy pictures. Approximately $20,000 in rubber-banded bundles of $100 bills fell out in my lap. I put the money in the glove compartment and tucked the folder into the seat beside me.

So, she actually had been trying to hire me.

Weird.

Now, I know about weird, but even for me this was a first.

The engine of the Comet roared to life as I turned the key. In my world, nights that started strange usually crash-landed in the town of Fucked-Upville before they were said and done.

The stereo connected with my phone and kicked in with the winsome sound of a dark guitar run. John Lee Hooker started singing about a long night full of danger. Dropping the Comet into Drive, chain-link steering wheel sliding coolly under my fingers, I moved out into the night to see if old Mr. Hooker knew what the hell he was talking about.

TWO

I HATE STAKEOUTS.

Not stakeouts like vampire executions. Those suck too, but mostly because they're messy. I mean, seriously messy. During the day while they sleep, vampires turn into giant bags of blood. It quickly becomes blood-a-palooza when you go to stake the undead sons of bitches. Seriously, I usually wear a poncho.

No, I hate sitting on my ass waiting for the person I'm after to come out of where they are supposed to be. Some cheesy writer would call me a man-of-action and say that 'being idle goes against my nature'.

Mom just said I had a short attention span.

Either way, on a stakeout, you can't really read a book or knit or anything else because you have to keep watch. If you have a long wait, it leads to severe boredom.

And I don't get paid by the hour.

The *good* thing about a stakeout is that you have plenty of time to think.

And listen to music.

I was in the Comet, fifteen songs deep in a playlist titled Blues Ain't For Pussies, at the head of an industrial park that a report in the folder said was a probable location for Nyteblade's base of operation. According to one of the sticky notes inside the folder I had, Nyteblade would be in an alley between buildings D and E at 10 PM on today's date. I had no idea who wrote the note or how they knew he would be there, but it was the only time written in the folder, so that was where I planned on meeting him. There were a few minutes to kill before I headed to the meeting place. That would still get me there early. I didn't want to be the last one to arrive.

Sometimes, in this business, that will get you killed.

Looking around the industrial park, I was sure the alley would be just lovely. This would never be mistaken for the best part of town.

The buildings were old. Red brick faded to a drab pink by weather and time. Bushes that were once features of the landscaping had been allowed to run their course and now stood sentinel with branches overgrown, gnarled, and tangled. Jutting out haphazardly into the parking lot, they waited to grab you if you walked too close. More lights were out than on around the buildings, barely breaking up deep shadows in the corners with their baleful, jaundice glare. Litter danced with dry leaves in the night breeze.

I watched a plastic sack from a liquor store swirl around a dead light pole for a few minutes until it fell victim to the out-of-control bushes.

Glenn Kaiser and Darrell Mansfield pulled voices together to sing a cover of Blind Willie Johnson's 'Nobody's Fault But Mine' softly through the Comet's speakers and I thought about vampire slayers.

There are a lot of people who find out vampires or monsters are real and decide to fight them. It's a lot more common than you might think. Once you discover that the monster in your closet can and will eat your face off, the normal person has one of three reactions.

One, you live the rest of your life in fear of the dark. You never go out at night, you are never alone, and you go to church much, much more than you ever did before. You may have survived your encounter, but you never truly *live* again. PTMD, Post Traumatic Monster Disorder, it's like PTSD but with something that shows you this old world is nothing like you thought.

Two, you embrace it. There are people who try to assimilate themselves with monsters. A lot of nightclubs are gathering places for vampire lovers. The lycanthropes get their stalkers too; people who want to be furry or feathered or scaly once a month. This reaction usually happens with the monsters who are predatory but do have the ability to blend in with humans to hunt. Vampires, lycanthropes, Nephilim, and Fey—those are the ones with the biggest fan clubs.

I mean, you never find a fan club for a Chimera or a troll.

Trolls get no play at all.

And it gets more complicated.

Lycanthropes are people most of the time, and like people, they are good and bad; but being a lycanthrope doesn't make you evil, just dangerous, especially a newly made one or some of the more animalistic breeds during a high lunar cycle.

Vampires are always evil. I have never met one that wasn't a monster. Fey can even be good. In fact, most of the problem with the Fey is that they're mischievous and they don't think like humans. They are like aliens, and even though they've been fascinated with humans for centuries, they just do not comprehend how we work. They also suffer a lack of understanding about how fragile humans can be.

Which brings me to choice number three.

You decide that you are going to mount up and fight the good fight against evil.

This is what I did. People find out monsters exist and then decide that they will become monster hunters. The problem that they soon discover is a normal human is no match for a monster. Quickly, they get themselves killed in their pursuit.

I should know because that's what happened to me.

I'll get to that.

Vampires seem to inspire the most monster fighting in this world, probably because of all the books and movies about them. I've taken out my fair share of vamps, but it's not the only thing I do. There are few proclaimed vampire slayers and they range all kinds. Anita out in St. Louis, but she has a lot of stuff going on, not just vampire executions. Bubba does many monsters, including vampires, and does a fine job of it. I hear whispers about the Blue Woman now and again, but it's hard to pull the fact from the fiction on that one. There's some folks in California, in L.A. and a small town east of it who do mostly vampire slaying, but I haven't met them yet. The black guy and old man combo who roam around do nothing but vampires. From what I hear they have a personal stake in it, so to speak. Sam and Dean will tussle with a vampire, but usually they're chasing down demons.

There are some more monster hunters scattered across the country and the globe, but really, very few considering just how many monsters there are out there.

Most of us don't specialize in vampires only.

This Nyteblade guy seemed to.

That's one reason why I was there. This guy should know that the vampires had intel and were gunning for him. I would like someone to tell me if the shoe were on the other foot, professional courtesy and all. I was also hoping he would be able to help me find out exactly what the hell happened earlier. Honestly, I was a little stoked to meet this guy. Even though the notes were sparse and some even unintelligible, they made him sound like a true badass.

Almost as good as me.

Now, I know that sounds cocky, and it probably is, but the fact stands that I am *very* good at what I do. Years ago, after I discovered that the world was not just people and all the monsters didn't hide under the bed, something happened to me.

Something that left me not quite human.

While in the midst of hunting the monster that killed my wife and children, I rescued an Angel being held captive by the bad guys. Yes, a real, honest-to-God **Angel of The Lord**. The bad guys had her hooked to machines coded with sorcery, trying to impregnate her and create more Nephilim. Nephilim are the offspring of humans and Angel or demons, usually they come out powerful as hell and evil as shit.

It was a Nephilim bastard named Slaine that ritualistically slaughtered my family.

I don't want to talk about that part right now.

Some things are still too painful. After my mental throwback earlier tonight I can feel the brittle edges of my mind and it would be too easy to fall into that hole.

Anyway, I couldn't walk away from seeing the Angel in that position, so I rescued her. Being just a human against the monsters, I ended up getting myself killed. She returned the rescue and healed me with a transfusion of blood, or whatever it is Angels have for blood.

It worked. Sometimes I think too well.

Now I'm faster and stronger than a regular human. Not much, not like toss-a-car-around strong, but enough to hold my own. My night vision is near perfect, and I have a sense about magick and other things supernatural. High resistance to magick and monster powers came with the benefits package also. I still get outmatched by the monsters sometimes, but not being completely human keeps me from getting dead. I know I will die doing this one day, but after losing my family, I just don't give a damn. When death does come I can finally go be with them.

No, I can't kill myself to get to them. That would be a mortal sin.

This isn't a theology debate. I don't give a shit if you disagree with my assessment of mortal sin, I'm not taking any chances with the afterlife. So, I'll keep hunting monsters until that day comes.

Finally, I had to get out of the car.

Turning the ignition off killed the music. I can't stand to leave keys in the car. Call me paranoid, but it keeps me sane to have them in my pocket. Standing, I stretched and leaned on the Comet, rolling the situation around in my head one more time. Why would a vampire even think that I would work for them? I'm not a vampire hunter. I don't seek them out, but I've killed every one of the evil bastards I've run into. Most people have a romantic view of vampires. They picture them as the eternal lover full of longing and dark passion. Thank you very much Hollywood, but that is *not* the way it is in real life.

And vampires never sparkle unless they just ate a stripper.

I think it makes people feel better than knowing the truth. The truth is, vampires are all evil. Some are annoying, small-time evil, and a few are serious, big-time evil, but they can't fight their nature. Evil is as evil does and all. I've heard the same stories as you about good vamps who still have their souls, but I haven't met them and don't really believe they exist. If ever I do meet one, hopefully I won't shoot his ass before he can prove it.

It really bothers me that a vampire tried to hire me.

I'm a man who gets paid, but I do not work for the monsters. Never have, never will. Plus, reading the file, unless she was completely off the mark, they had this guy's base of operations pinned down. Why not just take him out themselves?

Sure, his HQ could be fortressed up like mine is but he seemed to be a solo operation. I have a family of misfits to circle the wagons if need be. It's harder when you're a one-man-band.

Vampires are like the mafia of the supernatural world. They run in packs, families, and blood lines. Hell, any crap reason they can find to band together and make power plays are taken advantage of. I haven't really had a reason to make enemies with any of the families yet, but I'm sure that will change.

Maybe it had and I didn't know it.

Vampires usually do not work alone. The one in the parking lot was by herself, but I had serious doubts she was alone. Being a fairly freshly turned one by the way she became dust, she had a master somewhere. I needed more information, which is why I was going to find this Nyteblade guy. He was in the equation somewhere and now so was I.

I looked down at my watch—big hand on the nine, small hand on the ten. My hands skimmed down my body, checking to make sure all my weapons were in place and to make a mental check of anything I might want to get out of the trunk of the Comet.

Always the CZ rode under my left arm. The right side of the shoulder holster had a row of pouches that held extra clips for the pistol. The weight of the clips helped balance out the weight of the gun. Four clips of fourteen bullets gave me seventy bullets for the pistol with the clip in the gun and one in the pipe. That should be enough for a meeting that was supposed to be just talking.

Hey, I like to be prepared. The old southern saying 'It's better to have it and not need it than to need it and not have it' definitely applies to ammunition. Across my lower back lay a Taurus Bulldog .44 Magnum snub-nosed revolver set for a left-hand draw. The Taurus is my backup gun. It's small, only holds five shots, but because it's a revolver, it's dead reliable. The CZ is a great gun, but automatics jam and they always do it at the worst possible time. If that happens to me, I want my backup to be fail-safe. Revolvers fire every time, guaranteed. Pull the trigger and a bullet comes out. I picked the Taurus Bulldog because it was a small revolver that held .44 caliber bullets. I love my 9mm, but the backup gun is a worst-case scenario option, and in my opinion, there is no better manstopper than a .44 caliber bullet.

Of course, they were from Orion Outfitters. Silver jacketed, but these bullets have a drop of phosphorus sealed in the hollow point rather than the silver nitrate the CZ carries. Phosphorus is dangerous stuff, even a drop of it. Exposed to air, phosphorus burns and keeps burning.

Almost everything supernatural is vulnerable to fire.

Everything except demons, that is; but bullets don't work on demons anyway.

Since a vampire started all of this, I also had a pocketful of small plastic vials with wax-sealed rubber stoppers in my coat. The kind that shooters come in at a bar and look like little test tubes.

Owning a bar, I have a shitraft of them available. They were filled with holy water.

Blessed crucifixes hung around my neck and curled in my other pocket, making me as ready as I could be.

Cool air ruffled through my beard, tickling my nose. Fall in the South, where the day may be 75 degrees, but when the sun goes down, so does the temperature. Pulling my leather jacket closed, I settled it around the straps from the shoulder holster. I had killed as much time as possible, so I began heading to building D.

The alley was everything I imagined and then some.

Buildings D and E sat close together, back-to-back. The alley between them was about ten feet across and filled with garbage. I entered the open end, the other blocked by a brick wall that had an overflowing dumpster in front of it. Trash bubbled out over the top and spilled to the ground where it spread like water. From the looks of it, the other residents just began throwing bags of garbage *at* the dumpster once it had filled, not worried about it piling up. The stench of rotting food filled the alleyway, making me breathe through my mouth.

I said a quick thank you to Jesus, Mary, and all the saints above that it wasn't the dead heat of summer. If it were, the smell would have been unbearable. The trash wasn't all in bags either. Scattered down the length of the alley were wads of paper, old carpeting, and empty and broken bottles. Here and there were piles of what looked like spoiled meat. Wooden pallets had once been stacked neatly but now sprawled across the midpoint. The only light spilled from one floodlight down the mouth of the alley. Deep shadows covered the nooks and crannies created by piles of trash and the doorways along each building.

Tension sang across my nerves as I tried to look at everything and listen to everything. My steps were slow and careful as I walked in staying near the wall and shadows. I did not draw my gun, but I wanted to. My eyes darted here and there, searching shadows for anything dangerous.

Because I wasn't really watching where I was putting my feet, occasionally something sticky would pull against the sole of my boot. I did not look down to see what it could have been. Broken glass littered the alley floor, crunching and tinkling underfoot, so I didn't even try to be stealthy. I just moved slowly, every sense wide open, nerves tingling with adrenaline.

About halfway down a shadow moved in a shadow.

The dark shape of a man crouched atop a stack of wooden pallets just a few feet from where I stopped. In the dark I couldn't make out much about him. He was big, bulky with his black coat spread around him. My hand was sliding slowly under my jacket when the shape spoke.

"Are you Deacon Chalk?"

The voice from the shape was deep and raspy. Why the hell did everybody know my name tonight?

"Are you Nyteblade?" My hand stayed in my jacket, fingertips just touching the grip of the pistol.

"I am the one called Nyteblade."

The figure leaned a little forward, shifting toward me. "Answer me, are you Deacon Chalk?"

I'd already had a weird night. Now this asshole was freaking me out by acting bizarre. Freaking me out is not a good idea. It tends to make me shoot people. But he should not have known my name. Then again, maybe he should; the note in the folder didn't say why he would be in this alley.

Maybe he was sent to meet me.

By the vampires?

Who else could it be? I was sent by them.

Suspicion tightened my scalp and I started looking around the alley because the whole situation now had a whole new tilt. I was on edge coming into this. Now? Now, I was over the precipice and free-falling.

"That's me, man. Look, this isn't adding up—"

Wooden pallets rasped against each other and flew away as he launched himself at me. Black fabric swirled out from his body like wings as he jumped, popping and flapping in the night air. A large, pointed object filled his hand and stabbed at my chest, banshee howl flying from his lips.

"DIESOULLESSUNDEADCREATUREOFTHENIGHT!"

The CZ cleared leather, swinging around. I didn't have time to shoot because we were too close and he was too fast. Instead, my hand holding the gun lashed out, knocking the object away before it could impale me. My left hand clenched into a fist. Without thought, I slammed it into his chest, knocking him back on his ass. The pistol's laser centered on his form sprawled out among the garbage.

On his back, large black duster bunched up underneath him, he was smaller than he looked on the pallets. Maybe 5'10", the man on the ground was thin. Stick thin. He couldn't weigh more than a buck fifty. Everything he wore was black. Black boots, black leather pants, and a black T-shirt all hid under a long black duster. Pale, freckled skin and bright red hair gleamed in the night. Big black sunglasses covered his eyes, making him look like an insect.

Who the hell wears sunglasses at night to hunt monsters?

The thing he tried to stab through my chest lay next to him, still spinning lazily from being knocked out of his hand. It was a three-foot-long wooden stake as big around as my wrist. A bandolier of them clung tight across his chest. The biggest freaking crucifix I had ever seen hung in a contraption of straps on his thigh.

"What the HELL is your PROBLEM?" Spit flew as I screamed at him.

Laying on his back, he looked up at me with his mouth hanging open.

"You tried to fucking stake me?" The stake clattered down the alley as I kicked it with my booted foot. "I'm not a vampire, you dumbass."

He lay unmoving, every muscle tense and the deer-in-headlights look that people who are not familiar with guns get when one is pointed at them. In my head, I was debating on shooting his ass when the skin on the back of my neck started prickling.

What. The. Fuck.

Some supernatural mojo was happening. The Angel blood in my veins began to rush in a boil. Every second the mojo built, pressing into my skin like a weight. Heat radiated from the back of my head and neck. In the corner of my vision, wisps of steam from the temperature change of my skin and the cold night air swirled around my face. I quit looking at Nyteblade and began to try and see the entire alley at once. The night breeze shifted and the smell of garbage passed away from me and was replaced with a different smell.

A musty, dry smell of shed skin and tainted venom.

Fucking vampires on the wind.

THREE

MOVEMENT from the end of the alley made me jerk my gun up. Sighting down my arm, I watched as the garbage began moving. Bags, boxes, and clumps tumbling down from the heap like lava from a volcano. Vampires rose, shedding garbage like a second skin. I quickly counted twelve of them.

Twelve preternaturally strong undead predators.

This was bad, really fucking bad.

Nyteblade jerked back when I kicked his leg. "Get up, dammit. We have to go now or we are totally screwed."

The vampires were out of the garbage now and slowly walking toward us. Nyteblade stood to his feet, his head crossing in front of the gun barrel as he moved beside me. Damn idiot. The extra clip I took out was heavy in my left hand, but I would need it if I had to start shooting.

My head was on fire, angel blood lighting up in the presence of so many supernatural creatures. I shook my head, trying to shake it off, to keep it from distracting me from staying alive.

A hand touched me on the arm.

Glancing quickly at Nyteblade, I noticed that he had lost the sunglasses and his eyes were wide open. White showed all the way around pupils that were a bright cornflower blue. His pale, freckled hand pointed up in the air behind me. As he drew my attention, a low, hissing began to fill the night air, buzzing and snaking its way through the alley's acoustics. A fast look around and I saw that the tops of both buildings were lined with vampires. Numbers tumbled in my head as visually I grouped them in rough tens. I didn't perform an exact count, but easily fifty bloodsuckers surrounded us.

I had seventy bullets for the CZ. Another five in the Taurus put me at seventy-five total. To kill a vampire by gun meant two bullets per, one in the heart and one in the head.

Not enough bullets and no way could I hit every shot fired. Nobody is 100% when it comes to shooting, hell, if you're good you hit 40%. Especially if you add in the fact that no vampire was just going to stand still and let me cap their ass. So, I would not be killing all the vampires in the alley. I just couldn't. I might be a lot of things, but I am not a damn superhero.

Head shots only as much as possible.

A bullet in the brain wont kill a vampire. They will heal it eventually. But it would put them on their bloodsucking ass for a few minutes, and a few minutes might be enough for me to get us gone.

Pointing Nyteblade toward the open end of the alley, we began to move.

Slowly.

Inching our way out, the air was heavy with tension. It vibrated like the strands of a spider's web when an insect has been caught. It was like swimming in a pool of hungry sharks. One tiny drop of blood and it would be a feeding frenzy. It was only going to take one small break to rain vampire hell down around our ears. The vampires were posturing, hissing and snarling, the pack of them making their presence a threat. Predator behavior, trying to spook the prey into running. Every step we took, the vampires took one also, closing the ranks of their pack. Mirroring our movements, they were acting like zombies.

Or puppets tied together with one string. I knew it would happen. It had to. But I still didn't see it coming when it did.

Nyteblade cursed as he stumbled on something and fell against the wall, just ten feet shy of the alley's opening. He cursed again as the rough brick tore open the skin on his palm. I couldn't smell the blood from the scrape, but the vampires reacted like they had been plugged into a live wire.

Their hissing soared into a cacophony, high and shrill, drilling into my eardrums. Thunder from the barrel of my gun rolled across the alley's walls as I shot into the mass of vampires. My ears closed and everything became muffled. Recoil ran up my arm and into my shoulder as I pulled the trigger. Fifteen bullets spit out in as many seconds. Burned off nitroglycerin swirled the air in front of me as I popped the clip and let it fall to the ground, no time to catch it as I slammed a new one home.

Pushing Nyteblade with my shoulder, I kept firing into the vampires who were scrambling down the alley. The ones on the roof let out a chorus of screams. Most of them began crawling down the wall like lizards and a few launched themselves into the air, swooping up as the wind caught them.

I hate flyers.

They are the hardest to kill and they are fast as hell. No way did I want to be lifted off the ground at their mercy. They became my focus as I pushed against Nyteblade. He was dragging ass, fumbling inside his coat.

Bullets flew from the end of my gun as fast as I could get a bead and pull the trigger, smoke curling into the space around me.

This is why I use laser pointers on my pistols; they make a huge difference when you have to find your target fast. I'm a better-than-average shot, winging many of my targets, making them spiral out of control to slam into the garbage on the alley floor. Another two clips down and I spared a glance to both Nyteblade and the end of the alley.

He had hauled that huge silver crucifix out from under that coat and was holding it above his head. It was easily two feet long and probably weighed at least thirty pounds. Holy light blasted out from it in a halo that covered Nyteblade like a spotlight. On the other side of him a gang of vampires who had crawled down the wall to block our exit were a snarling mass of undead bodies, held at bay by the glow of the cross.

Vampires hate crosses and religious symbols. It doesn't matter the faith of the person holding the cross either, it is the symbol itself that hurts them. Vamps make holy objects glow in their presence, and the light will cause intense pain and even eat their flesh away like radioactive waste.

Now, this doesn't mean that you can just grab two sticks and hold them up in the shape of a cross. That does not work. But if you take a few moments and lash or nail those sticks together, then they have power against vampires. It's the intent to make a cross that gives the shape its power. And the cross can be made of anything: Wood, steel, silver, plastic, frozen holy water, even chocolate all work.

Trust me on that last one, I don't have time to get into that story.

My last clip slipped into my gun like a lover and I began eyeing up the vampires left behind us in the alley. They were advancing slowly, shuffling like zombies. A quick count was twelve vampires still in the alley with us. I had fourteen bullets for the Desert Eagle and five in the Taurus, enough for each of them, but then I would be completely out of ammunition.

I really didn't want to be out of bullets if I didn't have to.

The twelve vampires were injured by my shooting, but their bodies were healing and they were moving faster with each step.

Time to get surgical.

Taking a second, I put the healthiest one in my sights. Sighting down my arm to the barrel of my gun, the laser's dot danced on his face. I matched the rhythm of my breathing with the rhythm of his shuffling.

Once we were in sync, I squeezed the trigger. The bullet took him in his cheekbone, just under his eye. A blink later and the vampire behind him was splashed with watery brain mush. He didn't react at all as the one I shot fell at his feet. A squeeze of the trigger and I took him out with a head shot next. Seven bullets later and I had thinned the advancing vampires down to the three most injured ones.

The gun was hot through the leather holster as I slid it under my arm.

Nyteblade still waved his giant cross at the mass of vampires on his side of the alley. He was wearing down, though. His arms were visibly shaking, even through his duster. Every so often, the cross would dip down and a snarling vampire would try to dart over the glow, only to be driven back to the group as Nyteblade swung the cross in their direction.

My hand touched his shoulder.

"Hold them off just a few more minutes." My mouth was right next to his ear because I knew the concussive noise of the gunfire had to have made him mostly deaf. Holding him steady with my left hand, I used my right to pull two of his wooden stakes from the bandolier around his chest.

They were good, solid pieces of wood. About three feet long, smooth and sharply pointed, their weight told me they were made of hardwood. My guess would be hawthorn. That was the traditional wood for stakes. The backs of both were carved into a notched handle so that the best grip possible could be maintained, polished on the pointy end so they would slide in as friction free as possible, and unpolished on the handle to help you keep it in your hand.

This was important for two reasons. One, it is next to impossible to shove a piece of wood into someone's chest, so you want the tip to be sharp and slick. Two, if you do get the stake in, it is a bloody process and makes you prone to losing your grip, so you want the handle to be rough and absorbent.

I have no idea why a wooden stake through a vampire's heart will kill them, I just know it works. Silly as it sounds, a piece of wood in the heart will turn a vampire to dust quicker than anything. And any piece of wood will work. One day I will tell you the toothpick story, but for now, just trust me, wood plus heart equals dead-ass vampire.

I spun the stakes in a circle to loosen up my wrists and forearms. The last three vampires on my side were still closing the gap. They were in rough shape. I've seen zombies move faster. Watching them, I noticed that they were moving weird even for being shot up.

All three vamps were drawn and stretched thin. Thinner even than the girl vamp from earlier tonight. Like her, they reminded me of pictures of the concentration camp prisoners from World War Two. I never heard of anorexic vampires, but there is a first time for everything. The most important part of the description was the vampire part. Along with the rabid mass of vampires Nyteblade held at the end of the alley and all I was worried about was making them dust.

Shuffling to the right three steps helped me cut the first one from the group. Short and dark and still wearing a dirty chef's apron and smock, his face was gaunt, all fangs and hollow eyes. As I drew near, he stumble-lunged to grab me. The stake in my left hand flashed as it crashed into his cheekbone. Black blood flew out of his mouth as his head turned sharply away and splattered down his filthy formerly white smock and apron. Hooking upward with my right hand, I drove the stake under his ribcage and through the rubbery diaphragm.

I must have hit the heart on the first thrust because his eyes got wide and he froze in mid-attack. The transition to a pile of dust took seconds.

When staking a vamp by hand, you have to go under the ribs to hit the heart. You cannot just drive the stake through the sternum. Nobody can without a hammer. The sternum is thick, very tough, and made of a flexible, fibrous cartilage. It's like Kevlar over your heart. If the stake you are using is thin enough, you can slip it between the ribs, but then you have to travel through the lungs and that shit apparently hurts. Most bloodsuckers won't stand still for that.

The next vampire scrambled toward me. She was a young one when turned and, apparently, a hippie. She looked about twenty, with long brown hair that hung below her waist. Tiny, round, purple glasses rested on a perky nose above thin, colorless lips. She was even wearing a tie-dye shirt with bell-bottom jeans and no shoes. Her hair was a rats nest, clumped with garbage, and stuck to her shirt in several places by some unidentifiable substance. She swiped a thin arm at me that had talons extended. They rasped along the leather of my coat. My left arm knocked hers away and my right drove the stake into her side. Wet fluid shot over my hand and the smell in the alley actually got worse. I had hit an intestine in a dead body that drank blood to survive.

Gross.

The shriek that tore from her mouth was shrill and ear piercing. A twist of her body yanked the stake from my hand. Spinning, she launched herself at me like a homicidal rag doll and whirlwinded into me. Even though she was small, her weight knocked me down, driving me across the alley floor. Scrambling like an insect, she skittered on top of me before I could catch my breath.

I landed on my right side with my arm trapped under me. My left hand still held the stake, but the arm was between me and the vampire. She was trying to get to my throat and open a vein. My arm was the only thing keeping her back. Fangs latched on to my arm through my jacket. She didn't have a good grip with her mouth, but the puncture wounds her teeth caused burned like acid. If I hadn't had the leather coat on, her fangs would have scraped on bone.

The butt of the other stake scraped her eye socket as I jammed it in her face. Her shrieks of pain were muffled behind the thin hands covering her eye.

It was the opening I needed.

My hand closed on the stake still jutting from her side. Pushing down to change the angle, I shoved it up and into her body cavity. The wooden stake slid like silk, hitting her heart and exploding her into dust. I closed my eyes and held my breath as it rained down on me.

Relief flooded in and a shudder ran through my body. Adrenaline painted my nervous system. I got to my feet a little unsteadily, using the alley wall to help me up. Blood made my arm stick to the inside of the jacket from the bite. It throbbed with every step over to the last vampire on this side.

This one was a caricature of a vampire. The once-expensive three-piece suit hung on him like a joke. He was so thin he looked like a skeleton. His walk was the shuffle of a zombie, not the predator glide of a vampire. Putting my hand on his head to hold him back, I put the stake under his ribcage.

Dead eyes looked at me, glazed over in a sickly yellow cast. His jaw worked mechanically, the half-exposed fangs chomping up and down slowly. He wasn't really trying to get to me, just going through the motions. There was a bit of wiggling the stake to hit his heart, I'd guess it was shriveled in his chest cavity, but he just stood there until I dusted him.

It was pretty pathetic.

The vampires on the other side of Nyteblade were in a frenzy. They leaped and crawled over each other like a mound of rats. Still howling, hissing, and spitting, they boiled in a knot of undead fury. They were frustrated at being held off by the cross. I knew they could smell the blood under my jacket. I knew they were pissed off that so many of their kind had been killed tonight.

I knew I didn't care about any of that.

The blessed crucifix from my pocket wrapped around my right hand. It sparked into white light in the presence of the vampires. Next out were the shooter tubes full of holy water. There were five of them, and they held about an ounce each.

That may not sound like much, but holy water acts like acid on the undead, and for some reason, it even works through the clothes they wear. A few drops would repel a vampire, no problem. The tubes were hard plastic and the lids were rubber corks sealed with a ring of wax. You could pop the top on them with one hand. Sliding back behind Nyteblade, I put my mouth by his ear again. He smelled sour, fear pouring through his sweat, pulling all the acidity out of his skin. He jumped when I spoke.

"Keep that cross held high, but you follow me. You have to keep up. If they separate us, you *will* die."

I snapped my fingers to make sure Nyteblade heard me. He nodded, dripping sweat into his eyes in spite of the cool night air. His arms flapped and shook from holding the cross up for so long. That cross had to weigh at least twice as much as my gun, so I knew he was nearing the end of his stamina.

I hoped he was up to running after me, because if he fell behind he would be dead before I could turn around. We just had to make it past these vampires and around the corner; then it was only a short run to the Comet. If I could just get him to the Comet, I could get his ass out of here.

Then I could start making headway on what the hell was going on with this weird ass night.

One of the holy waters went between my teeth, then two in each hand. I had the tubes separated by a finger so that a quick open-and-close motion with my hand would drop one; then I could flip the cap from the second one. Moving in front of Nyteblade, I used my thumbs to snap the caps off the first two tubes.

The vampires were frothed like dogs at the end of a chain, held back only by the edge of holy light from the cross Nyteblade held and the crucifix in my right fist. Teeth clenched on the tube of holy water, I screamed to let Nyteblade know I was ready. My legs tensed in a sprinter's stance. I raised my hands and brought them down in an X, crossing across my body, and then throwing them back up and out to the sides of my chest.

Moonlight glittered on the holy water as it flew from the tubes and out onto the mass of vampires.

The effect was instantaneous.

What little hearing I'd recovered from the gunfire was stolen in a dash of undead screams. The mass parted like the Red Sea as vampires flung themselves from the path of the holy water. Bloodsuckers convulsed and jerked as it ate into them. They were so tightly packed when I flung the holy water that, in their flailing, the ones I hit rubbed it onto the ones I didn't. Smoke rose from the vampires and there were small flashes of flame where some got an especially strong shot of it. They roiled back against the brick walls and spilled out of the alley end. Some ran off, but most fell to the ground.

Opening and closing my hands, I dropped the two empty vials to the ground. My thumbs flipped the caps on the other two tubes in my hands and I flung more holy water onto them. Now every vampire left had smoke coming from their bodies, and they were clawing at themselves and screaming.

I pushed off and began to sprint.

Running, I threw the last of the holy water in my hands as I passed vampires. Those tubes dropped and I snatched the one from my teeth. Looking over my shoulder as I cleared the corner, I saw Nyteblade was right behind me but dropping a step or two as we went.

Some of the vampires that had not gotten good doses of the holy water were rising up, shaking off the effects. They would be hot on our trail shortly. We still had to get down the side of the building and across the lot to the Comet. Reaching back, I grabbed a handful of Nyteblade's duster and hauled him in front of me. Holding on to his coat, I ran as if our lives depended on it.

Because they did.

I still had the last vial of holy water, half a clip in the CZ, and my Taurus with five bullets. It wouldn't be enough to save us if we were overtaken, but it might be enough to get us to the car.

Legs pumping and my shoving got Nyteblade to the end of the building. My lungs worked like bellows, burning like a forest fire. I'm built for power, not speed. I can run, faster than you would think for a man my size, but I am not a marathon man.

At least not when it comes to running.

Nine vampires had overcome the holy water enough to begin chasing after us. Over my shoulder I saw them charging down the side of the building. With a shove to keep Nyteblade running, I popped the cap on the last vial of holy water in my left hand and slid to a stop.

"Keep going to the black car! I'll be there in a second."

My right hand dug for my keys as I flung the holy water in the direction of the vampires. They fell back immediately. I didn't hit any of them, but they had learned their lesson. It was almost like a comedy act as they tripped over each other not to get splashed. My left hand went behind my back and came out with the Taurus .44 Bulldog. It's a small gun. Not much bigger than my fist.

I began to run again as I punched the electric key fob I held. The engine of the Comet roared to life and the driver's side door popped open. The doors on a Mercury Comet from the sixties are heavy suckers. If they are unlocked, they swing out on their own. I had put in the electric engine start and the door opener for situations just like this, where I need to get in the car on the run. The '66 model Comet I have is the two-door version and had the largest door opening of any car in that year. It yawned forth, waiting to swallow me. I am a big guy and I need as much space as I can get to jump in and out of a car.

Nyteblade was at the car when I got there, vampires still a handful of steps behind me. He had the cross held up like he had in the alleyway. Grabbing his coat, I shoved him into the open door of the Comet. He sprawled across the bench seat in the front. My boot went on his ass as I kicked him across the leather and dumped him into the floorboard.

One leg in and one leg out, I leaned on the door of the car and fired at the leading vampires. The phosphorus in the bullets left streaks of light in the dark. One of them exploded into dust as I nailed its heart and head. Two more fell from catching bullets, the phosphorus blazing to flame where it struck them. Bending my knees, I slid into the car, pulling the door closed behind me. I dropped the Comet into DRIVE, stomped the gas, and took off leaving a trail of smoke behind like the car's namesake. In the rearview mirror, vampires were screaming at the night in frustration as we got away.

Fuck 'em.

FOUR

THE COMET WAS a shark gliding through oily water as I pulled up to Polecats. The parking lot was packed like usual and cars of all kinds lined the lot. Some customers were going into the club and one guy was leaving.

Nothing looked suspicious as we cruised slowly through.

Nyteblade had crawled out of the floor boards and was pressed against the passenger door with his coat pulled around him like a shroud. His eyes were unblinking, staring at me like he had been the entire drive over. Once I got behind the club I spun the car around and backed into the alley behind the building so that the nose pointed out. The alley was narrow and provided cover for the car. I turned the ignition off but left the car in NEUTRAL with the parking brake engaged in case I had to crank it up and get the hell out of there quick.

Flipping open the glove box gave me a box of ammo. Practice let me reload the CZ without looking, so I used the time to check my surroundings through the windshield.

There were no vampires that I could see. The area looked clear.

Nyteblade made a noise as if to speak and I quickly cut him off with a slash of my hand. I needed silence to think and to listen. He stilled immediately, probably because of the gun in my hand. All the way to the club I'd been rolling events through my mind, trying to figure out what the hell was happening.

Obviously, I was set up.

It was the only thing that made sense. This Nyteblade guy was no threat to anyone whatsoever, especially not a can-control-fifty-vampires-level threat. That was a lot of supernatural firepower to throw at someone. From everything I had seen since meeting him, he didn't warrant it, so that left me. Nyteblade had been both bait and part of the trap, a hinderance that could have cost me my life.

I didn't know why someone, or something, had tried to take me out, but I was damn sure going to figure it out. That came later, though. Right this moment I wanted to be safe and secure and then find out what Nyteblade knew.

Survival first, answers second.

The loaded gun was a comfortable weight in my right hand as I pulled out my cell and punched the top contact with my left. It rang twice and the voice that answered was all business.

"Polecats, this is Kathleen, how can I help you?"

Kathleen, Kat to her friends, is the manager of Polecats. Answering with her name meant things were normal at the club. No trouble. If she had just answered, "Polecats," no name and no "How can I help you?" then I would have known to come in quiet and ready to shoot someone or something.

Truth is, I own the club, not just use it as an office. It's a good moneymaker and helps fund my war on monsters.

Bullets be expensive, yo.

Kat and all the folks who work for me know just what I do and why I do it. In one way or another, they have all been touched by the monsters. Some of them I saved and they work for me to pay it forward. Some of them I was too late to save and they work for me to feel safe or to help seek revenge. Some of them are family members and friends of people who have been touched by the darkness. Whatever their reason, they all know what I do and help me in this mission to keep humans safe from monsters.

Like Kat, for example. Kat's sister was killed by vampires years ago. It was a vicious, evil kill. I found her while hunting something else entirely. She had been playing groupie and letting vampires bite her to try to find information on who killed her sister. The bloodsuckers found out what she was up to and enslaved her, forcing her to be a one-woman blood bank for a really twisted sonnuvabitch named Darius. For months she endured physical sadism on a level most would not survive.

I found her while hunting down a witch who had gone on a finger amputating spree in an Atlanta suburb. I took her out of that and helped her get justice. She has been by my side ever since. Dedicated and faithful, but she has a deep-seated, violent and virulent hatred for anything vampire.

Yes, she loves me. I love her. No, we are not together. It's not like that between us.

There's nothing wrong with her looks, in fact she's really pretty, but from the beginning it was clear the trauma from what I took her out of has kept her from any romantic relationships. Plus, I'm not ready to move on from my wife's death, not by a long shot. Most of all, Kat is a sister to me and there has never been an attraction between us, not on either end. I love her, but we will never date. It would be too weird. Instead, we have a kinship that lets us work closely together. She also keeps me organized and maintains the operation of the club in all its facets.

Polecats is a good, old-fashioned honkytonk club. It is also my main base of operations. I converted an abandoned warehouse into the club about five years back, after the loss of my family and the madness that came afterward.

Before opening for business, I fortified the damn thing. Steel doors and shutters on the windows. Recessed bolted frames around them. Bulletproof Lexan in the windows and doors. Every opening and space covered by digital and infrared cameras, motion detectors, and proximity alarms.

In short, the works.

A trunk line carries the electricity and the Internet that is hydra branched into the surrounding systems of my neighbors. So, there is no way to cut the communications or power to the building without killing the entire block, which most bad guys won't do because they do not want that much attention drawn to them.

Or they simply can't.

It's hard to think about things like that if you are not even human. Point is, once I'm inside and the club is locked down, I am safe as houses.

"Kat, are there any vamps in the club?"

"No."

"Double-check."

"Give me a second."

I knew what she was doing, switching the security cameras to infrared, looking for cold spots in the club. "No, we're clear."

"Lock it down, Kat. All of it. Customers out without creating a panic, employees in the break room. Tell Father Mulcahy to get out the Sweeper and be ready. I am coming in the back door with company."

The phone went dead as Kat went into action. She didn't question or even waste time on good-bye. Good girl, Kat is. Stowing the phone, I jacked a shell into the chamber of the CZ.

"Let's go," I growled at Nyteblade, "and be quick about it."

The door to the Comet opened slowly and I slid out, gun at the ready. Nyteblade stumbled out of the car behind me, tripping on his damn coat and the bandolier of stakes around his bird chest. Grabbing his collar, I hauled him to his feet and pushed him to the door of the club. It is a plain gray steel door with a simple handle bolted to it. The bolts go all the way through the door itself and come out inside the building. Inside, they are held on by wing nuts. A few quick spins and the handle would come off, leaving anyone on the outside trying to get in with nothing to grab on to.

My foot pushed the door to the Comet shut and my finger punched the key fob to lock it down tight. The keyhole for the club's back door is recessed. Still keeping my eyes on our surroundings, I had to use touch to feed in the key. It slid in and turned the heavy lock.

The steel door was heavy enough to make me grunt opening it. It is a solid sheet of three-inch steel. Most steel doors are a frame covered with an eighth inch of steel sheeting. Not this one. It's like a bank vault door. I put my back against it, held it open, motioning Nyteblade inside with a quick head jerk. I backed in after him and the door closed behind me on oiled hinges.

The inside of the steel door has a round spinner like you see on a bank vault mounted on it. Giving it a quick twirl, I heard four clicks as the bolts it controlled locked into each side of the frame of the door. Two-inch-thick steel bolts sunk six inches into the steel frame and surrounding wall. Nothing was coming in behind us without a rhino.

Or a Sherman tank.

We were now in the back part of the club. It is the only part left that still looks like a warehouse. Bare brick for walls, no windows because of the back alley, and a stairway made of metal and concrete that leads upstairs. It's mostly used for storage. Kat keeps it clean and tidy. Boxes of supplies were sorted into stacks for the club and stacks for me. The club got the stacks with alcohol, glasses, and peanuts. I got the stacks with shotgun shells, bullets, and grenades. Go figure.

Heading up the stairs to the break room with Nyteblade in tow, I heard the customers being asked to leave over the PA system. The break room is at the top of the stairs and is the most central room of the club. The entire thing is as secure as a bomb shelter and is where all the weapons in the club are kept.

Okay, not all of them, but a good part of them.

It isn't actually used as a break room either. That's what it was used for when the place was a factory, so that's what we call it. Employees take breaks in the lounge behind the main area of the club. It is pimped out with couches, a stocked fridge, state-of-the-art microwave, foot massagers, and anything else needed for the employees to relax.

The break room is large and well lit, consisting of a big open room lined with metal cabinets. Inside, the cabinets are weapons, and each one had the kind of weapons they held stenciled on the door. A long metal table with chairs takes up the center of the room.

I deposited Nyteblade in a chair and began pulling guns and crosses out of the cabinets and lining them up in pairs along the table. All of the crosses were silver and blessed each day. The guns were all CZ 75 9mm, like mine, and were identical. I provide them for the employees so they are interchangeable. I never want anyone to feel crippled if they lost 'their gun,' so everybody's gun is the same.

They're loaded with the silver-jacketed Orion bullets and they are all 9mm because it is a good size for someone with smaller hands but packs enough of a punch to get the job done. You might have to use two or three rounds for that job, but that is why you have fourteen in the clip.

The unmistakable sound of cowboy bootheels on tile announced company before the first person entered the room. We have a thing going with the name of the club being Polecats and all, a semi-western motif. In twos and threes they began to line up along the wall.

I kept working, making sure I laid out a cross and gun combination for each employee. Owning a club is fun but it's also all business. It makes money, a ton of it, and it's mostly untraceable. Plus, you can do things like throw everybody out with no notice and they will line back up tomorrow to see the show.

Nobody interrupted me or ask any questions, they just let me work. Like I said, they all know what I really do. Voices murmured as they talked amongst themselves quietly and a few of the waitresses waved or smiled at Nyteblade, which turned his face scarlet and made him study the floor.

Finally, Kat walked into the room. I didn't hear her coming because she wore Dr. Marten's instead of cowboy boots. Kat doesn't work the floor. She's pinches in when and where needed, but her demeanor is all wrong. It's not that she has no humor, but it is so dry that most people have a hard time connecting with her. She is all business and that business is serious.

Her hair is long, blond, and bone straight. She keeps it pulled back in a ponytail that shows her Midwestern, corn-fed, girl-next-door looks. Big green eyes, with high cheekbones and a straight nose., She looks like the stereotypical high-school sweetheart. She's compact, built like a cheerleader, the kind that throws other cheerleaders in the air. Her gun was out and in her hand, the CZ 75 9mm gleaming in contrast with her black Arch Enemy shirt and dark jeans. An ever-present array of blessed crosses hung around her neck.

Father Mulcahy, our head bartender, followed her in. He held a modified Benelli shotgun we call the Sweeper because it was loaded with hand-packed silver shot, so fine it was almost like pepper. The hand packing made the birdshot spread dramatically when fired. Two rounds from it could sweep the entire room and slow down any supernatural critter, but any humans not directly blasted would basically be mostly unharmed. It was a tool Father Mulcahy brought with him when he started working with me. He loads the shells himself and he loves the damn thing.

He's an odd cat, our Father Mulcahy is.

He is actually a bona-fide Catholic priest, and one of the exorcist order at that, with a face that looks like Robert DeNiro got the shit beat out of him.

Really, I'm not being mean, and it's not just because I am so pretty, but Father Dominic Boru Mulcahy is a rough-looking man. He's a foot shorter than me, but probably only fifty pounds separate us. Cut into the shape of a square, he has thick dockworkers' arms attached to a barrel chest. Coarse salt and pepper hair rides over a square face marred by a boxer's nose, cauliflower boxer's ears, and scar tissue masquerading as eyebrows.

He smokes, drinks, cusses, and believes in God, His Son Jesus Christ, Holy Mother Mary, and all the saints in Heaven with all his heart and soul. Proficient in Shaolin Kung Fu, Brazilian jujitsu, Ninpo, Kenpo, and Muay Thai, he can shoot like a sniper and knife fight like a hardened convict. The priest is one of the toughest son-of-a-bitches I know.

I met him when I first started on this road, shortly after I lost my family. He serves bar downstairs at night, performs Mass in the mornings, and is there for whatever I need to fight my war.

Sometimes it's advice.

Sometimes it's cover fire.

Either way, he's as reliable as cancer.

Once everybody was in the room I stopped working and turned to the group. The employees fell silent and became attentive. Most of our floor crew were women, working the bars, the beer tubs, and entertaining with stage shows of various sorts. Two of the security staff were women and half the kitchen crew. All of them good folks who worked in my honkytonk. A lot of people would dismiss them as low-class.

Most people wouldn't know their ass from a hole in the ground either.

These were good soldiers. Yes, there are some people who worked the club who are damaged goods. Hell, we all are in one way or another. Every single one of us had our lives touched by the evil in the night. But that didn't make them less, it made them more. More determined to do what they could to fight it. More determined to help me stop it from happening to anybody else. I kept them safely back from the monsters. I protected them as much as I could, but I knew without a shadow of a doubt that they would all kill for me if it came to that. Pride and love toned my voice when I spoke to them.

"All right, I want you to all to pack up for the night. Grab your crucifix, and your guns." They moved forward to form a line at the table. "Father Mulcahy will take you downstairs and see you all in your cars, and out. Of course, Kat will call you about working tomorrow, and if it is going to be a few days, we will compensate you the money you are missing. So, you have at least the night off."

A slender hand rose in the air. The hand was attached to a slender arm that led to a small brunette with a body that would give eyesight to the blind. Ronnie. I nodded for her to speak. Her voice was clear when she did.

"What's going on, Deacon? If you need our help, just say the word."

I smiled. "We have a bloodsucker problem. But we haven't figured out exactly what that's going to wind up entailing." I reached out and touched her bare shoulder. Her skin was smooth, silky under my calloused fingertips. "If I need you, I will call."

Ronnie leaned into my touch. Her thick, brown ringlets shimmered as she nodded. She was a sweet girl who had lost her brother in a Santeria gang war a few years back. He had given his life to try and save her, but it hadn't been enough. Thankfully, I had been able to pull her from the fire, literally. The scars on her palms were still shiny, and if you hugged her, occasionally you would get the slightest whiff of lit matches in her hair. Those slender arms moved to reach for me when Kat's voice cut in.

"Okay, y'all stay in, and watch for vampires. If you so much as see one, call me and I will tell you what to do." Kat has a pleasant voice, but it is a pitch deeper than you would think from looking at her. I mean, she looks damn near dainty, but she uses her voice to her advantage, putting authority into her words.

Ronnie stepped back into line. Kat nodded to her with a smile and kept talking. She lifted her own gun up for emphasis. "Be safe, and remember, if you are in doubt, shoot first, and call here before you dial 911."

One by one, everybody picked up a gun and a cross from the table. Most of them hugged me and a few of the girls kissed me on the cheek as they went by. We are all family at Polecats. When all were armed and sorted, Father Mulcahy followed them out of the room. He would make sure the coast was clear in the underground parking deck and lock it back up after releasing the cars.

One of the reasons I chose this particular building to open the club was because it has an underground loading dock from its earlier life as a shipping business. It wasn't hard to secure that and make it a parking garage for employees. I had narrowed the opening to one-car access with a heavy-duty steel gate that worked on an electronic system.

An employee pulled up, clicked her opener, and that sent a signal to Kat's office. She looked on the monitor to see whether they were alone. If so, she passed them in the gate; if not, she alerted me or Father Mulcahy.

Kat pulled up a chair and waited without questions. She would catch up as we went along. I had called her earlier and told her about the vampire in the parking lot and meeting Nyteblade. She had put her gun away in a shoulder holster, but the strap was unsnapped for quick pull. She wasn't the best with a firearm but could more than handle herself. Sitting in the chair with her feet up and her nice, girl-next-door appearance, she looked pretty normal.

Normal may be a strange description, but it fits. Hey, I am far from normal. Before my life went crazy and I discovered there really were monsters, and not just under the bed, I was a tattoo artist and a part-time bouncer in slow season. My preferred mode of dress is lots of black and silver, lots of leather and denim and t-shirts, and I am usually armed. Heavily armed. So yeah, take my look, the employees and their working clothes, Father Mulcahy in his Roman collar and priest attire, and normal is the best description of Kat there is.

It was time to get to the bottom of what was going on and how it related to this Nyteblade character. I wanted to know why he had been expecting me, why he had thought I was a vampire, and why vampires were trying to kill me.

First things first, I needed one thing cleared up.

"Is your name really Nyteblade?"

His eyes were wide and crystal blue when his head jerked to look up at me. He had pulled a pair of thin, wire-framed glasses from a case in his coat and they rode on a freckled nose on a small face. The makings of a thin red goatee framed his mouth and sharply pointed chin. The same red–orange hair bristled up on his head in a short, clean cut.

Sitting with the gigantic duster on his small frame made him look like a high-school kid. Truthfully, he looked kind of like he was joking, dressed as a bad TV show's idea of a vampire hunter for Halloween. His big eyes flashed a little anger and he drew a deep breath.

"That is the name the creatures of the night know me by."

He actually managed to look indignant.

Kat, God bless her soul, snickered, and I tried, I swear I tried, to keep the sarcasm out of my voice.

"Really?" I asked. "What creature of the night gave you that name?"

For a moment he thought about getting angry, I could see it in his eyes. Then his shoulders slumped and he deflated like all the air had been taken from his balloon. I'm not sure if it was my sarcasm or Kat's snicker.

"My true name is Larson."

"That's better."

Yep, I liked Larson a lot better than Nyteblade. It was easier to say and fit him a lot better. He looked like a Larson. More like a librarian or a computer programmer, less like a super-mega-awesome vampire hunter.

"So, tell me what you know about the vamp attack tonight."

"I don't have to tell you anything. I don't even know who you are."

Now his chin did raise up and point at me.

I smiled and tried to make it friendly, really I did. I can't help it that on me a smile usually looks like the grin of a pit bull.

"You already know my name is Deacon Chalk. This here is Kat. The guy in the priest robes with the big-ass gun who will be back here in a moment is Father Mulcahy." I needed to get a point across to Larson and I wanted to get it across fast.

My foot hooked a chair and kicked it around so that I could sit backward in it but still face Larson. The CZ slid out of its holster under my arm and into my hand. I didn't point it at him, just held it casually. A naked gun makes a nice subtle threat on its own. It would be especially effective after he had seen the fighting with the vampires earlier.

"Now you know who we are."

The CZ waved around, the ruby dot of the laser indicating me and Kat.

"And while I appreciate that you think you don't have to tell us what you know, I will have to respectfully disagree."

The CZ tapped the face of my watch.

"Time is of the essence, so tell me why those vamps set me up using you."

The CZ draped in my hand off the back of my chair, pointing in the general direction of his crotch, red dot dancing on black denim like an exclamation mark.

The gun was decocked, I promise.

Larson's eyes were really, *really* big and really, *really* focused on my gun. Snapping the fingers on my left hand to get his attention made him jump. His eyes flickered to meet mine.

"I don't know why I was attacked. I assume I must have made an enemy in the vampire realm."

"You killed some vampire and this was retaliation against you?"

His ears burned bright red and he sheepishly turned his head away, refusing to look at me anymore.

"You've never killed a vampire, have you?"

I knew the answer before he shook his head. It was the only answer that made any sense at all. The gear he had was the most ineffective way to take out a vampire. You use wooden stakes when they are in their coffins and you are trying to be quiet. Any other time you blow them apart using the proper ammunition.

"So, what? You've been snooping around vampires and getting in their way?"

He shook his head again. "I have asked around and done field research but have not taken action as of yet."

Well, that explained how they knew about him, his damned research. He probably had been poking around at some of the clubs owned by vampires and the Goth clubs that catered to wannabes, asking a million questions and acting like a vampire slayer.

So that brought the events of tonight back to me. I was the obvious target because Nyteblade, sorry, Larson was *zero* threat to the vampires.

He was weak, inexperienced, and from the look of his gear, didn't know his half-ass from a hole in the ground. This whole thing had been a hit on me. I was set up, put in the crosshairs by some vampires where I would be outnumbered *and* distracted trying to keep this bumbling idiot alive.

This was not good news. I hate it when I haven't done anything and people still try to kill me. It really pisses me off. I mean sure, I've dusted my share of bloodsuckers in my time, as I've come across them, but I haven't targeted any in quite a while.

That would change as soon as I figured out who was behind this.

For the time being, I put the gun away and turned in Kat's direction.

"Okay, let's think and tell me if you know of anything I have done recently that may have pissed off a local vampire with the pull to have fifty disposable bloodsuckers to throw at me."

Her blond ponytail waggled back and forth as she shook her head.

"I can't think of a vampire with the power to command fifty other vampires to do anything, much less have them to spare."

She was right. Vampires organize and work together in bloodlines and clans to run a lot of underground crime and other shenanigans. However, the basis for all of that is a kiss of vampires, which is a small group of three to ten. A kiss is usually centered around one sire and a few that he, or she, turned into vampires.

Sires have some mental control over their fledglings, especially when they are freshly turned, but even the most powerful vampire will usually be able to hold only a few before they start to lose control. Individual vampires have minds of their own and are unpredictable. Plus, vampires have varying levels of intellect. The larger the group, the more likely it will fracture. For someone to send out fifty other vampires, we were talking big-time power.

Either that or all the vamps that attacked were pissed off at me personally.

That couldn't be it. If that were the case, they wouldn't have worked together without one vampire calling the shots.

Being undead really boosts your ego. Turns vampires who were nice when alive into raging undead dicks.

Kat's feet hit the floor and she stood, lifting her hands over her head in a stretch. Her black T-shirt rode up, exposing a pale curve of hip over the waistband of her jeans. I caught Larson watching her and he quickly looked away.

Like I said, Kat is real pretty.

Done with her stretch, she pulled her shirt down and started for the door.

"I'll go figure it out for you."

Kat headed out of the room as Father Mulcahy came in. He sat on the corner of the table. Laying the Sweeper down, he shook a cigarette out of the pack he kept in his shirt pocket and put it between his lips. The sharp tang of matchstick flared as he snapped a thumbnail over one from a book of matches.

I knew without looking that the matchbook was black or red with silver writing on it. Father Mulcahy uses the matches for the club. POLECATS—LIVE MUSIC FOR LIVE PEOPLE, the front of the matchbook would read. We didn't always have live music, like tonight we were band free, but it made for a good slogan. Menthol-tinged smoke streamed from his nostrils. Father Mulcahy smokes Kool brand cancer sticks.

"All the lads and lasses are off and away. It's all quiet out there as far as I can tell."

Father Mulcahy was a mix of Italian and Irish descent. It gave a strange sound to his voice, a mixture of accents that rolled into an odd cadence. Plus, his voice was gruff from years of black coffee, cigarettes, and whiskey the man consumed; but that same voice could coax tears from the congregation at Sunday Mass, just like angels singing. I had experienced it myself.

"So what world of shite did you stir up this time, son?"

I shook off my jacket, peeling the left sleeve away, where it was stuck to my arm. Dried blood left a pattern of rusty brown over my tattoos. Pushing the sleeve of my T-shirt up exposed the two puncture wounds from the vampire in the alleyway. They were clotted black with blood and stuck to the sleeve. I'd mostly been able to ignore them until now. Looking at them, giving them attention, made me aware of how much they hurt. It was a deep puncture and throbbed like only a vampire bite will.

"Vampires. Other than that, I have no idea. That's the problem. Kat's going to see if she can sort it out."

Moving over to the sink, I slipped my shoulder holster off and peeled the T-shirt over my head. Wadding it up, I tossed it into the trash after rinsing the blood down the drain. You don't leave blood lying around in my business if you can help it. Sure, this is my headquarters, my safe house, but it's always good to keep the habit up of being careful.

The antibacterial soap was cool in my hands and arms as I lathered up. The warm water ran black into the deep stainless-steel basin, the soap cutting away the dried blood and the gunpowder residue from my hands. It burned a bit more as I washed it deep into the fang marks and then rinsed it away. Luckily, being dead, vampires don't have communicable diseases. Well, other than vampirism, anyways.

The priest handed me a large adhesive bandage from the first-aid kit by the sink and took another drag of his cigarette. Squinting one eye, he gave Larson a look over.

"Who is this one?" he asked, nodding his head toward the man in the chair.

I took the bandage and slapped it over the bite.

"His name's Larson, used to be called Nyteblade. He tried to stake me earlier tonight."

The priest snorted, shooting gray smoke out of his wide nostrils.

"Well, you have been looking a bit pale lately."

"Hardy-har-har."

I flipped him the middle finger and opened another cabinet. Reaching inside, I grabbed a 3XL T-shirt from a stack of promo items for the club. It was a black shirt with a traditional tattoo-style pinup dancing on a pole under the word POLECATS. The back had the same slogan as the book of matches. I slipped it on and then put my shoulder holster back in place and instantly felt better.

"After he tried to stake me, we were attacked by an assload of vampires. That's why I brought him back with me, to find out why he was there to start with."

Father Mulcahy's humor died with the update. His head nodded once up and down. The end of his cigarette flared orange as he took a drag. He walked over to Larson and put his hand out. Larson flinched, but then stuck his own out and shook the priest's outstretched hand. When he did so his coat fell away, revealing the large ornate silver cross strapped back on his thigh. The priest froze, staring at it.

Still holding Larson's hand, he asked, "May I see that cross, son?"

Thin fingers scrabbling on the straps, Larson pulled out the cross and handed it to the priest. Hands calloused from years of wielding weapons and praying the rosary caressed the surface of the cross. I stepped closer to see what he was examining.

The cross was made of silver and covered in ornate filigree. A masterfully detailed figure of Christ crucified was worked on the face. There were small square pieces of ivory embedded in the four ends of it. Father Mulcahy turned it over in his hands. Along the back was an inscription I couldn't read that looked to be some European Slavic-based language, but languages ain't my strong suit. The words HEXE AUFGABEBRECHER were deeply etched in the silver. Under his breath a curse rolled from the priest's lips. His eyes blazed as he looked back at Larson.

"Do you know what this is?"

Larson leaned back and gulped, his Adam's apple bobbing. "A cross?"

Father Mulcahy scowled.

"Not just a cross, this is *The Witch Breaker*."

He said it like it was supposed to mean something. Larson just shook his head, not understanding any significance.

"It is a cross that was designed specifically for fighting against witchcraft. St. Augustine of Hippo forged it himself after much prayer and fasting." Blunt fingers stroked the squares of enamel. "It contains the teeth of St. Peter."

Now I could follow. Father Mulcahy is a member of an Exorcist Order of priests, sanctioned by the Vatican and blessed by the Pope himself. He holds Mass at St. Augustine of Hippo. Most people did not know that St. Augustine of Hippo is a Vatican stronghold that keeps safe much of its anti-occult arsenal.

There is a reason Father Mulcahy works with me, it's not just my winning personality.

"Teeth of St. Peter?" I chimed in. "Interesting."

The priest ignored me; it's okay, he does that sometimes. His gruff voice was full of wonder, like a child on Christmas.

"Where did you find The Witch Breaker?"

"Um, eBay. Forty-two dollars including shipping."

Father Mulcahy looked like he had been slapped. He stared at Larson, who turned red around the ears again and looked away. I reached in my wallet, pulled out a $100 bills, and handed it to Larson, who took it gingerly, as if it were going to bite him.

"Here, call it even." I did not leave room for argument in my tone.

Larson stuffed the money in his pants pocket and the padre looked me over, nodding his thanks.

Father Mulcahy has done a lot for me, and it was the least I could do in the situation. I paid him for tending bar, but he gave it all over to his parish so they could run a soup kitchen and battered women's shelter. He thought the cross was important, and thusly, he needed to have it. I didn't mind; besides, who knew when I might run up against some witches that needed breaking.

Kat's voice rang out from the hallway for us to join her in the conference room. Father Mulcahy wrapped The Witch Breaker in a T-shirt and put it away in one of the cubicles. After checking the door three times to assure himself it had locked, he began to move toward the conference room. I followed suit.

At the door, I stopped and turned. Larson just sat in the chair I'd originally put him in.

"You, too, son. I don't want you in here alone."

He held up his hands in a beseeching manner. "I would like to go home. I don't know any of you and I don't want to be caught up in your situation. Please, just show me the way out."

Striding over, I stood in front of him. Planting my right foot between his brought me close enough to make him have to lean back and crane his neck up to look at me. Counting to five before I spoke added weight to what I was saying.

"Understand *this*," My finger pointed down at his face. "You may have information I can use. Until I figure out if you do or not, the *only* place you are going is with me into the other room." I leaned forward, making him crane back even farther. "Have I made my stance on the situation clear?"

Nodding, he got to his feet slowly after I stepped back to give him room. Once more I walked to the door, stopped, and turned toward him.

"And for Pete's sake, take off that silly-ass coat."

FIVE

THE CONFERENCE ROOM is just that, a conference room.

It has a big-ass table and big, comfy chairs; Internet access; conference phones; and a wall-mounted video screen perfect for PowerPoint presentations. I just let Kat put in whatever tech stuff she felt she needed. I can find things on the Internet like most folks, but compared with Kat?

That was like Larson being compared with me as a vampire hunter.

Mostly I work alone because I'm the one who started all this and I am the one most likely to survive a fight with a monster, but I do rely on my people.

Kat can organize anything to within an inch of its life and can research like no one's business. Father Mulcahy has a lifetime of Vatican-sponsored study about all kinds of occult subjects that he brings to the table. Plus, sometimes I work with other experts I know from this weird war I am in.

I even consult the police occasionally.

When I haven't been too violent.

This room is the central place for gathering information and translating it into the most effective tool it can be. If there was a strategy to be had, this is the room it would be born in. The majority of the time for me strategy is to just go in shooting, but occasionally I needed a more developed plan than "kill every monster I see."

Kat typed furiously, clicking her mouse dramatically as we entered and took seats. I tossed my jacket on the back of a microfiber chair and sat down. Leaning back, I put my feet up on the conference table.

Speaking of jackets, Larson had left his duster and the bandoliers in the break room like I had asked. His arms were pale, freckled sticks coming from the sleeves of his black T-shirt. I would have to scale his height back to about 5'6" also, because the boots he was wearing had about a 3-inch rubber sole on them. They were the clunky, strappy, combat-styled boots that a lot of Goth kids used to wear. You've seen them. They come up to the wearer's knees, have lots of flashy silver buckles, studs, and grommets, and look like they are from the wardrobe department of a bad apocalyptic movie. They're meant to be intimidating, and I guess they are if you don't know any better.

The thing is, they are held together with the equivalent of Elmer's glue. Try one roundhouse kick and the sole of your boot will be flapping around like a blown tire on a car.

That's why I wear a practical pair of German tanker boots. They have a high-density rubber sole that is stitched on properly, thick leather straps, and a steel shank. Designed for kicking a slipped tread on a tank back into place, they are durable, comfortable, and admittedly, do look pretty badass.

The screen on the wall flickered to life and information began to fill it, fed in from the computer Kat was using. I recognized some of the names and addresses on the list as vampire power players and businesses that were vampire friendly. Pictures popped up and started pairing up with names. Like I said, Kat can organize like nobody's business. She would also have every scrap of information available on these vampires. She keeps close tabs on them after what happened with her sister.

Hatred will motivate someone like few other things will.

Ask me how I know.

Once done, Kat sat back and picked up a laser pointer. The screen was filled with pictures. Different faces of different ethnicities, ages, genders, and time periods. She twirled her chair around and pointed at the screen. A red dot swirled around the screen, circling them all.

Kat turned in her chair to face us.

"Okay, these are the most likely candidates that we know about. Still, none of them has the power or persuasion to make fifty vampires do anything."

I agreed with Kat's assessment. Looking at the names and pictures up there, I saw heavy hitters, even a few major leaguers, but no one who had enough pull to do what was done tonight.

I looked at Kat and the priest.

"Can either of you think of what I may have done to get them all, or even most of them, out for my blood?"

Father Mulcahy lit another Kool from the one he was finishing and shook his head. Kat thought for a moment, her tiny chin in a small hand.

"Unless there's something I don't know, you haven't done anything to make the entire vampire community hate you." She smiled. "At least not more than they already do."

I waved my hand in the air to show a negative. "Other than tonight, I haven't run into any vampires recently. The last vampire I dusted was over six months ago. But I do hate the concept of them as a community."

"That would have been that thing at the zoo?" Father Mulcahy asked.

About a half-year back, the local zoo had a rash of animals slaughtered, skinned, and left in trees. No one could figure out what was happening to them, so the cops called me in. It was a Nosferatu who had made a nest inside and was using it as a hunting ground.

Nosferatu are vampires, but they are the most primal of them all. They cannot pass for human and actually have batwings and rodent hair on their body. They are nasty bastards, fierce and vicious like rabid dogs.

That had been a long night.

"Yep, but that can't be it. Nosferatu are the bottom-feeders of the vamp community. No other bloodsuckers would posse up to revenge them."

Pushing with my feet spun me to look at Larson sitting in his chair. He looked really uncomfortable. As my dad used to say before he left this shitty world, he looked as uncomfortable as a nine-tailed cat in a room full of rocking chairs.

"How did you wind up in that alley tonight to meet me?"

A thin hand rose from his lap and rubbed the side of his face. Nervous gestures dominated him. Touching his face, adjusting his glasses, licking his lips. All of them done over and over, almost like a habit. Hell, it might make me anxious just watching him be anxious.

He swallowed and said, "I was listening for information at Varney's when I was approached by a girl who offered to tell me where I could find a vampire to stake."

Fucking Varney's.

Varney's is a tiny Goth club on the southside of Atlanta. It's a hole in the wall, full of all the Goths who were still stuck in the nineties scene. Imagine a tiny room where everything is painted black and red full of sweaty, overweight middle-agers dressed in black, wearing greasepaint makeup, heavy mascara, and black fingernail polish. It was more of a place for swingers than vampires. I had never, ever heard of a vampire even setting foot in there.

"Did you get the name of this girl?"

Larson shook his head.

"What did she look like?"

Larson scratched his chin.

"She was young. So young I don't even know how she got into the club. She had long, messy hair."

"Looked like a cat could get lost in it?"

"It was pretty tangled."

"Let me guess, she wore a bright yellow sundress?"

Larson nodded.

I turned back to Kat.

"I bet this was the same vampire who sent me to see Larson here. Did you pull a match from the picture I sent you?"

She popped back into her chair and began typing and clicking again.

Larson leaned over to me. His Adam's apple bobbed as he swallowed. "That was a vampire I talked to?"

No wonder he tried to stake me. He didn't even recognize a vampire when he was just a few feet away from one. I looked over at him and raised one eyebrow.

"Yeah, it was, but don't worry, I took care of it vampire-hunter style. She's a pile of dust now."

I turned back to Kat and she shot me a look. I smiled big at her. So what if I yanked Larson's chain a little? He tried to stake me earlier, so I felt real justified.

A picture unfolded on the screen. The face staring out was the same vampire who had sent me into that alley earlier tonight. In this picture she was a smiling, happy girl posing for the camera.

She still looked remarkably like my daughter.

My head swam for a second as the memories tried to surface and I shoved them back in their box. Father Mulcahy tapped on the table to get my attention. The scar tissue he uses for eyebrows lifted over one eye at me. He knew how close the picture was to my daughter, hell, he had performed her funeral along with my wife and son, and he also knew how I am about that.

To distract myself, I pointed at the picture and looked the question at Larson. He nodded and pushed his glasses back up the bridge of his nose.

"Alyssa Burton, age fourteen, disappeared from Cross Plains, Texas, approximately three months ago. There is a reward of one hundred thousand dollars for information leading to her return." Kat turned and looked at us.

"A hundred grand is a decently hefty reward. Are the parents wealthy?" I asked.

Kat shook her head.

"From my research, no. Dad is a hardware store owner in Cross Plains, but it isn't a very big town. The reward has apparently come from her family, friends, and the community as a whole. Her family is stable. Father and mother still together, two younger siblings ages twelve and seven. I found pages of hers on a few social network sites and they all indicate she was happy. There are also almost twenty pages on those same sites looking for information about her and offering the reward that was set up by her friends and maintained by them even now."

Three months is a lifetime for teenagers. If they were still maintaining those pages, then she must have been loved by them. The big reward put up by them and the community was a sign of love too. Why had she gone missing? Most runaways do so because of trauma from home, this girl was well loved and, by all indications, happy. How did she get to Georgia as a bloodsucker?

"Did your research turn up anyone in her circle of friends who disappeared with her?"

Kat shook her head.

Happy runaways generally leave on an adventure, but they almost always take someone with them. Where's the fun in an adventure alone? I'm no real expert and it's a generalization, but it's based on life experience.

"Any ties to Georgia you can find? Friends or relatives in the area? Interests she had that might lure her here?"

"No, she has no family or friends who are from here. There is no reason she would be in Georgia that I can find."

If Kat couldn't find a reason, it wasn't there to find. She is a magician at data mining.

"Okay. Isn't Western Jim still in Texas?" I asked.

The blond ponytail bobbed up and down.

"We should call him and see if he knows anything."

"Done and done," Kat said. "I left a message on his phone about two hours ago when I found Alyssa in the National Center for Missing and Exploited Kids network. He hasn't called back yet."

This was not worrisome. Western Jim is a monster hunter like me. He had been a Texas Ranger in the seventies when he ran up against a Thessalonian bloodcult and had to shoot it out with an ancient entity bent on reinstalling human sacrifices. He was a crotchety old bastard and quick as a rattlesnake with his six-gun. We'd worked together a few times when we were chasing monsters and wound up in each other's territory. He would call when he was free, but it might take a bit if he was knee-deep in a hunt.

Kat's face turned sad.

"I called Detective Longyard and let him know that the girl would not be found so he could contact her parents. He wanted to know if you needed any help."

"Not yet. Tell him I will call if I need him."

Detective John Longyard was the lead investigator on the murder of my family. He is a good man and knows what I do. He is my go-to guy on the police force and helps me cut around them when needed. He gets me information if I need it, gets me into crime scenes, and gets me out of complications that come from having to skirt the law when things get hairy.

Or scaly.

Or fangy.

It was hard on him sometimes, but he did it out of duty to his fellow man. My feet dropped to the floor as I sat up.

"So now we have a newly turned girl from Texas who came to Georgia and acting as a setup to try and get me killed." I looked around the table. "Anybody have any ideas how to start figuring this one out?"

Larson coughed and cleared his throat. His cheeks burned red. A pale hand drifted over his forehead as he began talking, the words stumbling from his mouth in nervousness.

"New vampires don't travel very far, not by themselves. They don't have the control over their urges to feed. From all evidence she was turned in Texas and then came here, so she didn't travel alone. She would have had to have a stronger vampire to keep her in check or it would have been a bloodbath between Texas and here."

He sat back with pride on his face under the flush of his embarrassment from when he started.

Sounded like he actually knew a thing or two about a thing or two.

That's fine, but it was all book knowledge. He had no practical knowledge whatsoever. He'd actually sat and talked with a vampire without being able to spot her for what she was. It was a little like saying he had been petting a puppy and not noticing that it had rabies.

Father Mulcahy blew smoke toward the ceiling.

"So, we are talking about a new big vampire in town."

Kat looked at him shaking her head.

"No, that is not possible. If there were a new powerful vampire in the territory, there would have been a turf war. I would know about it because vampire activity would have spiked."

She definitely would have known. Because of Kat's past with vampires, she kept closer tabs on them than on any other supernaturals in the area. Hatred will make you obsessive sometimes.

"In fact," she said, "just the opposite has happened. The vampires have been really quiet the last few weeks."

A lull in vamp activity? Normally the vampires mind their p's and q's. They are evil, but with the plethora of victims that can be seduced into giving blood, they rarely kill anyone. Usually they stay involved in their crimes and misdemeanors, keeping themselves occupied.

It's almost like a game for them. Because of this, the cops actually keep them in check pretty well. They don't know what they are dealing with usually, but it just works itself out somehow. It also keeps them out of my line of fire for the most part.

I am just one gun in a war, so my focus is always on the monster at hand. For an area the size of Metro Atlanta, vampires are almost like a rat problem. They are there, and they need to be exterminated, but you don't see them, so they fall to the bottom of the priority list.

Well, tonight's attack changed all that. Vampire equals top-of-the-priority-list.

Number one with a silver fucking bullet.

"Have there been any reports of vampire activity on our social media?"

Kat shook her head no.

Larson looked over at me.

"You have social media?"

I snorted through my nose. "Of course."

I didn't ask: who doesn't?

"It's how we get work sometimes."

I turned back to Kat and she shook her head.

"The problem as I see it is that there is a ton of stuff we don't know." I ticked my points off on the fingers of an upraised hand. "We don't know who the bad guy is, why they tried to kill me, how they accomplished the setup, why Larson here was used as bait... In fact, all we know is that the problem is a vampire-related one, and someone tried to take me out." I stroked my beard, thinking. "Does anybody know of any big happenings in the vampire world, anything that maybe has nothing to do with us yet, but will?"

They all looked at me. I could see them reaching for conclusions and could also tell that they were not going to come up with any.

Time for a different tact.

"Okay, Kat, find out if there is a major vampire player that may have recently dropped off the radar. Maybe the person setting me up has had a new development in their unlife and are blaming me for it."

Kat's quick typing caused the screen to change to the Internet. Web sites popped up and dropped off as Kat worked the way only she can. She would stop on a site for a second, rapidly read some bit of information, switch screens, and go off on another search. Follow a link. Cross reference. Do a reverse search on an image.

It really would be amazing if you could keep up with it.

I can't, so I just let my eyes go unfocused and dropped into my head to think about the problem at hand.

A lot of folks get scattered when someone tries to kill them.

I don't.

Panic does no one any good, except for the people who are trying to kill you. I only care *why* someone was trying to kill me so I could figure out *who* was trying to kill me.

Process of elimination. One problem at a time.

Also, since I know and have come to grips with the fact that I will not live to a ripe old age and die in my sleep, I will always be proactive.

One, find the bad guys.

Two, kill their ass.

That was my goal, figuring out why was just a means to an end. I had a plan forming in my head to smoke the bastard out. I just needed a name and a place to start. For that, I waited on Kat.

Looking over at Father Mulcahy, I saw that he was sitting still and quiet, like he normally did. Years of monastery training ensured he could sit like a rock. That and being an army sniper somewhere in the world that had gone to shit before joining the priesthood.

Larson also sat stone still, enraptured by the screen as Kat worked. He wasn't blinking and his mouth hung open slightly in awe. I told you it was amazing if you could keep up. Maybe Larson could. My eyes slipped closed so I could think some more, and I didn't open them until I heard Kat give a quiet, but triumphant, "*aha,*" and stop typing.

A picture of a vampire filled the screen. He looked pretty normal for a corpse. Vampires are always a bit off, especially the older they are. The vampire in them doesn't quite get the human part, and when you throw in fashions through the ages… Well, let's just say they usually act and look a bit *dramatic*.

This one had long, wavy black hair with sharply trimmed sideburns that met across his face into a thick, Fu Manchu-style mustache and a soul patch. Pale, he had a heavy brow and a sharp nose. Dark eyes rimmed in red sunk over sharp cheekbones, one of which had a strange star-shaped scar on it. He must have gotten the scar before becoming a vampire, or he had been wounded with a blessed object.

Vampires can close any wounds, unless they're caused by something holy. The picture was taken from the waist up, a kind of sitting portrait. He looked like he was slender, but broad of shoulder, and dressed in a high-dollar pinstripe suit. Admittedly, he was a good-looking corpse. I didn't recognize him, but he looked like a player.

Kat's voice cut across the room, clear and concise.

"Gregorios, no surname. Owns a vampire dance club downtown called Helletog. That's his legitimate business. Illegal businesses include several vampire bordellos tucked away in different parts of the city. They also double as distribution centers for dealing various illegal pharmaceuticals and finding victims." She clicked some more. "Supposedly over six hundred years old, and with the largest kiss in the city. He normally keeps a pretty high profile and is a minor celebrity in the Goth and fetish scenes, but very recently has dropped out of sight, only making minimal appearances at his club."

This bloodsucker fit the bill as much as one could. A big player, but laying low. It was as good a place to start as any.

"Send the addresses to my phone and me and Larson here will go knocking and see if we can find this asshole and figure out what he knows."

Larson looked at me sharply, eyes wide.

"Why am I going? I don't want to go anywhere with you."

I held up my hand to stop him from speaking.

"You don't get a choice on this either, pal. You are in this and I want to know why. They used you to get me in a trap, so you are stuck with this until the end." I waved my hand in a flourish as I stood up. "Besides, you wanted to be a vampire hunter. Here's your chance to see how it's done."

I knew he'd probably changed his mind about being a vampire hunter after the attack earlier. Seeing the monsters in action will do that. They are not nearly as horrible in theory as they are in real life.

Fiction paints vampires as cool and sexy.

In real life, they are vicious, deadly creatures and we are their food.

I was taking Larson with me to learn more about why he was involved, but I also wanted to turn him away from wanting to hunt monsters. He wasn't up to the job.

Hell, I am a little more than human and some days I'm not up to the job. Going down this path, I am going to die. I have made peace with that, but that didn't mean I was going to just let him follow the same path to the same end.

I mean, I'm an asshole, but I'm not a fucking asshole.

SIX

WE WERE in the Comet cruising down Interstate 75 heading into the city of Atlanta where Helletog was.

Here in the South you do a lot of driving. It's like the city is where you go to do certain things, but most of us live outside of it in the suburbs, putting the Metro in Metro Atlanta. There is space in the South for us to spread out and we take advantage of that. We have MARTA, which is public transport consisting of a few trains and buses, but there is no true subway in Atlanta, and if there were, it damn sure wouldn't go to the suburbs.

So, we drive. Parking is plentiful, the streets are wide, and we love our cars.

I have a few vehicles, but I mostly drive the Comet. I love this car. It was built back when cars were meant to go fast and last a long time. It's older than I am. A '66 Mercury Comet, it's two tons of metal. Long in the hood and with a wide set of doors, it looks vaguely like a shark, menacing and sinister.

The engine is a 351 Windsor, which is car talk for eight cylinders built for nothing but power and speed. Of course, the car is painted black. The interior is from a Lincoln Continental, so it is plush and soft. You can ride in comfort for hours on end. I am a big guy, and I need a big car to ride for any length of time.

I can drive anything, but the more comfortable I am, the better I do so. It gets jack for gas mileage, but I am okay with that. I don't drive this car to save the environment. I drive it because I love it.

You may not understand, but if you ever got behind the wheel of a car like this you would. It's a hotrod. I love the sound of the motor as it roars to life. I love the rock of the car in idle because the motor is like a beast chained to a stake, waiting for the links to break so it can roar forth and wreak havoc. The rich smell of gasoline and oil that comes through as you drive, the scent of metal and leather inside the car, these bring me peace. There are no antilock brakes and very little power steering. When you brake, you brake all of a sudden. When you swing into a curve, you hold that car or it will get away from you. The Comet is the loudest, fastest, most dangerous car I have ever driven.

And I love it.

Larson and I were in the front seat. He was seat belted in and his knuckles were white as he held on to the door. I would bet it was the first time he had ever ridden in a muscle car being let loose to do what it was made for, which is eating highway miles. Highway 75 is a wide, sweeping stretch of asphalt. Up to sixteen lanes on each side and smooth as silk. The Comet was wound up in her high-range and we were cruising down the road just a peg over a hundred miles an hour.

I fiddled with my phone, scrolling the playlists, looking for music. It took a second, but I finally found what I wanted. One tap sent music flooding over the noise of the motor.

An electric organ started off with a light blues boogie run. It danced lightly above the sound of the engine. After a few seconds, a slap bass, guitar, and drummer kicked in, driving the organ into a blues funk corner. That's when she started singing, whiskey-tinged gospel voice cutting in, carrying with it the promise of everything that is woman.

Larson's eyes got wide and he leaned over to me.

"Who is *that*?"

I smiled.

"Susan Tedeschi." My fingers rested on the volume knob. "Sit back, shut up, and learn something."

Turning the knob pushed the music through the speakers, filling the inside of the car with the blues.

Susan Tedeschi sang about having evidence that her man was a two-timing dog. Her voice was proof enough for me. Nobody else can touch her, the only one better was Koko Taylor. She ain't a torch singer, naw, Susan Tedeschi is slinging napalm.

From there the music shifted to the blues rock of the Allman Brothers Band and their "Whipping Post" all about a man done wrong who isn't putting up with it anymore. Then Son Seals sang out how he just wanted to go home, his guitar driving the point in front of his smooth vocals. By the end, of that we were cruising off the highway onto North Avenue and we were right around the corner from Helletog.

Pulling to a stop at the end of the off ramp, the road in front of us was crawling with college kids walking to somewhere. One of the South's biggest colleges is on North Avenue, so seeing wandering groups of kids is not uncommon.

Waiting for the light to turn, I watched them pass by a homeless man with a sign that just said PLEASE in shaky marker on dirty cardboard. His clothes hung on a frail body in tatters. Grime and dirt filled the creases on his face while a new trucker cap gleamed on top of dirty gray hair. The cap was white and red, and he obviously hadn't had it long. It probably came from a homeless shelter just that day. Reaching out a thin arm that held a cracked plastic cup, he beseeched the groups of passing kids for change.

Most of them ignored him and kept walking. A few kind souls waved or nodded at him as they shuffled by, their high-dollar jackets pulled close against the evening coolness. At the end of a group one frat boy took notice of his fellow man.

Frat boy was big, not muscular, just bigger than average. Dirty dishwater blond hair and a chin that was weak all sat on a thick neck. He was dressed in hundred-dollar jeans made to look like they came from Goodwill and a red sweater. He moved toward the homeless man with a bad look on his face.

I've seen the same look on the face of a dog that is getting ready to bite.

A sharp push on the horn of the Comet made the frat boy's head snap up and look at me in the car. I held up my finger and shook it at him, telling him no. Mouth breathing, he stared at me for a moment. Scowling, he flipped me off and walked away to join his friends.

Tough guy.

The homeless man smiled and gave me a little bow of appreciation. His teeth were black and his clothes were rags on his thin, dirty body, but he was polite. A glimmer drew my eye to his hand. He held a box cutter with the razor extended. I hadn't seen it before, and I knew the frat boy hadn't either. Instead of saving the homeless guy, I saved the asshole.

Seems about right.

The light turned and I goosed the pedal to pull out onto the road.

We were not on the road very long before I pulled off at a small, stand-alone restaurant that looked like a miniature pagoda with a drive-through. Neon flashed on the sloping tiled roof and the words BENTO BOX blinked and buzzed into the night. The restaurant had no dining room, it was drive up only. There was a walk-up window in front and a few tables with benches outside, but the weather was a bit chilly for folks to be out, so they were empty. All the customers were in the drive-through. Pulling into line, I turned down the stereo and turned to Larson.

"Hungry?"

He looked around at the strange-looking building. "What is this place?"

"Bento Box. Drive-through sushi. Best damn sushi in the state of Georgia for that matter."

"I don't eat sushi."

Turning back to him, I studied his features. "You don't eat sushi because you don't like sushi, or you don't eat sushi because you have never tried it?"

"I just don't think I would like it. Raw fish doesn't sound good to me."

The car ahead of us pulled away. A tap of my foot pulled the Comet up the speaker box. It sat on an even more miniature version of the restaurant itself. Behind it, a huge sign with colorful pictures of sushi and writing along with prices washed us in light. The bulbs were kept fresh so it was almost blindingly brilliant.

"I'll order for the two of us," I said.

Before he could say anything else the speaker box squawked and a woman's voice called out of it, tinny and staticky. "Welcome to Bento Box, can I take your order?"

Leaning on the door, I spoke into the round speaker. "Hello, Katsumi, how are you and your honorable father tonight?"

A loud click sounded through the speaker and the static disappeared.

"Deacon! It has been too long since you came by. Father is well, and I know he has missed you also."

Enthusiasm filled the smooth tone of Katsumi's voice.

"It has been too long indeed," I replied. "I will come back soon to visit. Unfortunately, I cannot stay tonight."

"That is unfortunate. Will you be having your regular order?"

"I will, and if you could double it, that would be great. I have company in the car with me."

Silence poured palpably from the speaker.

"It's okay, Katsumi. It is good company."

If Larson had been bad company, then when we pulled around to the drive-through Katsumi would have been holding an Uzi out the drive-up window to distract him while one of the ninja sushi chefs came around to slit his throat.

The Takakage family take my safety seriously.

"Very good. Pull around."

The Comet rolled up to the cleared drive-through window and we pulled even to see Katsumi's smiling face. It was a good face. The Takakage family is a family of beautiful daughters. Katsumi had glossy black hair piled on top of her head and held in a thick bun with ornamental chopsticks. Her big brown eyes were outlined in heavy kohl eyeliner, making them appear liquid and unreal. The skin on her perfectly heart-shaped face was flawlessly smooth. Blood-red lipstick outlined full lips that would make a priest bite his knuckles.

Just ask Father Mulcahy.

She wore a ridiculous sheath dress with a mandarin collar that was painted-on tight and showed her shapely torso. I knew there was a long length of just as shapely leg under that skirt. She looked like a young, vibrant, Japanese woman.

She looked human.

She wasn't even close.

The Takakage family were Tengu.

Tengu are figures from Japanese folklore. There they are called demons, even though they are anything but demonic. What they truly are is some form of raven shape-shifters who gave birth to all the ninja legends. To my knowledge, Katsumi and her family were the only Tengu on American shores.

A few years back, I helped her father, the patriarch of the clan, get his daughter back when some dumbass mafioso had kidnapped her. Jimmy Legbone was a feral little two-bit gangster who thought he could climb the organized crime mountain if he could harness some heavy firepower. He kidnapped Katsumi's baby sister, trying to force Maasakki to kill for them. I helped them get her back, and ever since they never let me pay for my sushi.

Katsumi handed out a large paper bag, which I took and passed off to Larson. When I turned back she had two large cups filled with sweet tea. I took those, too, and handed them over as well.

"Any chance you will let me pay this time?"

She waved a perfectly manicured hand in a shooing manner. The nails on it were about three inches long, painted blood red, and I knew could turn diamond hard and razor sharp.

"You pay for it by promising to come visit my father as soon as you can."

See, they never let me pay.

I used to feel bad about it, but the sushi is just too damn good not to come here. I promised I would visit soon and told her we were eating in the parking lot before leaving. Katsumi leaned out the window, the edge catching her dress as she bent at the waist, pulling the fabric even tighter. Those blood-red nails lightly touched the back of my head and my chin. Strength vibrated down those shapely arms as she pulled my face close and kissed me on the cheek, leaving a thick imprint of lipstick. I left it there as I pulled away. I would wipe it off after I parked.

I didn't want to insult Katsumi in any way.

Once the Comet was parked facing out into the lot with a brick wall to the rear I unbuckled my seat belt and took the bag from Larson. Inside were two beautifully painted wooden boxes. The black lacquer on them was broken by colorful paintings of feudal Japan. Samurais, geishas, and mythical creatures swirled across them in breathtaking designs. Both of them were hand painted and unique. Usually, the food comes in preformed plastic Bento boxes, but they always give me the fancy ones.

I have a whole collection of them at home.

Handing one to Larson, I opened mine on my lap. He watched warily as I slid the top open to reveal the contents. Inside, the box was divided into sections, each compartment containing different forms of sushi.

I love sushi.

The only kind I don't care for is octopus or squid. Both are too chewy for me. The sushi in the box on my lap was all of my favorites. Eel, salmon, and tuna arranged on tiny beds of rice. Also, a veggie tempura roll and a dragon roll. Opening the soy sauce, I poured it into the space provided for it and grabbed the chopsticks that were stuck in the side. They were lacquered black to match the box but sharpened on the end into fine points. I used them to pick up a portion of my favorite sushi from the box, dip it quickly into the soy sauce, and pop it into my mouth.

Delicious.

"What the hell was that you just ate?"

Swallowing, I looked over at Larson.

"It's a Southern Deacon Roll. It's tempura, which means 'fried.'" I held up another piece for his inspection. "It's a fried catfish sushi."

Maasakki Takakage had created the roll just for me. It was incredible. A lot like a tempura California roll, but with catfish instead of crab meat. Popping the piece into my mouth, I chewed and swallowed before speaking again.

"You should eat up. We have a long night ahead of us."

"You couldn't have just picked a burger joint?"

I picked up my sweet tea and took a sip of it. Larson was being pretty damn annoying.

"Look, slick. This is good food. Open your horizons a little. Plus, it's perfect for the night we have ahead of us. I doubt everything is going to go smoothly. This will give you plenty of protein in a package that won't sit heavy in your stomach." My chopsticks tapped the crucifix of the rosary hanging from the rearview mirror, making it sway to and fro. "Besides, it's Friday, which means no meat for us Catholics." I pointed at his box with the chopsticks in my hand. "So shut the hell up and give it a try."

Larson's mouth pulled tight into a line as he slid the lid off his box. He did what I had and opened the pack of soy sauce, emptying it into the space provided. He surprised me by using the chopsticks properly. Avoiding the Southern Deacon Roll, instead, he chose a piece of eel. Gingerly, he dipped it into the soy sauce like I did and then put it in his mouth. Slowly his jaw worked as he chewed it.

It took only a second or two for the surprise to show on his face as the flavor hit him. He swallowed and picked up another piece, this time the veggie tempura roll. He ate that piece without hesitation.

"This is actually good."

"Told you."

We ate in silence after that. When I was done, I put the empty box on the back seat and turned to look at Larson. My back was against the Comet's door and I had my sweet tea. He was about halfway done with his meal when I broke the silence.

"Tell me why you are hunting vampires."

The chopsticks in his hand closed over a piece of the Southern

Deacon Roll. He held it wavering over the soy sauce. It trembled on the end of two pieces of wood until he decided against dipping it. He popped it in his mouth and chewed thoughtfully. Taking a drink from his tea made his Adam's apple bob up and down. Blue eyes cut over to me and then back down to the box on his lap.

"I just think they are evil and somebody has to."

He didn't even *sound* convincing.

Taking my own sip of tea, I felt the sugar rush into my system. It was sweet enough to be syrup. My blood pressure rose slightly and I felt it tight in my temples. The Styrofoam cup squeaked when I lowered it.

"Bullshit," I said. "There are people who hunt them. People like me, not people like you." Again, those blue eyes cut over at the emphasis I made. "Something made you decide to get involved, even though you have no training to help you survive."

His eyes were back to staring at the box of food in his lap. "When I was in school I did a paper on folklore in ancient cultures, specifically on burial superstitions. My research led me to book called the *Morbius Manifesto*."

I had heard of this book. It was a subsection of the *Darkhault*, a book so full of evil and satanic knowledge that no one could pinpoint which occultist in the dark ages had spawned it. The *Darkhault* had been broken up into the subsections and kept separated by the Vatican so that its evil power couldn't be fully accessed.

I'd asked Father Mulcahy why the Church didn't just burn them, and he explained that some occult books actually have demons trapped in their pages, bound into the physical copy of the book and kept imprisoned for the safety of humankind. If they were burned, then the demons would be released to wreak havoc. The Vatican tried to keep them all secured, but being evil, demon-possessed books, the slippery bastards were always getting away.

My hand came up to pause Larson. "Wait, where did you read the *Morbius Manifesto*?"

Larson got that look that scholars get when dealing with the uneducated. You know that look, like the answer is so obvious they cannot even believe they are having a conversation with you. It's the same look teenagers perfect when dealing with anyone over the age of twenty-two.

"Online." The unspoken "duh" hung in the air.

See what I mean?

"From that you learned vampires were real?"

His head bobbed up, then down, and he continued eating. "I didn't believe it, of course. But the *Morbius Manifesto* did outline the characteristics of vampires, what one would look forward to if they were working with a vampire, and how to kill them if they got out of control."

That explained the crosses and the wooden stakes earlier. The *Morbius Manifesto* would have been written long before semiautomatics and silver ammo. But reading some old occult handbook wouldn't convince anyone vampires were *real*. Taking another sip of my sweet tea, I gestured at him with the cup.

"Tell me how you know they truly exist. You obviously had never met one until Varney's, and then you didn't know what she was."

Larson's ears burned bright red at this.

"What convinced you?"

"There was a newscast one night about an unsolved multiple homicide in South Georgia. Four people all died from having their throats 'cut.'" Larson made air quotes with his fingers here. "They showed crime scene footage, and the four people were just slaughtered. I don't even know how they showed the footage they did, except that there was so much blood it looked like an art exhibit. It didn't even look real."

His eyes glazed over as his mind took him back to that image he saw. I shifted and shook the ice in my cup. It was enough to bring his attention back to me. Motioning, I encouraged him to continue.

"In the midst of this footage I noticed that the bodies were surrounded by huge piles of dust, and the biggest pile had a wooden two-by-four that had been sharpened and driven into the floor." His eyes were wide as he looked at me. "In that moment, everything clicked, and I *knew* that book was true and vampires did exist."

"So *that's* when you decided to strap up some stakes and hunt the damned things?"

Larson flinched at the heat in my voice. I didn't give him time to respond.

"I can't tell you how incredibly stupid that was."

My hand swung his way. I wasn't going to hit him, I swear I wasn't, but he flinched again. My finger jabbed into his face, emphasizing my words.

"You are damn lucky some bloodsucker decided to use you to bait a trap for me instead of draining your blood *after* you led them to every person you ever loved so they could slaughter them in front of you."

The bag rustled in protest as I started gathering the trash from our dinner and shoving it inside.

Pale hands came up between me and Larson as if he were trying to shield himself from my anger. "I did more research before I went hunting."

The paper bag sailed over the back seat, narrowly missing his head in my anger. Now it wasn't just the sweet tea that had my blood pressure up. My voice was hard and cold even in my own ears.

"Research? You did some fucking research? You know that scene you saw on the news? The one that gave you your 'revelation' about vampires?"

It was my turn to air quote. Larson shrank back against the door from my bunny-eared fingers.

"Let me tell you something that the news left out, slick. I hunted that kiss of vampires for three damn nights. They killed that family slowly. The entire time they drank from one of the family, they made the others watch them do it. Every member of that family was tortured because vampires like the spice of fear in their food. Once I got there that family was lucky to have died after what they went through."

My hand grabbed the edge of my shirt and pulled it up to my chest. On the right side of my stomach, just past the words tattooed there, is a fist-sized knot of scar tissue. It sat fat and slick in my skin.

Grabbing his arm, I pushed his hand against it. I couldn't feel anything on the actual scar tissue, but his fingertips were cold and moist on the skin around it. The bones in his hand moved as I ground his palm into the scar tissue so he could feel its rough texture and hardness. His eyes darted from his hand to my face and back again. Sweat beaded along his eyebrows and upper lip.

"Before I could kill them all, one of those bastards sunk their fangs into my side and tore this chunk out. I almost died dusting those satanic cocksuckers. Then I had to do the same thing to the family, who turned vampire while I tried to not bleed out."

In disgust, I shoved his hand away from my skin and turned to the steering wheel.

"That's *my* fucking research."

Flicking the key brought the engine roaring to life. I hit the volume to blast music into the car so I wouldn't have to hear him apologize. Dropping into gear, I launched the Comet out into the night like its namesake.

SEVEN

TURNING THE STEREO DOWN, I spoke to Larson, somewhat calmed down by the time we got close to the club, but my voice was still harsh. My throat, still tight from the rage I had swallowed. I wanted him to understand the ground rules for the night so he didn't try to bolt.

"All right, you stick with me. Don't get separated and don't speak. I will do the talking and you will keep quiet. If you have any questions, you keep them to yourself until we get back to the car. If it all goes to shit, get to the car. Clear?"

I saw him nod out of the corner of my eye as I was pulling into the parking lot for Helletog. It was a massive building made up of a series of cubes stacked one on another. Neon screamed the name of the club out into the night and traced along the top of the roof. Leave it to a vampire to name his nightclub a Chaldean word for demonspeak.

The whole building squatted on the parking lot like a gargoyle. That's not just a descriptive turn-of-phrase, gargoyles really do squat when they are not in motion. If you can get them to stop moving for even a second they drop to their haunches. Make them stop for long enough and they solidify into stone.

We drove slowly through the rows of cars until I found a spot where I could point the nose of the Comet toward the exit. The lot took up about half a square mile and was surrounded by a ten-foot chain-link fence. Cars huddled up next to the mass of the club itself like chicks under a hen, but the asphalt lot stretched out empty and wide around them. The Comet slid into the opening smooth as silk. I killed the ignition and reached into the back seat to get my coat.

It was a real version of what Larson had on earlier, a lightweight leather city jacket that hit me about knee length. Pulling it on in the car was awkward, but I hate driving in a coat, which is why it was in the back seat. However, I did need the coverage to hide my weapons.

The CZ rode under my left arm in a shoulder holster and my backup Taurus .44 in a lower back holster set for left-hand draw like always, my standard carry set up. I'd added a Benelli pump action .12 gauge shotgun in a modified thigh holster on my right thigh. The Benelli had been cut down and sported a pistol grip, so it was short enough that the coat would hide it as long as I paid attention and did not break concealment. The custom holster for it held the shotgun in a spring steel clamp so I could tear it off and use it in a flash.

An ASP extendable baton rode in a pocket on the shotgun holster, held in place by Velcro. Collapsed to eleven inches, it fit just fine beside the shotgun, but extended it was a thirty-one-inch steel rod. Inside each boot were knives, two matching stilettos with eight-inch blades that had silver wire hammered into them. My St. Benedict cross hanging beside the St. Michael medal around my neck, blessed rosary in my pocket, and I was loaded for vampire.

Larson's hand on my arm was feather light. "What kind of plan do you have?"

"We go in, ask for this Gregorios guy. We talk to him and see what he knows about the attack. If he won't talk, or tries to lie to us, then I begin hitting him in the face until he does." Sarcastic, but this was about my normal plan for getting information.

"Are you planning on killing him?"

I turned and looked at him to see if he was being serious. By the look on his face, he was.

"When dealing with vampires it is usually for the best. You don't go fucking with them unless you plan to take them out. So, no, I don't *plan* on killing him tonight, but it is a viable option I am keeping on the table."

"Why do you need so many guns if we are just getting information?"

I was growing a little tired of Larson. He had watched me load up, so he knew how much hardware I was carrying. He'd also been in that alley with me earlier, so he knew it was all justified, but still, he was acting like a civilian.

"First of all, someone is already gunning for my ass, so I'm making sure I'm ready for what they might do next. Remember how close things were in that alley when we met. Secondly, we are about to go knock some heads together at a club owned by a six-hundred-year-old vampire. There is a pretty good chance shit will get out of hand."

Light from the parking lot gleamed on his glasses as he fidgeted with them.

"Well, since you are dragging me into this, can I have a weapon too?"

Ah. Here was the reason for the twenty questions.

He had a point and it made me think better of him. I was making him go into what I knew would probably be a dangerous situation. For his own safety, he should have a way to defend himself. Would I give him a gun? Hell no. He was way too much of an amateur to trust with a firearm. Thankfully, there are a lot of ways to deal with vampires.

Opening the glove compartment, I pulled out a handful of rosaries and two plastic bottles of holy water. They were the sport drink kind with squeeze tops. I had an unlimited supply of holy water, blessed crosses, and rosaries thanks to Father Mulcahy. Handing them to Larson, I looked him dead in the eye.

"Listen to me. Put the holy water in your jacket pocket and the rosaries around your neck, under your shirt. Keep them hidden and do not pull them out until I give the word. Things gets scary, I don't give a damn, keep these hidden."

The last thing I needed was for it to get a little tense and Larson to panic and pull out a cross. That would make shit hit the fan quickly, just like it had earlier in the alleyway. I leaned in, getting close to stress my point.

"Maintain your cool, no matter what goes on here. Got it?"

Larson nodded and put the rosaries over his head. Pulling on the neck of his T-shirt, they slid under safely out of sight. He leaned over and put the holy water bottles in a pocket of his big coat.

Once he was settled, I gave him the nod and we got out of the car.

Night air blew cool around me, rustling across the back of my skull. My hands slid into the pockets and kept my jacket held closed so the wind didn't blow it open, breaking concealment.

Even I couldn't walk around openly displaying this much hardware.

I have all the applicable weapons permits, and have worked with the police enough that they look the other way when I do my job. Most of the time anyway. The monsters do a good job of hiding, but cops still run into the weird stuff if they are on the job any amount of time. If things got too bad for them, they had my number and they used it.

Assuming Larson was following, I turned and headed toward the club. We should be able to walk in, question our guy, get our answers, and hit the road.

Yep, it should be that simple.

Yeah, right.

Vampires always have a way of screwing up your plans.

EIGHT

MUSIC PULSED in the night air as we walked up the concrete slope leading to the club. *Thump-thump* house music with a frenetic electronica edge. I guess it was good to dance to if you were in a certain frame of mind, but it wasn't my cup of tea. My music has to have more than just bass to make me happy. I like bass and I even like electronic music at the right time, but I never was one for nightclubs like this.

Walking up to the door, we met the bouncer who was checking the IDs of people coming and going.

He was taller than me, which does not happen very often. I would have guessed him at 6'7", maybe 6'8". I was broader and heavier, but he wasn't a lightweight. There were enough muscles that you could tell he worked at it. How did I know he was the bouncer? He was dressed like a bouncer.

No matter where you go, bouncers all look like they shop at the same stores. Black jeans, black boots, and a black hoodie. White-blond hair was held back by a black beanie. I was a bouncer before; I am familiar with the uniform. Hell, most days I still wear the uniform.

As we walked up, he stopped slouching against the door and became alert. Even behind the sunglasses covering his eyes I could tell he was eyeing me up. I'm used to it. I look like trouble and I know that. I'm okay with it, I cultivate it.

We kept walking to the entrance with him eyeballing us, but he didn't say anything. No questions or comments, no request for an ID. Either he wasn't very good at this job, or the club didn't pay worth a damn. I hoped it was the latter; then everything would go smoother inside. People who work at clubs that don't pay much are usually there for the scene and don't take their job very seriously. It makes them not care enough to really question you or stop you from doing what needs to be done.

Inside the door the music went from a pulse on your skin to a fist that thumped you in the chest. It was so loud you couldn't even make out any sounds, just bass. The vibrations rode in the floor and up through the bones in my legs.

I *hate* clubs like this. The air hung heavy with the chemical smell of a fog machine that burned in my nose like medicine. The undercurrent scent was of humans packed tightly together. It was the sweaty, meaty smell of exertion, dancing, and desperation mixing sourly, then cut across with the medicinal copper tang of recreational drug use.

We entered the lobby, a small area just inside the door. To the left was a booth that had a girl taking money. Just past that was the actual entrance to the main room of the club and the dance floor. Another bouncer stood there with his back to us, framed in the double doorway. Light pulsed in time to the music in front of where he stood watching the dance floor. The girl waved us over to the booth with a smile on her face.

She was small, probably about 5'2" and slender. She had a cute pixie face, with big blue eyes, but the eyeliner around them was heavy and black, and her full lips were painted dark crimson that looked almost black in the dim lighting. Thick hair had been straightened to within an inch of its life and dyed black with blue highlights.

She wore a threadbare Patty Smith t-shirt that looked less vintage and more hand-me-down, either bought second-hand or given to her by someone who bought it new decades ago. A narrow black collar with small silver spikes and a steel ring hanging from it circled a slender neck. The same kind of bondage belt slung around hips swathed in an extremely short black-and-pink plaid skirt, below which were fishnet stockings more holes than net. From the knee down she had the same boots as Larson, all black straps and silver buckles.

The chain attaching my wallet to my belt slid through my fingers smoothly as I pulled it out to pay the cover. She motioned for me to lean over. I did and turned my ear to her so I could hear what she was saying. Her hand cupped my ear, lips next to my head. Warm breath brushed my skin when she spoke.

"Are you here for the bouncer job?"

Well, well, well, my night was looking up. Leaning close to return the favor, my fingers brushed thick hair back from her ear. It was heavy, but soft and luxurious. I softly touched the nape of her neck where the hair was fine and felt her shiver. As I put my mouth by her ear to speak, I caught her scent. Under the makeup and hair product, close to her skin, she smelled like honeysuckle in the rain. It was a sweet smell that made my head swim for a second. My voice dropped to a low purr before I could stop it.

"Yes, I'm here for the job. Who do I need to see?"

I felt her shiver again as she pulled back from me and my fingers slipped across her skin. She held up a delicate hand telling us to stay put and went around the side of the booth she was in. Larson and I both studied her as she moved past us. It was an easy job, watching that skirt flip in time to the sway of her hips. She may have been wearing Gothic combat boots, but she sashayed like she was in heels.

Walking over to the bouncer at the dance floor entrance, she had to touch him to get his attention. He was spellbound by the inside of the club where people were bouncing and swaying to the thump of the house music. See, low pay makes shitty bouncers. If you don't notice someone who looks like me in your nightclub, then you are not doing your job worth a damn.

Standing on her tiptoes to get close enough to be heard over the music, the girl said something to him. He shook his head violently, dismissing her with a flick of a chubby hand. Anger flared on the girl's face and her fist wrapped in his shirtfront.

Eyes wide, he leaned back in surprise. I couldn't hear what she said to him, but the snarl on her mouth showed that she meant it. A quick turn on her boot heel and she came back with him in tow.

Annoyance sat sourly on his face, but I could care less. I had his number as he looked me up and down with beady eyes. They were so far in the folds of his face they looked like tiny black dots. He was used to being the biggest, scariest guy in the room. He didn't have a muscular build; he was just big. A thick, square chest over a big barrel of a stomach with two beefy arms attached. Most people would look at him and be intimidated just because of his mass, but he was soft.

Mushy.

Not that he couldn't hurt you. He could, and he would. In fact, he would enjoy it. There was a sadist's gleam in his beady eyes, but at his core he was also a coward. The look on his face said he wasn't happy about the fact that I was bigger and scarier looking than him. He was just a bully. If I were actually here about a job, he and I would have issues. I knew by looking at him he became a bouncer just so he could beat people up. I would bet money that he got in a lot of fights, but I would also guarantee he never fought anyone even close to his own size.

How could I make such definitive statements?

Experience.

I worked as a bouncer for years when I was younger and dealt with dumbasses like him on a constant basis.

Taking her place at the booth, he dropped heavily on the stool she had used. Sullenly, he glared at me and ignored Larson. I gave him the dead eye back.

If the bouncer's pissy attitude bothered the girl, she didn't show it. Making a 'follow me' motion with her hand, she led us to a hallway beside the front counter. It was a pretty narrow hallway, dimly lit and covered floor to ceiling in posters and fliers for bands. I followed the girl with Larson close enough to me to be my shadow. As we walked down the hall, the brightly colored bits of paper desperately fluttered at us, hanging on to the wall usually by one sad staple or tack.

The farther we went, the more muffled the music became. The girl swayed down the dim hallway, hips moving with the careless grace of a dancer. Those hips led us to a door with the word OFFICE painted across it. Drawing up short, she turned to me. Her blue-toned hair feathered along her cheekbones and she fidgeted with her belt. When she spoke, she looked me in the eye and I heard her clearly over the far-distant music.

"You don't remember me, do you?"

Of all the things she could have said, I was not expecting that question. Looking at her, I concentrated on her face and eyes, and searched through my memory for any trace of recognition since I apparently knew her. My mind ran through all the girls associated with all the cases I had been involved with in the last five years, mentally comparing her with everyone I could bring to mind.

I came up with nothing.

In my defense, I had no idea where I would know her from. Hoping she would not be offended, I shrugged.

"Sorry, darling, no, I have no idea."

Her hands went to her belt and began to unbuckle it. The bondage rings on it jingled against the spikes sticking out beside them. Once it was unfastened she dropped it to the floor with a thud. Lifting her shirt with one hand, she pulled down the edge of her skirt an inch or two with the other to expose her hipbone.

On it was a small tattoo of a pink unicorn.

Ah, I didn't remember the tattoo, but it looked like my handiwork.

Before my life exploded, I was a tattoo artist. It's one of the reasons I have so many. No, I never tattooed on myself; that's just not something I was ever interested in. I always wanted to concentrate on dealing with the pain of getting it or doing a good job, not both.

Looking at the girl again, I adjusted her age in my head. She looked to be in her early twenties, but if I did her tattoo it was before I lost my family, and that was five years ago. She had to be in her late-twenties at least now because you cannot get tattooed in this state unless you are eighteen.

"This was my first tattoo. You did it at World Famous Tattoo."

Yep, World Famous was the name of my shop. Told you I never lacked confidence.

"I was nervous and a bit scared, but you were really nice to me. I love this tattoo."

Her big eyes got soft and a little sad. That tiny chin pointed out as her full lips turned down at the corners. Stepping closer to me, she put her hand on my arm. With the pressure of her touch I felt my heart get heavy. My chest grew tight. I knew what was coming next. Her hand slid down, fingertips lightly stopping on the wedding ring I still wore.

"I read about your family online. I am so very sorry for your loss."

Dammit, her eyes glistened with unshed tears. If she cried, I was sunk. Her sympathy would touch that raw spot left by the loss of my family and I would break down. Already I could feel the fist of pain in my chest pulsing. I couldn't do that.

Dammit, I could not break. I had a job to do. My chest tightened even more and heat filled my cheeks. Drawing in a deep breath to maintain my center, I took a tiny step back.

Instead of crying, she threw her arms around my neck and hugged me for all she was worth. My arms automatically went around her and both her feet were off the ground. I could either grab her or let her fall to the floor. She seemed to weigh nothing in my arms. A line of warmth stretched between us and one of her arms locked across my back as the other cradled the back of my neck. Her face was next to my ear when I heard her whisper again how sorry she was for me.

That was all it took.

My face grew swollen and tight around my eyes. I felt the tears fill up and spill down my cheeks. They ran hot and salty down my face. I always miss my wife and children, but this stranger's kindness and sympathy had touched a knot of the sorrow I held deep inside and let it loose. My throat thickened and my heart felt like a stone as I let the sorrow and loss roll through me. Small hands smoothed along my head, cool and soft against the flush of my pain. The weight of her in my arms was a comfort.

We stayed like that for a long minute as I cried and she clung to me, in a dim hallway in a vampire's nightclub, soothing whispers of comfort in my ear. If the monsters came for me at that moment, I would be dead.

Finally, with a deep, ragged breath of release, I pulled it together and lowered her to the ground. Glistening tears cut trails of mascara down her cheeks. Tracks of it led to stains on the collar on her shirt. Sniffing, she rubbed her eyes, smearing even more makeup. A bashful smile made her look young and innocent again. Wiping her palm on her blouse, she then held her hand out to me. Her palm was warm and moist against mine as we shook.

"My name is Tiffany, or Tiff, if you want."

Seeing her sweet smile helped me pull myself back together, to put my armor back in place. Reality came rolling in.

A vampire owned this place.

This was a nightclub owned by a vicious, evil predator. What the hell was this soft girl doing working here? This girl with her big eyes, her pink unicorn tattoo, her shy smile, and empathy was working for a monster. A monster that would drink the blood from her throat and steal the innocence from her heart if he could.

I thanked her for her compassion, and I meant it, but my mind was back on the job. No matter what else I did tonight, I was getting this girl the hell out of this club.

Tiff watched me intently, her hand still in mine. Standing hipshot and running her free hand through her hair, she parted her lips to say something. Larson cleared his throat. Color filled her. She swallowed whatever it was she was about to say. A quick glance toward Larson and her fingers trailed out of my grip.

Larson had the good sense to try and look nonchalant. Hands deep in the pockets of his coat and boots scraping the floor where he shuffled his feet, he looked embarrassed for interrupting. Tiff turned to the office door with a last look in my eyes.

Her tiny fist made a sharp knock on the door and she stuck her head in to say something. I saw her nod and then turn, waving us into the office. Larson and I walked in past her. A bashful smile, a touch on the arm from her as she left the room, and the door shut behind us.

Once closed it was absolutely silent on the other side of the door. It was worth noting that the room was soundproofed. That opened up a world of options for the evening. A soundproof room is your friend when you are up to violent ends.

The office was very nicely decorated, if a bit small. Framed photos of musicians covered pale blue walls. A modern black couch sat along the wall beside the door, and two matching leather chairs sat in front of a large oak desk.

The desk wasn't new. No, it looked to be almost as old as Gregorios claimed to be. Made of thick oak planks with thin metal filigree on the front-facing surfaces, it was a beautiful antique. It was also everything a desk should be. Heavy and imposing, it gave the illusion of strength. I am sure any musicians the club was screwing out of their cut from the door were suitably impressed.

Behind the desk, a wall-length aquarium gave the only light to the room, emanating a greenish blue glow. Shadows flitted through it as fish swam to and fro. They were all colorful and exotic and alien looking the way ocean fish can be.

Between the aquarium and the desk sat a man in a chair. He faced the aquarium, so all we could see was one arm out to the side of the chair back, holding a cigarette. The arm moved behind the chair and we heard the sound of inhaling and saw the exhale of the smoke move to the ceiling in a stream of gray. It disappeared in the dimness and then rolled back down as it hit the ceiling.

"Young Tiffany tells me you are here about the position we have to fill."

The voice was deep, rich, and accented. The office chair gave no sound as it spun to reveal the man before us. He looked just like the picture Kat had pulled up. Same hair, same sideburns and mustache, same dark eyes, same flair for the dramatic. A black silk tuxedo shirt with ruffles on top of leather pants and, I swear to God, thigh-high boots.

He gestured with a long-nailed hand.

"Please, have a seat."

His eyes were deep pools of black in the backlighting of the aquarium.

I took a deep breath through my nose. Musk from incense, some sharp, astringent cologne, the tang of saltwater from the aquarium, and cigarette smoke.

That's all I smelled.

He was good.

But he was no vampire.

He looked like a bloodsucker, but he wasn't. Vampires don't move like the rest of us. They are dead, and because of that they are either too still or too fast. Rarely do they act completely human. The man behind the desk didn't move right to be anything other than human, but the fact that he didn't smell like a vampire confirmed it.

"You are not Gregorios."

Sighing, he waved his hand. "And you are not here to work as a bouncer."

Leaning forward over the desk, he lit a candle with a long, slender lighter. It flared slowly to life, the orange light from it lending a predator gleam to those dark eyes.

I didn't know his name, but I knew his game. He was a renfield—a human familiar to Gregorios. Renfields share power with their vampire masters. Different vampires and different renfields have different abilities. He would be connected to Gregorios mystically, and by his appearance, he was also Gregorios's stalking horse—a daytime double to throw people off the vampire trail.

"No, I am not here for the job."

"Then please tell me why you have come to my place of business?"

Long fingers steepled in front of his face, dark eyes glittering in the candlelight. Sitting there, he was the personification of everything dark and sinister. I'm sure it made all the little Goth girls go all trembly in the loins, but it was doing jack for me.

Tiff popped in my mind and, instantly, my old friend anger swept through me in a flashfire.

My mind quickly stacked up possibilities on how to handle this. I didn't know if he and Gregorios were powerful enough to communicate mind-to-mind. I actually didn't know what abilities I might be up against. That thing inside me that let me feel vampires and other monsters was quiet, so I was confident they weren't telepathing at the moment, but that could change instantly.

Probably the wisest course of action would be to tread lightly until I could get a better handle on the situation.

Know exactly what I was up against.

Yep, I should definitely be cautious.

But where would the fun be in that?

Dropping myself heavily into the chair closest to me, I threw my feet up on the desk. My boots made a thud against the wood and my coat fell open, revealing the CZ and the shotgun. Adjusting my position with my elbows on the armrests, I slouched like I had not a care in the world, but my hand landed near the trigger of the shotgun strapped to my right thigh.

With my knee bent up like this, I could probably get a shot off through the holster without damaging my leg too much. The end of the barrel should be just past the front of my knee, so all the silver shot should clear me. There was a shell in the chamber, and at four feet away, the shotgun would pulverize his skull; but if you weren't paying attention, then you might not notice how ready I was to fire. If he pulled some metaphysical crap, or hell, pulled a gun from the desk drawer, I would shoot first and doctor my leg up later.

Priorities.

"I am here so you can explain to me why your master tried to kill me earlier tonight."

Whatever he thought I was going to say, that wasn't it. I watched his face change for just a second before he smoothed back into his act. He knew who I was, but he did not know about the attack on me earlier.

"Why would my master waste his time trying to kill you? You are no threat to him."

He took a drag off his cigarette and blew the smoke to the ceiling. He was going for nonchalant, but something was up.

I hate not knowing who I'm talking to. It really bothers me.

"What's your name, pal?"

"You can call me Gregorios. My master and I are one. To speak to me is to speak to him."

Pretentious bastard. Renfields never understand the truth of their situation. They tie themselves to a vampire, and in exchange they gain powers and abilities, plus some longer life, but they are bargaining with a creature they do not understand. It's like having a lion for a roommate. Yes, your house is safe, and yes, your neighbors fear you, but the day comes that the lion is hungry and you are not a roommate anymore.

All of a sudden, you are just lunch.

No matter how fond a vampire may be of a renfield, they will use them up. They don't care. Bloodsuckers are not human and do not have human emotions. If their renfield is killed, they are furious, but it's more a wounded pride than a sorrow over loss of a loved one. It's kind of like the anger you feel when someone scratches the paint on your new car. It is not the same as true sorrow.

Trust me, I know the pain of losing loved ones.

This guy had probably been with Gregorios for a long time—years, if not decades. But at the end of the day, he was a tool and a lackey. He was not and would never be equal to his master. He just did not see that he was replaceable. I sighed, pulling the air deep in my lungs and letting it out in a slow stream.

Delusions of grandeur are very tiring.

"All right, Greggie. You know who I am."

It was a statement, but I paused to get confirmation. He nodded to the affirmative.

"I leave you guys alone unless I have to."

Not entirely true, I kill them every chance I get, but that would be over-sharing.

"Tonight some vampires tried to kill me. Being the biggest player in town, your master is the likeliest candidate for being responsible, so here I am. I want information. If it wasn't him, then he needs to tell me who to go after. He's too big a fish in this pond not to know why something like this went down."

Twisting my foot to the left, it tapped against the phone on the desk. Vampires keep old technology like landlines in business.

"Call him in and I'll talk with him about it."

"My master is not here and would not come just because you called on him. He did not try to kill you; if he had, you would be dead."

See, there were those delusions of grandeur again.

"Why isn't he here? See, you *need* to start talking or I am going to assume that your master *did* order the hit on me and when it failed, he hit the bricks and left you here to take the fall."

I stood up and leaned over the desk. I know how big I am and I do use that to my advantage sometimes.

"Trust me, Greggie. You do *not* want me to start making assumptions."

Larson made a noise that sounded like he was trying to get my attention. I ignored him. I was busy, what could he need that I should stop paying attention to the renfield in front of me to find out what the wannabe behind me wanted?

The door to the office crashed open and there were the two bouncers from the entry to the club.

Ah, maybe that's what Larson was trying to get my attention for.

I had a moment to look over my shoulder to see them shoving Larson out of their way, moving toward me. He stumbled and crashed into the wall, slumping down to the floor in a daze.

My fingers curled as I grabbed the edge of the desk. Tension sang in my arms and shoulders as I heaved and flipped it toward Greggie. It was a heavy damn thing, probably weighing close to a thousand pounds. If I had tried to press it, I would not have been able to make it budge, but I just needed it over, and that was just a matter of leverage. With my height and size, I had leverage in spades.

The desk landed on Greggie's legs, knocking him and the chair he was in to the ground. It had the effect I wanted, he was pinned to the ground and I could deal with the bouncers.

I spun around to face them, my hand snatching the ASP from its pocket. A quick flick of my wrist and a loud *snickt!* extended the baton to thirty-one inches of hardened steel in my right hand. The ASP is a collapsible steel baton. It opens like magick and locks in place. Why did I grab the ASP and not either of my guns? Because I was now dealing with humans.

I really try to only kill monsters. The only thing I had on these two was the fact that they were human; besides that, I knew nothing about them, so I opted for relatively nonlethal force.

You can crack someone's skull with the ASP, but you have more control to avoid lethality. On the left was the one who was taller than me but thinner; on the right was the shorter but wider bouncer. They looked a little Mutt and Jeff, but these bozos could hurt someone.

I remembered their actions outside. The one on the left had picked up on what I was; the one on the right had just been pissy because I'm bigger than him. I assumed Lefty was the more dangerous of the pair because Pancho, the one on the right, was a bully. Bullies come with their own set of problems. They are usually sneaky and vicious if they do attack you.

The real danger I faced was that there were two of them.

Anytime you are outnumbered, you stand a good chance of losing the fight, especially if you are limiting yourself on what you will and will not do, like not killing anyone. That was my plan, not killing either of them, but I was holding the option open. The only solution was to take them out as quickly and as efficiently as possible. Which one to choose first, which one?

The decision was made for me as Lefty moved forward in a martial art stance and the bully Pancho stepped back. He was going to wait and let the other one get started before jumping in. He was a bully, but he wasn't stupid.

The tall one stepped forward and faked a front snap kick to get my attention, then moved into a fluid straight punch to my head. It was good. He was muscled enough to put a lot of force behind the punch and long-armed enough to make it difficult to avoid. I would bet he was hell on unruly club patrons.

His problem was that I am not a club patron.

I am stronger and faster than stock humans. Worst of all for him, I know how to use that strength and speed from years of martial art study.

Hurrah for full-contact combat karate.

My left arm came up to block the punch. Muscle and bone hit muscle and bone. Using what I was taught, I snaked my hand around his forearm, sliding to his wrist and clamping my fingers down on the bones.

Most of the time in a fight when you block, you simply knock the punch or kick away. I was taught trapping. Someone extends a limb to you in a punch or kick, you grab it and take it from them.

Let me get my hands on you and you're fucked.

Grinding the bones in his wrist with my left hand, I twisted, using my mass to pull him forward. I was strong enough to jerk him off balance and into my body. My left hand had his right arm and it was pressed across my chest. I threw my right elbow into his face and it caught him flush on cheek below his eye. Bone-to-bone contact hurts. His head whipped to the right and I smashed my elbow into the side of his face again. It connected with the cluster of nerves in the side of his jaw and I felt his knees go. His body slid down mine and he fell into a boneless puddle.

Out cold.

I let go of him as he fell, stepping over his body and turning on my heel. Using my own momentum, I whipped the ASP into the neck of the other bouncer who was coming up behind me, knife in hand. The steel rod sounded loudly as it smacked into the side of his neck and drove him to his knees. The blade sailed from his hand and skittered across the floor under the couch.

Chubby hands flew to the side of his neck. Stepping around him, I swung the ASP into his exposed side, just below his ribcage. Breath flew from his lungs with a grunt. He collapsed on the floor gasping for air, his face turning purple. I leaned out the office door to check if the hallway was clear. It was. Apparently these were the only two bouncers coming to help Greggie. Two bouncers for a club this size? No wonder they were looking for help.

Stepping back into the office, I closed the door. Now all I could hear was the gurgle of the fish tank, the gasps of the Pancho, and Greggie cursing me from under the desk that pinned him to the floor. Another smell joined the others in the room, the ammonia stench of urine from where the bully pissed himself.

What a tough guy.

Larson had been thrown to the ground and was getting back to his feet, scrambling to avoid the spreading puddle the bully was laying in. Greggie was trying to move the desk off of himself and was still cursing me. Wires trailed from one of the feet of the desk, probably from the button Greggie pushed to call in the bouncers. Stepping over, I put my foot on the desk. Leaning my considerable weight on it caused him to stop moving.

His face had gone white as a sheet and sweat stood like crystal beads across his brow. I would bet he had a broken bone under that desk. Everybody gets the same sick look on their face when they break a bone. It hurts in a completely new way, driving nausea through your guts, making you feel like you will puke your asshole up through your throat.

I felt him reach out to his master mind-to-mind. It's hard to explain, but that thing inside me that recognizes magick felt the brush of it. It was as if there were moths beating their wings against the inside of my head.

I leaned harder on the desk.

Greggie paled to the color of wet paper and the moths ceased. He turned his head and vomited bile from his mouth, missing his chest but covering one shoulder and soaking into his long, black hair. I was right about the broken bone, that's the only thing that makes you react the way he was. The pain of applying pressure on it had cut his concentration and prevented him from making the connection with his master.

I spoke to Larson without turning my attention from Greggie.

"Go ask Tiff if they have any rope or anything we can use to tie these three up so we don't have to worry about them."

He moved to the door without question. I heard it open, the music blared in, and then it closed and we were back to the quiet of the office. I looked down at Greggie; he had stopped cursing me and now just glared as oily sweat dripped into his eyes.

"Soooo…" I said, drawing the word out in sarcasm. "We should revisit the conversation we were having earlier. Before you invited these two for company. Where can I find the real Gregorios to ask him some questions?"

He glared at me more. His long black hair swirled in disarray around his head and stuck to his face with sweat and vomit. His lips pulled tight in a line of refusal.

I leaned on the desk again.

Dark eyes rolled back in his head and sweat broke on his forehead into rivulets that ran down the waxy skin. A small, pitiful moan slipped through his lips. His pupils were tiny dots when his eyes opened. They jittered around with pain. When he finally focused on my face, I looked the question at him.

The door behind me opened and closed quickly; the music flared and died. I spun around, ASP still in my hand and ready at my side.

It was just Larson.

He held a long orange extension cord, a roll of gray duct tape, and a pair of chrome handcuffs in his hands.

He didn't flinch when I turned on him, so I guess he was getting used to this kind of thing. I looked at the stuff in his hands.

"Okay, the duct tape and extension cord I can see, but where the hell did you find a pair of handcuffs?"

He actually blushed a little.

"They belong to Tiffany. She wanted to know what we needed them for, but I convinced her to stay where she was instead of coming back here."

"Good job."

I took the duct tape and started using it to secure the two bouncers, careful to avoid the puddle of piss around the bully.

"She doesn't need to be involved in this, but we are not leaving her here when we go."

He nodded, and stood holding the handcuffs and extension cord.

He had actually done well at getting the stuff. Duct tape, properly applied, is plenty strong enough to hold a normal human. Most renfields, however, share some of their master's strength and it would not be enough to hold Greggie. The extension cord, because it's a bunch of wire bound together, is extremely strong. It and the handcuffs should be more than enough to secure Greggie. It made me wonder if Larson had gotten lucky, or if maybe, just maybe, he was figuring out what we were up against.

After the two bouncers were bound and gagged, I grabbed the desk and moved it off of Greggie. With the desk out of the way I could see that his femur was indeed broken. The break formed a strange lump on his thigh, the bone sticking up at a weird angle.

Compound fractures are one of the worst ways to break a bone. Being a renfield it had the same pain level as it would for a normal human, but he should heal much faster. Fast enough not to need a hospital if the break was stabilized.

Greggie was a bit of a quandary for me. I have killed renfields in the past. Usually they are evil on their own, and that is why they are tied to a vampire to start with. Unfortunately, I didn't know Greggie well enough to say that. Renfields, no matter how connected they are to a vampire or how many powers and abilities they received from that, are still fundamentally human.

Again, I really do try not to kill humans.

Now, in my experience, if I killed his master, he stood a good chance of dying with him, especially if he was older than a human should live. Just like the age of a vampire catches up with their body once you kill them, the same thing happens to a renfield. If he was not older than he should be, then he might die from the psychic shock of his master's death.

But those were all could-happens, for now, he was human.

A strong, supernaturally powered human who was mystically tied to a blood-sucking fiend from hell and tried to take me out a minute ago, but human nonetheless.

I picked up one of the leather chairs and smashed it against the floor until it broke into pieces. Then taking the duct tape and two chair legs, I splinted his thigh to hold it steady. He tried to grab me once during the process, but some pressure on his leg and a good dose of glaring from me made him settle down. I picked up the chair he was in and then lifted him into it. He didn't weigh but about 120 pounds. Some quick work with the handcuffs and the extension cord and he was completely immobile in the chair.

Larson watched all of this quietly.

Once Greggie was in the chair and secure, I sat on the side of the overturned desk and pulled his chair over to me. The CZ came out. Again, a gun, naked in your hand, makes a nice threat.

"We need to come to an understanding. I want to talk to your master tonight. Dawn is coming and I do not have time to play around."

I tapped his broken leg with the barrel of the gun, making him flinch deeply.

"Now, here is the part you need to understand. I know I set your leg. I know I didn't pull out my gun earlier and cap those two bouncers on the floor. I know that these two facts might lead you to think that I won't kill you."

I leaned in so that our faces were an inch apart. His eyes were dilated to the max with pain, and those almost-black pupils locked on my eyes. Oily sweat stood out along his cheeks and forehead, and his breath ruffled my goatee.

I had his undivided attention.

"That would be a very bad assumption for you to make. Tell me where your master is and I will walk out of here with you alive. Refuse and I will shoot you in the face and then go door-to-door on Gregorios's other businesses. Your choice."

Leaning back, I crossed my arms, keeping the gun out.

"Now talk."

Greggie took a shaky breath.

"If I tell you, then you will simply go kill him."

"Only if he makes me."

The lie slipped from my mouth easily.

"You said he didn't try to have me killed, so I just want him to point me in the direction of who did."

He stared at me as if trying to see if I was telling the truth. My eyes were blank. Windows to my soul with the shades pulled down. After a moment, he dropped his head as if he were defeated.

"He has retreated to his brothel on Cheshire Bridge Road."

"Thank you."

I stood.

The moths began beating frantically against the inside of my head as he reached out for his master.

Damnit Greggie.

Spinning the CZ in my hand, I slammed the butt of it into his broken thigh. The moths blinked out of metaphysical existence. Greggie mewled like a hurt cat, a scream strangled in his throat, and then he passed out. His body slumped bonelessly, held upright against the orange extension cord.

"Why the hell did you do that?"

Larson was almost as pale as Greggie was and his voice shook like his hands.

"He was trying to contact his master metaphysically. The pain cut his concentration and stopped him."

I slipped the gun back inside my jacket.

"We need to go now, because I am sure if he wakes up he will call out to Gregorios, and I don't want that son of a bitch knowing we are coming. Cheshire Bridge is only about fifteen minutes away, so hopefully he'll stay out until then."

Larson reached around his neck and pulled out two of the blessed rosaries I had given him earlier. Slipping them over Greggie's head, he tucked them into the renfield's fancy shirt. I looked a question at him.

"If he wakes up, the holy object should keep him from using any vampire powers, which means he would not be able to contact his master as long as they are touching his skin," Larson said, looking at me. "Right?"

Made sense to me.

Actually, I should have thought of it myself.

I nodded my approval, adjusted my coat to cover my weapons, and we were off to a vampire whorehouse.

NINE

TURNING down Muddy Waters on the Comet's stereo, I looked over at Larson. We were zipping through the city streets, heading over to Southern Dolls, the vampire whorehouse. We had cleared the club of people by cutting the music and turning on the lights. Larson had suggested the fire alarm, but I nixed that plan. It would have brought the fire department and police to check on the club. With my plan, we just had to wait for the people who were completely stoned to realize they had to go. Tiff had been hustled out of Helletog and put in her own car.

I told her to go home and never come back, her job was done there. She looked at me with her big eyes and nodded without question. I also told her to go see Kat tomorrow about a job at Polecats.

If she could work at Helletog she could work at Polecats.

Anyway.

A call to Kat had garnered directions to Gregorios's place on Cheshire Bridge. She informed me that it was a vampire jack shack, stocked and manned by vampire chicks who serviced their clientele with sex and bloodletting. It also had a dungeon for customers with kinkier tastes. I told her about Tiff and ended the call.

"That was a good move back at the club, with the rosary. Thanks."

Larson glared at me.

His spoke and his voice was heated.

"Look, don't mock me. I know what you think about me. I thought once I could be what you are, but I know now that I'm not cut out for it." Thin, sparrow hands flitted around his duster, adjusting it out of nervous anger. "But just because I'm not some gigantic, gun-toting maniac doesn't mean I'm worthless." Turning to the window, he watched traffic and lights streak by in the nighttime. "I realize that I can't beat information out of people like you, but I do know a thing or two about vampires. I can help you until this godforsaken night is over."

He had a point. I had dismissed him and kept him with me only to figure out why he'd been chosen as bait. He had some knowledge, even if it wasn't from experience, and so far, he had not been the liability I had first thought. To be perfectly honest, even back in the attack in the alley, he had helped. Keeping those vampires off my back with his cross had turned the tide in our favor.

It was one of the reasons we'd made it out alive.

Well, shit.

"Okay, you're right. From here on out, I put you to work. You should be of help, but you still listen to me. You still do what I say, when I say it." I slowed the car and began looking for the entrance. "And you still don't get a gun."

Larson stared at me for a long moment. His head drifted up and down, nodding in agreement. I slowed the Comet as we came up on the jack shack. The big car bounced when we left asphalt and hit gravel pulling into the parking lot of the whorehouse.

A small muscle in my back gave a twinge of protest as I swung out of the car. I had pulled something at the club, probably tossing that big-ass desk over. It would only get worse as the night wore on, that's the way strained muscles are.

Reaching into my coat pocket, I pulled out some naproxen in a little pop cap bottle. I stood beside my door and dry swallowed six of them. They would help once they got in my system.

I fought through the bitter aftertaste, taking stock of the area and staying ready to drop back into the Comet if need be. Larson followed my lead and stayed next to his. The jack shack was a low, one-story cinderblock building with a flat, tarred roof. It had a few windows that were all painted black and covered by bars. The building itself was understated. Painted gray and with no decoration to indicate it was a business.

The sign was a big, lit box with the words SOUTHERN DOLLS on it. It cast a pink glow across the cars in the lot. I began walking around the car to the front of the building. Larson joined me. Gray gravel under our feet crunched with every step. I spoke to him low and from the corner of my mouth.

"Here's the plan. You are my backup. Go to the door, ring the buzzer. They will look at you on the camera and buzz you in. You open the door and hold it for a second. I'll be right behind you." I grabbed his arm to emphasize the next point. "Once we are inside, just go with the flow and keep your mouth shut. If we get separated, just play it cool. You can be nervous in here; first timers usually are, so they won't think anything about it, but do not panic. When shit goes off, you follow my lead and watch my back. Don't let anything or anyone sneak up behind me."

"How will I know when"—he made bunny ears with his fingers—"'*shit has gone off*'?"

My hand patted my shoulder where my pistol rode.

"Trust me, you'll know."

He nodded and I let go of him. I stood back out of the line of sight for the door camera. I definitely didn't want to be spotted this early. Larson stepped up to the door and pressed the buzzer. After about thirty seconds there was a beep and a click as the door was unlocked. Larson pulled it open wide and stepped out of the way. My coat brushed him as I swept by quickly and we went inside.

Once through the door there was a narrow hallway that was completely bare of decoration. It quickly ended into an open room with couches, chairs, and half-naked girls. There were five of them. All different types. All trying their damnedest to look human.

Blond, brunette, redhead, black, and Hispanic, apparently, they were trying to have something for everybody.

The blond was tall, leggy, and spray-tanned. She couldn't have been turned long because she had some tattoos and implants, both of which weren't something an older vampire would have. Her face wasn't bad, too heavy on the eye shadow, nearly so on the lipstick, with hair by White Rain. She was trying to go for the southern girl-next-door look by wearing the absolute smallest American flag bikini ever made. Either that or she shopped in some really slutty juniors' sections. Even her six-inch heeled stripper shoes had an American flag motif. She stuck out her hand, and before I shook it I checked to see if her nails had flags painted on them.

Nope, just red.

"Hey, y'all, welcome to Southern Dolls. I'm Blair, have y'all ever visited us before?"

I smiled at her southern accent. It was real. Maybe she genuinely was a southern girl before she died. Could be, Blair was an extremely southern name. I shook her cool hand. Vampires are always room temperature. Cool, but not so much that the average person could tell. I took my hand back as soon as I could, even a chick vampire is strong enough to pull an arm off if she wanted to.

"I've been here a long time ago, but this is my brother-in-law's first time." I grabbed Larson in a manly arm-across-the-shoulder hug. I plastered a big loose grin on my face and really started pushing my own southern accent.

It bothers me when I see southerners on TV portrayed as having a thick drawl and talking like they are not very bright. We do not talk like that. There are folks here with southern accents, yes, some really thick and heavy, but those folks are usually still intelligent.

Normally, I speak clearly and with little accent.

My southerness shows in the fact that I do use the term *y'all*, and when I am tired, drunk, or around others with heavy southern accents, my own comes out to play.

For Blair's sake, I was putting on a show of it.

"I figured since I'm getting married this weekend we should go out and live it up. Y'all treated me so good last time, I figured my buddy here needed a dose of your southern hospitality."

One perfectly cultivated blond eyebrow rose over Blair's crystal blue eyes.

"And should we treat your friend as well as we treated you last time?"

I laughed, playing along.

"Aw, we should start him off a little slower; as you can tell, he's a bit nervous. But if he enjoys himself, then by all means, give him the works, it's on me tonight."

I reached in my coat pocket for my credit card, careful to keep the guns all covered. No need to show a gun too early, it kind of kills a conversation.

Blair smiled and took the card in her long-nailed hand.

"Well, then, sugar, I'll just scamper on back and run this card for the basic while your friend picks one of us for company."

"Go ahead and run it for two, darlin', as long as you can be my pick."

A brilliant, nearly human smile flew over her shoulder. No way in hell did I want her behind us when it broke off. She was clearly in charge, and that meant she was probably the most dangerous one of the five.

It was bad enough I was going to leave three behind and one with Larson. Not knowing where Gregorios was in the building I still had no plan. Hell, for that matter, I didn't know for a fact that he was in the building at all. I felt pretty confident Greggie hadn't lied, but not 100%.

This could all pan out to be a bust.

Blair giggled and smiled as she turned her back and walked into a small room beside the one we were in, shaking her barely covered ass in the process.

"Go ahead and have your friend make his pick, I'll be out in a moment."

I watched her carefully. Dead or not, the girl knew how to walk.

Larson looked at me with a slight glare. I clapped him on the shoulder.

"Just pick whoever you like best, man. Don't worry about the cost, I've got it covered. It will all be all right as long as you remember the rules my sister gave you before we left."

I said the last in a light manner, but gave him plenty of eye contact so he would understand that I meant my rules. He stumbled a bit as I pushed him toward the four remaining vampires.

His face had gone completely bright red as he looked them over, from eyebrows down to his chin. I hoped he could tell they were vampires. I hoped the hindsight of knowing the vampire in Varney's was indeed a vampire would help him now. By the way he was acting, he didn't have much real-world experience with girls undead or alive.

Finally, he pointed to the brunette. She giggled and she wiggled as she held out her hand for him to join her. Looking her up and down, she was cute enough. Short and soft, but fine I guess. Her nearly black hair fell to her shoulders in a straight line, and her bangs stopped Bettie Page style an inch above eyes that were a bright green and surrounded by too much eyeliner. A round face had big, pouty lips slathered with bright red lipstick, and a straight nose finished her face. For an outfit, she wore a leopard-print corset that pushed her full breasts up under her chin, a tiny black miniskirt over very generous hips, and fishnet hose that ended in black patent stripper high heels.

It took a push on the shoulder from me to get Larson to take the step and take her hand. She led him away as he glanced back at me. Smiling, I waved him off. He was on his own for a minute or two, I had bigger vampires to fry.

Speaking of, Blair sashayed her way back next to me and handed me back my card. She was all smiles as she put her arm in mine. No, there were no flashing fangs. Vampire's canines extend before they feed, a lot like a cobra's fangs or, better yet, a cat's claws. Just before a vampire strikes, the muscles in their face and neck tighten and knot up to give them the most power available. This also makes their canines slide down and become longer and tilted back into their mouths, so that when they lock down on their victim, they have a death hold. If you tear a vampire off someone during a feeding, it will usually take a mouthful of flesh with it. That's what happened to my side to leave that fist-sized scar. Let me tell you, that was a crappy lesson on vampire anatomy right there.

Blair tugged on my arm and we walked the same way Larson and the brunette had gone.

The door we went through opened to another hallway. There were doors down one side of it with lights above them. Some of the lights were on, some were off. Years as a bouncer in my younger days let me know that this was how you could tell if a room was occupied.

All the doors looked the same. To the right of our entrance was a rack full of clothes and costumes for the girls. A nurse's outfit, a plaid skirt, and a catsuit hung limply on wire hangers like they had given up. The doors extended to the left. At the far left end of the hallway was a large set of double doors with iron bars on them.

Looked like the door to a dungeon to me.

"Which room do we go in?"

"Aw, sugar, any room with a light on will do."

She smiled and tilted her head as she looked up at me. Her eyes were wide and crystal blue. I knew then why she had been turned. She had the face of an innocent. Her eyes were wide and her features fine. She had the look of a china doll. All sweet southern charm and doe-eyed Dixie doll. However, from there down she was built like a pornographer's wet dream. The combination was intoxicating. Plainly put, she was a knockout. But Blair wasn't the newly dead, she was well in control of herself. The innocent act was just that, an act. That body was just bait set in a trap. No matter how many charms she had, they only masked the bloodlust in her vampiric heart.

I looked up and down the hall. The doors along it were cheap. Not a one of them different. They all had decent locks, but the doors themselves were cheap. If you look closely, you can always tell a cheap-ass door. They are made from a plain wood frame and covered with a thin eighth of an inch of Luan, which is strong but will splinter. You can spot them a mile away primarily because they soak paint up like a sponge and always have spots that look like the wood is showing through. The thing about those doors is they are no better than paper for protection. One kick from a normal guy and that door is coming down. That is, assuming he doesn't put his foot right through it and get stuck from the knee down.

Really, it's not as funny as it sounds when it happens to you.

The only door that was different was the one to the dungeon. It was made of metal. But it wasn't a cheap tin door, this was heavy-duty steel like the one on the back of Polecats. Over it was a light shining into the dim hall.

My brain, asshole-never-quiet-brain, tumbled over why they used the lights-on system to show when a room was empty. It seems more logical to turn the light on when someone was using the room, doesn't it? Most people, cops included, would assume that the people went into the room and flipped the light on to show they were there. By turning the lights off when someone was in the room, it might fool those who would make the same assumption.

Like cops who were raiding for prostitution.

An officer kicks open the door with the light on and everyone in the other rooms has a few seconds' warning. It wasn't foolproof, but it was pretty smart. In a police raid, when you are the criminal any little edge may help you get away.

Pulling Blair close to me, I leaned in to whisper in her ear. My lips brushed her neck and she smelled of a nice, expensive perfume.

And snakes.

Vampires always smell like snakes. I don't know why, they just do. Maybe it is the fangs. Her hair was soft as it brushed my cheek.

"This is my last fling before the big plunge." My lips actually touched her skin. "I'm feeling like being *really* bad. Let's do the dungeon. The light is on."

There was a blink, a tiny fraction of a moment, with her becoming motionless like only the dead can. It was less than a second, but she stiffened and her skin became like stone. In a breath it was over and her imitation of life flowed back into her like magick. She acted like she was breathing, and her skin became soft and pliable again. If I had been a normal guy or maybe not holding her so close, I would have missed it, but now I had what I needed.

If Gregorios was here, he was in that room, behind the metal door.

Now I just had to get in there without getting me or Larson killed in the process.

"I'm sorry, sugar, that room is not open right now; it's being remodeled."

She batted her long eyelashes at me. Sincerity glowed from her eyes. Yeah, right. Her voice dropped down to a throaty purr.

"If you want to spank my ass you can, though. I'll be as naughty as you want to make up for it."

To illustrate her offer, she turned and stuck her ass out, shaking it with an empty promise.

I did what I was supposed to do and lightly smacked her on it. Her skin felt almost alive under my hand. She squealed in mock pleasure and I laughed like a real customer would. We were both playing our parts, she just wasn't in on my act.

"Well, honey-child, if you mean that, let's get on with it. Any room will work, I don't care."

Grabbing my coat sleeve, she pulled me to a room. My mind was racing. I needed to figure out how to get rid of Blair, get in the dungeon, deal with a 600-year-old vampire and whoever he had guarding him, and keep Larson alive.

All before dawn.

Should be no problem for a big damn hero like myself.

Yeah, right.

TEN

BLAIR'S HEART-SHAPED ass moved in time to the bass line of the hip-hop thumping from a small stereo on a shelf in the room while I sat on a vinyl couch that smelled like sweat and disinfectant. The carpet in the room was blue indoor/outdoor, the paint on the walls gray and cheap. Beside the sagging couch sat a small table with lotion and Kleenex. The trash can underneath it was filled with crumpled tissues.

Hey, they don't call these places jack shacks for nothing.

I had slipped on my sunglasses so I could think without having to keep my attention on Blair. She danced, touching herself in time with the music. The swimsuit was long gone and crumpled in the corner. My mind raced, trying to figure out a way to either get away from Blair or make her help me without tipping off her master.

The walls were too thin for me to shoot her unless I had to. The big problem was I had no idea if Blair could do mind-to-mind communication with her master. If she could, then I would not be able to force her to help me.

Hell, even if she didn't have that ability, a scream from her would still bring vamps a-running. Then the gig would be up and I'd probably lose Gregorios.

The song had hit its last verse, I was going to have to do something or Blair was going to get suspicious.

She turned her back to me, ass still moving up and down to the beat of the music. I slid the ASP out as discreetly as I could. If she were anything but a vampire, I would use it to choke her to unconsciousness, but vampires don't need to breathe, so that option was off the table.

Keeping the ASP in the folds of my jacket, I slid down on the couch, putting my feet between her legs. She took the bait, thinking I was getting into her dance, and moved back so she was right over my lap. My right fist closed around the ASP and my left lightly smacked her ass, making a *pop* heard over the music.

Turning, she looked over her shoulder with a smile. My hand rubbed her where I smacked and she threw her head back in faked pleasure. Blond hair flew over her face, whipping back toward me. Leaning up, my left hand snaked into it. Her hair felt like thick and heavy silk between my fingers. I closed my fist, jerked her by the hair to the left, and used my outstretched feet to trip her. She lost her balance and I used my weight to ride her over onto the couch with me on her back.

She fought with all her vampire strength, but I had the advantage of leverage. Laying on her, I shoved her face into the couch and drew back my fist with the ASP. Using the ASP as a fist load will increase your damage potential by about 300%.

It makes a regular punch into a bone crusher.

My fist smashed into the back of her skull and it felt like I hit granite. Blair began to buck under me like she had been plugged into a live wire. I pounded her head as she bucked and fought and screamed into the couch. Finally, as my hand felt like it was going to break, she slumped loose and liquid against the couch.

I hit her a few more times to make sure she was good and out, and not faking it.

Slowly, fist still raised, I climbed off of her. It took me a minute to get my fingers out of her hair. The heavy locks of it were tangled in my fingers and sticky with black blood. The vampire didn't move the entire time.

Blair was out cold.

That sucked. Vampire or not, there is a something inside me that balks when I use violence on a woman. I will do it, and I get over it quickly, but it does go against my raising.

Unfortunately, I was going to have to leave her. I had nothing to bind her with and no way to kill her without her waking and raising bloody hell. I hated leaving her alive, but I didn't have a choice. Settling my jacket back over me, the ASP slid back into its holster.

Out came the shotgun.

The great thing about a shotgun is that the shell is just a shaped charge behind a payload. This means you can load a shotgun shell with a large variety of materials for a wide choice of applications. I pulled out some specialty shells and reloaded it. My first four rounds were loaded with Mini-Missiles. These were solid lead slugs with a steel core and a high charge. On impact, the lead peels away, driving the steel core forward and through to penetrate a hard surface.

It's used for lightly armored vehicles but also works just fine on steel doors.

The last four shells were Dragon's Breath, white phosphorus loads that ignited on being shot and created a 100-yard flamethrower for three seconds. Fire is always good against monsters. Few supernatural creatures are proof against fire.

Pretty much just demons, and dragons.

I wasn't planning on running into any of them tonight.

I hadn't figured out a way to sneak into the dungeon, so I was going in blasting. That was fine by me because at the end of the day, subtle is not really my thing. Given a choice, I usually opt for blowing a bunch of shit up and sorting it out later. They would know I was coming the second I tried the door, but I knew what Gregorios looked like, so anything in there that wasn't him was fair game.

Slowly, I opened the door to the room. Glancing right and then left proved the hall to be clear. I stepped out, pulling the door shut behind me. Ten long strides took me to the dungeon doors. Placing my feet apart to brace for the shotgun's recoil, I took aim and fired. The highly charged shells caused a huge kick that I let roll my arms back and then forward, jacking the slide to chamber another shell. Concussion from the muzzle rolled off the steel doors and blew back the flaps of my jacket. The top hinge of the left door peeled open like a banana.

Lining up the muzzle with the bottom hinge, I fired again. That hinge also exploded and the door sagged from the frame. I chose to shoot the hinges instead of the lock because if you don't completely destroy a high-quality lock, it will often still hold, and the lock side of a door is usually reinforced. People don't reinforce the side with the hinges very often. Kick in a few doors and you will find the hinges are the weak link of most of them.

Two more shots to the other door's hinges and they were hanging like two drunk friends trying to keep each other standing.

Shouts came from inside the doors, but I couldn't hear what they were saying or figure out how many monsters there were inside the dungeon. That's one thing about firing guns, especially shotguns, inside a building. It makes your hearing go to shit.

Leaning back, I balanced on one leg and threw the other at the center of the sagging doors. My foot met the disheveled doors and they crashed into the room. Shotgun ready, I stepped inside.

The dungeon had a Gothic-style waiting room. Black walls and blood-red drapes. The décor was faux Victorian and fetish leather. Candelabras and recessed fixtures provided dim lighting. Directly across from me, floor-to-ceiling drapes hung in a heavy crimson brocade, barricading the rest of the dungeon.

A flurry of cloth revealed two hulking vampires. They were muscle bound, their faces distended into predator mode. One of them wore black leather motorcycle clothing that looked like armor. Wicked steel spikes bristled from him, glistening in the candlelight.

Unfortunately for him, those spikes grabbed the red drape he had pushed aside. The heavy cloth wrapped around his arm like a trap. Jerking it like a fish on the line, he pulled the entire drape down onto him. Fabric fell over him, covering him like a net.

I used the opportunity to fire off the first Dragon's Breath shell I had. A huge lick of yellow flame and thick white smoke blasted from the end of the gun. The smoke made it hard to see, but the spiky vampire caught fire as the drape he was tangled in ignited. He flailed around, fanning the flames that ripped over him. Tongues of fire licked at him and began to burn with an intensity that cut through the haze. Phosphorus smoke and oily vampire soot began to fill the air, making my eyes water.

The second vampire scrambled away from his fallen companion. Turning to look at me, his jaw slung down in a howl of rage. Taloned hands came up as he launched himself at me, flying across the room. He was nearly my size and fast as hell.

He wore a similar getup as his partner, just minus the spikes. His face was distended, knotted with muscles as he tried to strike at me. His fangs were out, and spittle flew from them. Bulging eyes were shot through with blood, and ropes of veins stood out from his skin. He was a vampire at his most feral, all pretense of humanity stripped away, an animal, a monster.

I had just enough time to turn my shoulder to him as he slammed into me.

It felt like getting hit by a small car. The blow took me off my feet and drove the breath from my lungs. I managed to hold on to the shotgun, but just barely. Riding me to the ground, he grabbed my head, trying to force it to the side so he had a clear shot at the vein in my neck.

Taloned fingernails dug into the back of my skull. The pain was sharp and immediate, burning like only a scrape or scratch will, like there was a match lit in four places on the back of my skull. The only thing keeping him back was my big arm and shoulder. I wasn't holding him back, it was just in his way because it was trapped between us. While he lay on me, trying for my neck, I drove my knee into his ribs.

It connected solidly, lifting him up and off of me. Ribs caved under the blow, I felt them pop and sag into his chest cavity. They gave with enough movement I was sure that I had driven a bone or two into his lungs, but again, vampires don't have to breathe, so it didn't really help. He still slowly made progress to the vein in my neck.

I was in a bad position. He didn't care if he drank my blood before or after he broke my neck. I had to get him all the way off of me, because fighting to keep my head down while he pulled on it with that devilish strength had the muscles in my neck and jaw in full spasm. I would not be able to last much longer.

My other arm still had the shotgun, but it was pressed on the ground and I couldn't swing the gun to bear. I was out of options, so I did the only thing I could do. Driving my knee into his side again, I let go of the shotgun.

I hate letting go of my gun.

As he lifted up, I went for my cross. My fingers closed on the steel chain and yanked it out of my shirt. I pushed it hard against his cheek and the effect was immediate. My hand became outlined in white blue light as the cross flared to life. Heat grew where I pressed the blessed silver to vampire flesh. Against my hand I could feel the holy heat as discomfort, but the side pressed to vampire flesh smoked and sizzled. With a violent convulsion, the vampire flew off of me, headed to the ceiling.

My hand snagged the leather of his jacket and I clenched my fingers into a fist to hold him there. He wasn't touching the cross anymore, but the skin under his eye and down his jaw bubbled with blisters. A red and black cross-shaped hole had dissolved into his cheek, burnt there by contact. The cross still glowed its holy light, causing small sores to erupt on the vampire's skin where it fell. He jerked against my hold, trying to get away, but my grip held firm. German tanker boot met vampire knee. The joint gave with a wet pop and he slammed around to the ground.

I didn't try to stand up. Madly scrambling for the shotgun, I closed my free hand around its grip. Still holding the cross above him, I sat on his chest and shoved the short barrel of the gun into his mouth. Fangs cracked on the metal. His jaw distended like a snake's as I pushed the barrel farther in, causing the burnt flesh on his face to crack and some blisters to pop, running yellow fluid. There was bloodshot white completely surrounding his pupils as his eyes flew open in pain and fear.

"Go to Hell, fangface."

My finger squeezed the trigger. Recoil shuddered up my arm and I rolled off of him. The phosphorus load ran through his body, cutting trails of light through his skin. Bubbles formed on the surface, thinning as they expanded to pop, spitting molten flesh and sighing steam. Cracks ran across his torso and flames leaked through. With the smell of sulfur and spoiled bacon, he disintegrated before my eyes, crumbling into ash and dust.

Slowly, I rolled to my knees, crouching with the shotgun held steady. Reaching in my coat pocket, I pulled shotgun shells out and reloaded by feel. My neck ached from fighting with him. Twisting my head made the vertebrae pop into alignment with a satisfying sound, tension cracking out of the bones in my neck. It felt better immediately. My neck still hurt, but now I should be okay until I rested.

Once I rested, my muscles would stiffen up from lactic acid buildup. The scrapes on the back of my head burned like a son of a bitch. Carefully, I touched them and came away with blood on my fingertips. Worse, I felt that he had actually dug furrows of skin from the back of my head with his talons. I hoped he hadn't messed up my tattoo back there. Wiping my hand on my T-shirt, I stood to my feet. Fuck it. Do what needs to be done, worry about the pain later.

Priorities.

Speaking of, I still had to find the vampire I came here for. I started moving farther into the dungeon. The spiky vampire had revealed a dark hallway when he tore down the drape. My head swiveled left and right as I walked in, trying to see the danger I knew was in there.

It's a strange thing to walk into a room or area where you know for a fact there is something that wants to kill you and is waiting to do that very thing. You walk slower. Each step seems to take you only a few inches at a time. Every noise you can hear is magnified. Your heartbeat thuds in your chest and your breathing fills your ears.

Patterns in shadows seem to move on their own. You feel like you can't see all that is there.

All of which is true and a sensory illusion made by heightened fear and adrenaline.

This hallway was dark and had a fake stone surface on the walls. There were two doorways at the end: one on the left, one on the right. I had no idea which one to choose. I put the shotgun in its holster and drew the pistol from under my arm.

The room should be more confined, and Gregorios should be inside. I would need to be more precise with my shots, so I changed guns. Standing for a second, I flipped a coin in my mind as to which door I would take. I had decided tails, door on the left, when the decision was made for me.

The door on the left opened slowly. A huge, hairy shape ducked low to fit through the doorway. Its bullet-shaped head had thick, heavy brows. Covered in coarse black fur, wrinkled skin surrounded its beady eyes. It was a gorilla of gigantic proportions. A thick neck flowed into heavily muscled shoulders that attached long arms to a wide chest. Shuffling forward on thickly bowed legs, its enormous knuckled hands drug along the ground. It turned to face me and a roar tore from that throat. A mouth big enough to cover my head stretched wide to show yellow canines about the size of small daggers and just about as deadly. Even from ten feet away I felt hot breath wash over me from the force of its roar.

That thing inside of me that recognizes magick welled up. It curled through my body in response to this creature. That was bad news. It would be bad enough to be dealing with a gorilla, but my luck? My luck meant I was dealing with a Were-gorilla.

Hell's bells.

Normal gorillas are strong enough to tear a man limb from limb. Lycanthropes were insanely strong. Strong enough to tear steel. A Were-gorilla would be able to crush stone in his hands. Plus, he would be human smart.

Backing away, I kept the gun pointed at him. He roared again and shuffled forward. I had the same problem with him I'd had with

Greggie earlier. If this lycanthrope was being coerced by Gregorios's powers to attack me, then I didn't want to kill him. No matter what he looked like right now, he was essentially human. If he attacked me, all bets were off and I would put a cap in his ass; but for now, he was just threatening.

I lowered the gun slightly and raised my chin at him.

"Why are you working for a bloodsucking piece of shit?"

Yeah, it was obvious to ask, but still, I had to try.

"I know what you are, and I know you understand me. If you don't answer me, I will shoot you in the head."

The gun rose back level with his face, the laser dot focused on his eye, making him blink and move his head.

"All my bullets are silver, and you know what that means for your kind."

Silver hurts lycanthropes. They can absorb damage from regular bullets like it is nothing, but even a tiny amount of silver changes the odds to the damage being almost human level. Plus, if the silver stays in their system, it begins to poison their blood, setting up a violent allergic reaction.

The Were-gorilla shook his head and slammed his fist against his skull. His long arms wrapped around his body and his head threw back in a howl. It was a plaintive, desperate sound. Brown eyes turned back to me, staring past the gun I still had pointed at his head and looking into my own eyes. I watched his form began to change: coarse black hair thinned, his arms shortened, and his legs grew longer. He became a bit more human. It was fluid and fairly subtle. Gorillas look a lot like humans as it is, so his transition into a half man, half gorilla wasn't spectacular.

"His familiars are all simians. I don't have a choice. I have to kill you by his order." The voice was strange, not human. Partially because the throat and mouth were wrong, but also because he was struggling through what seemed to be a lot of pain. I wasn't surprised. Vampire powers are a bitch to fight against. They make your head feel like it going to explode and like your blood is going to boil in your veins. He was unfortunate that his form of lycanthropy made him susceptible to Gregorios's power.

Vampires sometimes have familiar animals, which means they have the ability to vampirically control that animal. Unfortunately for this guy, that extends to lycanthropes of the same strain. Were-gorillas are pretty rare, so I was sure Gregorios had been keeping this one for a while.

"If it weren't for him, would you attack me?"

That huge head shook sharply. A definitive *No*.

"Are you going to lose control soon?"

Again the head moved, this time up and down. Yes.

Black fur flowed back over his skin as his body shifted back to the mass of his animal form. Another roar shook the walls and vibrated against my skin.

"I'm sorry."

I meant it.

The bullet smashed into his knee, sending a gout of blood spurting against the wall beside him. The fur and flesh peeled away to reveal red muscle and off-white bone. The effect was immediate, and his bulk crashed to the floor. A loud, shrill scream from him made my eardrums vibrate. Flailing around in pain, a huge fist smacked the wall, leaving a hole.

His knee had become a ruin of blood and fur. Silver will kill a lycanthrope, and it damages like a normal bullet does to a human. He would heal the knee, but it would take a while. I hated to do it, but there was no choice.

Well, I did have a choice, I could have killed him.

Pulling a blessed rosary from my pocket, I stepped to him. As I got near, he swallowed his screaming in grunts of pain and his flailing had become shuddering convulsions. Fat rivers of tears streamed down his face, turning the fur on his cheeks into an inky darkness. Breath tore from his lungs like a ragged flag snapping in the wind. Carefully, I dropped the rosary around his neck. His fur ran with a shudder as the cross blocked Gregorios's powers.

"You're free now."

He nodded and rolled over toward the wall. His breathing was still uneven, sobs racking his chest, shaking his form, but I didn't have time to stop and nurse him. He was on his own. I had done all I could for him. Hopefully he would get somewhere to receive medical attention. I didn't think it would comfort him to know I was going to kill Gregorios.

Then again, after being a vampire's butt-monkey, it might have.

ELEVEN

THE ROOM the lycanthrope had come from was open but cluttered. The fake stone wall motif continued, but then what else would you expect from a dungeon? Paisley wallpaper? Low track lighting cast shadows around the room.

A kneeling bench sat on one side of the room. It was black leather and had a low cushion for someone to kneel on and lean over the higher bench portion. The bench had large eyebolts at each end that held chains and leather cuffs. A submissive would kneel and lean over the bench chained into place for the dominant to punish them.

Down the wall from that was a St. Andrew's Cross, a large X made of black painted wood. This also had eyebolts and chains ending in manacles to stretch the submissive in a standing position for punishment. The far wall had a rack that held canes and paddles of all sizes and shapes. The wall beside it was a smorgasbord of floggers, whips, crops, chains, and cuffs all on hooks. It was an S&M version of your grandfather's tool shed.

In the far right-hand corner sat a dark throne-like chair painted black and red. Metal studs traced all its edges. It was large and impressive. In front of it was a rug where the submissive could worship the dominant. There were more drapes on the walls in that red brocade material. Candle sconces added dim lighting that gleamed on the chains and oiled leather.

I didn't see any hiding places or doors for escaping. I didn't see Gregorios either. I knew he was there, somewhere. How did I know? I could feel the moths in my head again. He was calling his kiss, his group of vampires to his side. He was there, somewhere in the room.

And he was scared.

My arms were getting tired of holding my gun out but I still didn't see Gregorios anywhere. I needed to find him before any other vampires got there for backup. Unfortunately, the moths didn't act like a Geiger counter. It wasn't a hot or cold thing. I either felt them or I didn't. I knew he was in the room, but I couldn't use it to pinpoint his location.

I fired my gun into the drapes to the left of the throne. No movement or sound.

"Gregorios, come on out. You know you can't hide from me. I will find you."

I shot into the drapes on the other side. Same thing. Nothing.

"You can stop calling for help. All of your kiss is dead. I killed them just like I am going to kill you."

He didn't know that I was lying. The moths in my head blinked out of existence. Good, that shit was annoying.

I pointed my gun at the throne. It had to be the throne, there was nowhere else to hide. It was the only thing big enough for him to hide behind. I squeezed the trigger four times in rapid succession. Wood exploded from the back of the throne in a shower of splinters.

You would think vampires would avoid any wood they could.

Tensing, I waited for something to happen.

There was no movement or sound except the echo of the shots I had fired. Dread crept down my neck. I had never run into a vampire that could turn invisible. That didn't mean they didn't exist. If Gregorios was one, I was well and truly fucked.

Shit!

I spun around, pointing my gun in all directions, frantically looking for some sign of him, somewhere, anywhere. My chest had gone tight in a band and my skin prickled and crawled, waiting for him to be behind me. I'm good, but if a vampire gets the drop on me, it's over.

I'd be one dead-ass hombre if I got lucky and one dead-ass hombre if I didn't.

Taking a deep breath, I centered myself, pulling calm into my lungs. Panic would do me no good whatsoever. First things first, I swapped the clip in the CZ. I didn't know how many bullets were left, I hadn't been counting, but I'd shot a lot and I wanted a fresh clip.

As the clip slid home, I pushed that thing inside me, my power, out into the room.

If Gregorios was being invisible, then my power would feel it.

My power is a weird thing. I've had it since that angel I saved brought me from the brink of death with a transfusion of her essence. Since then, I have been able to tell when supernatural powers or magick have been used around me.

It's a strange thing that I have tried to get more comfortable with over the years. It feels like a feather-light blanket inside of me, and it curls and slides out of my body. You can't see it; hell, I can't see it either. It's a feeling, a sensation. It reacts in different ways to different supernatural shit. Like the moth thing, that's a response to some kind of mind-to-mind communication.

Anyway, my power shifted and pushed into the room and it found...nothing. I couldn't sense Gregorios anywhere. It meant that he was not using any vampiric power to hide, so where was the bastard?

It clicked.

Sometimes I forget just how unhuman vampires are. I knew exactly where the cold-blooded bastard was. My gaze turned up and sure enough, there he was, hanging on the ceiling. He was upside-down, fingers dug into the ceiling and holding himself with his own strength instead of vampire magick. The CZ tracked up as he screamed down at me, spittle flying off of his fangs.

The two shots I fired at him both missed as he launched himself at me. His outstretched hand hit my gun as he swooped up and landed beside me on his feet. An electric shock ran all the way up my arm. The CZ fired wide and stray as it was ripped from my hand. My right arm tingled, numb from the blow. It felt a lot like if you hit the wrong thing with an aluminum bat, a sensation like it had been electrocuted. Dead and weak, it hung by my side.

The vampire dropped to a crouch on his feet like a cat. He looked exactly like Greggie. Black hair flowed around him, his outfit a cross between Renaissance Faire and Goth club wear. He stood, staring at me with red, glowing eyes. A hiss rolled from his lips. His face and neck were knotted and distorted, fangs glistening in the low light.

Gregorios didn't stand there long. With a flash of vampire speed, he swiped a clawed hand at me. I ducked it clumsily and stumbled back a few feet. If he got hold of me, I would be done.

Lunging after me, he swung those long-nailed fingers again, trying to slash my flesh to ribbons. I shuffled back and snapped a kick to his shin. It connected solidly, driving his leg out from under him. Down he went, landing on all fours.

He was only down for a split second before he threw himself at me again. Clawed hands scratched wildly at the air as I sidestepped and kicked him in the stomach. My foot sank into his belly and lifted him up. He flipped in midair and landed on his back.

Scrambling away, he crouched, hissing and staring at me.

That is the one thing about vampires: They can't usually fight for shit. They are incredibly strong. They can pull a human limb from limb, and they are fast as lightning; but for all their strength and ability as advantage, most of them fight like schoolgirls.

Scratch that. I've seen some mean ass schoolgirls scrap.

See, vampires generally don't turn their victims. Being predators, they prey on the weak in society naturally—the homeless, the disenfranchised, the sick, and children. You know, people who are not going to put up too much of a fight, culling the herd of humanity like lions on the Serengeti.

Except the Serengeti needs lions. Humanity doesn't need vampires.

Every so often they will find one of their victims intriguing enough to make a new vampire. Now, this person is still a victim. Vampires, like muggers, will generally avoid a strong, confident person who looks like they will put up a fight. Then once they turn their victim, they create an incredibly powerful creature of the night. Because of this new gift of strength and speed, the new vampire gets overconfident, secure in its position as the top of the food chain. Vampires generally have no fighting skills whatsoever. They don't start with any and never take the time to learn them. Good thing, because if they did, they would be almost unstoppable.

It's one of the few reasons humans can survive. That, fast breeding, and sunlight.

I shook out my right hand. Feeling began creeping back in with pins and needles. Gregorios rose from his crouch. His hair was wild, alternately plastered to his skin with sweat and sticking out in all directions from static, and his eyes glowed red with vampiric energy. He tensed, drawing in his physical power to attack me again.

My left hand came out from behind me with the Taurus .44 Bulldog. It's not a very big gun, and in my hand it looks positively dainty. My fist is bigger than the whole gun is. But it holds five bullets, and .44 Magnums are powerful.

Extremely powerful.

It's a close-range gun; the one-inch barrel means you have shit for accuracy over about ten yards. But as I said before, it is dead reliable. It will fire every time I pull the trigger, and I did pull the trigger, twice, and put two .44 caliber silver bullets into Gregorios's stomach.

My ears closed again from the thunder of the bullets. Warm air from the concussion of the bullets leaving the barrel washed over me. Gregorios bent at the waist like he had been hit by a baseball bat. The two slugs exploded out of his back in a spray of black blood and gore.

.44 caliber Orion Outfitter bullets, in like a penny, out like a pizza.

Silver coating made them work on a vampire like they work on a human, and from just a few feet away they took their phosphorus load with them. Gregorios sank to his knees, arms crossed over his midsection. He was 600 years old and even now, even with all that damage, he wouldn't die from it. But it hurt like hell, I just knew it did. Striding over, I snatched a handful of his hair and leaned in close to his face.

"Tell me why you tried to have me killed earlier tonight."

His eyes rolled up at me, the red bleeding out of them from the pain he was in. His skin glistened, slick with sweat that beaded like melting wax.

"I did nothing to you."

The voice was everything you expected it to be. Thickly accented, deep, and smooth as buttermilk even through his pain. The accent wasn't familiar, something European and old country, deep and scary. Well, it would have been scary if it weren't for the thread of pain running through it, raising its pitch sharply.

My voice stayed even. Dull and cold with a lack of emotion.

"If you didn't try to have me killed, then tell me who did."

"I will tell you nothing."

My left hand slammed the butt of the Taurus between his eyes. Purple washed across the bridge of his nose, the bruise florid against his waxy skin.

"Wrong answer, asshole."

He gave no resistance as I drug him over to the St. Andrew's cross that was on the far wall. If he hadn't been so severely wounded, nearly disemboweled by the .44s, then the chains I clamped on him wouldn't stand a chance of holding him, but he was, so they would do.

I had just finished fastening the last cuff when a racket rolled in from the hallway, getting louder as it moved toward the room. It was a cacophony of noise—hissing, screaming, and high-pitched howling.

Picking up the CZ where it fell, I turned to the door to meet the rest of the kiss.

The noise got louder and louder as it got closer and closer. A light from the hallway grew brighter and brighter. The noises were worse. Whatever was making it was right outside of the room. I could hear nails scratching the walls outside in the hallway. The hissing sounded wet, sliding through the air; the howls were ear piercing. Popping in a new clip, I released the slide and pointed my gun at the door, shoulders tense.

Larson stumbled backward into the room.

He held up his cross and it shone like a star. Following him were three of the vampire girls from the lobby. The hissing became deafening as they spilled into the doorway.

One of them spotted Gregorios chained to the X. She got the attention of her sisters and the hisses became screams. Their clawed hands flailed around them as they worked themselves up into a frenzy.

Larson, God bless his soul, stood his ground and kept them corralled in the doorway. Good thing, if they actually crossed the threshold, they would have the room to get around the glowing cross. The vampire he had gone off with was missing, so was Blair.

The three vampires were the redhead, the Hispanic girl, and the Black girl. She was tall, most of it legs, and her skin had turned a burnished copper color from a lack of sunlight. It lent her an otherworldly beauty, as if she were a statue, a piece of art. Her hair was natural, and her eyes a bright golden brown. Makeup had been expertly applied for her human face and now looked strange on her vampiric game face. She was worked up and her fangs extended finger-length in a heavily lipsticked mouth.

The Hispanic vampire was very petite and slender. There was no visible makeup on her face, and her long black hair had been cut in a blunt straight cut, bangs thick over her large hazel eyes. She looked young, maybe thirteen when she was killed. She was dressed young also, in a schoolgirl's uniform that was a fetishist's dream, made of skintight vinyl that clung to her every line and plane.

She should have been the least scary of the three because she was the smallest, but it was just the opposite.

Children who are vampires are downright spooky. Vampires are against the laws of nature anyway, adding to that the perversion of childhood innocence being destroyed, and she was disturbing on a far deeper level than her sisters.

The redhead was fucking luminous.

I didn't know when she had been turned, but it had been a while. Decades or more of no exposure to ultraviolet light had made her pale skin glow and shine. She was almost translucent. I could see the faint blue lines of veins under her skin. Her red hair stood on end as if she were in a windstorm, the tresses whipping back and forth like snakes plugged into a light socket.

That one had some power of her own. Her bright green eyes glowed with unholy energy, and I felt it humming in the air.

I didn't know what it was, but her power felt hot, like fire. It was aimed at Larson and not me. Luckily for him, he had the cross to keep it from affecting him too much. The strength of it felt like it would have made his blood boil in his veins. She had on a black sheath dress, split way above a generous hip, flashing thigh and more as she leapt back and forth in her black spike heels.

Larson held the cross high, standing his ground, but he didn't look good. Maybe it was the redhead's power spilling around the safety of the cross, maybe it was the screams of the three—shrill, blood-curdling screams that grated on your nerve endings like sandpaper.

Maybe he was just tired. He had held them off all the way down the hallway and into the dungeon with only a cross. He had done better than I would have thought, but that didn't matter now. I could see him faltering, his strength waning. If he dropped the cross or stumbled, they would be on him like a pack of rabid jackals.

He'd done what I had asked, he had kept them from coming up behind me. Puny Larson had held the monsters at bay and it was time for me to relieve him.

I'd had enough of their damned screeching anyway.

Pointing my gun in their direction, I sighted down my arm and along the line of the laser. The world narrowed to just them, the end of the barrel, and the red dot. Whistling loudly, I got their attention. They turned as one and snarled in my direction. My lungs filled with more calming air.

"Shut..."

BANG!

A squeeze of the trigger and the Hispanic vampire's brains flew over her sisters and her body slumped to the ground.

"...the hell..."

BANG!

Another squeeze and the redhead flipped back to the doorway as the bullet took her in the cheek, turning her into a red mess inside her red hair.

"...up." *BANG!*

The Black girl's eyes were wide when the third slug went between them, taking with it the burden of the back of her head.

Stepping around Larson, I delivered three more shots, the bullets ripping holes in the chests of the corpses where the heart was. With the heart shots, each vampiress exploded into dust. If you leave a vampire you shot just in the head to heal, then you could wind up with a mindless, rampaging killing machine. I definitely didn't need three of those.

Gregorios screamed an animal cry of pain and despair. He began thrashing around on the St. Andrew's cross. Spittle flew from his mouth and he gnashed his fangs together chewing air. Long hair whipped around his face, strands of it getting stuck in tears of blood that ran down his cheeks.

"They were mine! I created all of them and I will kill you for what you have done! I'll have your blood! Your death will be mine!"

Gregorios kept ranting and screaming and thrashing. His voice climbing into a shrill scream that rivaled the hell-bitches I had just put down. That once-handsome face stripped away into a bestial mask, all pretense of humanity vanished in anger and pain. His power roared out, filling the room, compressing the air around us.

It wasn't specified or aimed at anyone, it just *was*. He was 600 years old, and that was a lot of power to unleash. It pressed on the skin like hot matches, but it had weight like snaps from a whip. It should have been frightening.

Hell, it should have been bone-chilling, heart-stoppingly terrifying beyond belief.

I didn't fucking care.

I wasn't scared or even angry.

God, this had been a long fucking night.

I was simply tired, bone tired, down-in-my-marrow tired. I

wanted nothing more at that moment than to shoot him in the head and be done with it, but I had to know for sure if he had been the one behind the attempt on my life. If Gregorios hadn't set me up, then I didn't know I could relax. If I assumed and relaxed, I might not see the next time coming.

Flipping the CZ over in my hand, I held it gripping the barrel. As I walked over to Gregorios, my thumb flipped on the safety. Little tip, if you are going to pistol-whip someone, make sure the safety is on and never, ever, use the barrel.

Once, twice, three times I smashed the butt of the gun onto his face. The skin over his eyebrow and the bridge of his patrician nose split, shooting little droplets of blood over the handle of the pistol. It got his attention and stopped his screaming.

"Tell me why you set me up to be killed earlier tonight," I demanded.

The red swirled in his pupils with rage and he shook his head violently. That raw power of his still weighed heavily on my limbs, pushing me like gravity.

"I don't know what you are talking about."

He spat the words and glared at me with those red, red eyes. Blood dripped from his eyebrow onto his cheek and ran into the tears on his face.

"Tell me who you think might have done it, then."

He continued to glare at me. Damn, I was tired of hitting him in the face. I needed answers, and I am not opposed to violence, but I get no real joy out of it. If my world had never been destroyed by the monsters, I swear I would have been a nice, normal person. Really. If they had left me and mine alone, I would not be where I am today.

I'd probably be raising puppies and painting sunsets.

Setting my shoulders, I prepared myself to hit Gregorios again. My arm drew back like it had before. He didn't even flinch. He didn't hiss, or move at all. Then I felt it. A new power flowed into the room. It wasn't moths in my head this time, though.

It was bats.

The new power had the weight of the ocean to it. It smothered the power Gregorios had been dumping into the room, snuffing it out like a candle in the night wind. The rising tide of it threatened to crush every one of us in the room.

Gregorios's eyes grew bigger and his skin began to crawl before my eyes. You've heard the expression "make your skin crawl," but this was the real deal. The flesh on his neck and face rippled, moving like it had insects under it. Convulsing violently, he vomited black blood on his chest and then went as rigid as brittle steel. Dark eyes rolled back in his head and then closed. Lolling forward, his chin hit his blood-covered chest, and when his lids parted to look at me, Gregorios wasn't home anymore.

Someone else had joined the party.

Gregorios's eyes bled from a brown so dark it was almost black to a bright yellow, honey color. A color so bright they shone like there was a light inside his skull. Those sharp masculine features took on a softer feminine cast. They didn't change or morph besides relaxing, but his expression was now rawly feminine; delicate, haughty, and predatory. He looked at me like a woman would.

A woman with sin on her mind.

I took a step back and turned the pistol around in my grip.

"Who are you?"

Gregorios's head flipped back and he laughed. It was a throaty laugh that was also not masculine in the slightest. It was creepy as hell, but not manly in any way, shape, or form. The voice that slithered from his throat *purred* at me.

"I am Appollonia. Are you the infamous Deacon Chalk I have heard so many stories of?"

I knew I had found the vampire responsible for the hit on me.

That was not good. Newly made vampires can be controlled by their makers for a while. Gregorios was 600 years old and nothing, I mean nothing should have been able to control him. Hell, this wasn't even control, it was complete possession—subjugation of his body and personality.

"I take it you are the bloodsucker who tried to have me killed earlier tonight?"

I am nothing if not thorough.

Appollonia laughed again through Gregorios's throat.

"I see now I may have been too hasty in that. I hope you can find it in your heart to forgive me."

Those yellow eyes traveled from my face, down my body, to linger on my crotch.

"I am sure I can do *something* to earn your forgiveness."

The word *something* spilled from Gregorios's mouth like a dirty piece of candy, sweet and filthy. She sounded like a phone-sex operator.

From hell.

"No can do, sweetheart. There is no room for forgiveness where you are concerned. I will find you and kill you for trying."

No way in hell could I let this pass. If she didn't try again, word would get out and someone else would. I have killed too many monsters for someone not to want revenge. If word of any softness got out, I was a target from then on.

The smile on Gregorios's face was sly and playful.

"Oh, goody, do it now. I can give you directions, you can come now."

Appollonia arched the back of Gregorios's body that was still chained to the St. Andrew's cross. She thrust his chest out as if she were used to having breasts instead of pecs. I stepped away to keep her from brushing up against me.

"Oh no. I'll come when you least expect it. You will get no more warning than I had tonight, but trust me, I will see you soon."

Appollonia stared at my face. Gregorios's features still held that flirty smirk of hers. I know she didn't flinch when she dropped the bomb. I was staring in his eyes when she spoke again.

"We have your family."

Those words struck me like a fist in my chest. I took another step back and put my gun away. Turning, I found Larson staring at me. Still white from his earlier encounter with the three disco sisters of the undead, his freckles stood out like they were painted on his face. Wispy red hair was rumpled and there was a streak of something dark on his cheek. It could have been dirt, it could have been lipstick. Hell, it could have been blood. Crossing the distance between us put Gregorios/Appollonia at my back. His hands rose to rest on my chest.

"What are you doing, man? She has your family."

Concern radiated off him. He still had my back just like earlier.

"What are we going to do about it?"

My hand fell heavy on Larson's arm. It looked huge compared with his thin bicep. A layer of sweat and dirt covered his skin. Blue eyes were earnest and his thin red eyebrows stitched together in concern for me.

He just didn't get it.

Damn.

"I have no family, they were taken from me over five years ago."

I softened my voice but couldn't soften the blow.

"She's talking to you."

His eyes slid past me and looked at Appollonia in horror. The arm I held began trembling.

"What? I, I don't understand."

Appollonia's voice piped up over my shoulder.

"Let me clear it up for you, human. We have your mother and your sister. They are here with us. If Deacon does not come to me, then I will kill them."

I threw a glance over my shoulder. The smile on her face was evil. Pure and simple evil that was unrepentant. Child molester evil.

"It will not be fast. It will not be easy."

She sounded sultry. If she hadn't been casually talking about killing Larson's family, it would have sounded sexy. As it was, it sent chills down my spine.

Gripping Larson's arm, I squeezed it. He looked at me sharply. My voice was low, even though I knew the vampire could hear me.

"Hold it together. We will do what we need to do."

I let him go and turned to face Appollonia/Gregorios. She had his head tilted to the side, looking at me. Looking at me the way a cobra looks at a wounded sparrow on the ground.

"Tell me where to go."

"I can only share the information psychically. Have Larson," she paused with a small giggle, "or should I still call him Nyteblade?"

More giggling.

"Have him touch this vessel and I will insert the destination in his mind."

"First tell me how you knew to find me here. Was Gregorios your stalking horse all along?"

I was fishing for information. I needed to know just how far this bitch's power spread.

"Oh, I have been looking for Gregorios since he went into hiding. I felt his power flare and call out to me a few moments ago, so I came to fetch him."

Gregorios/Appollonia looked at me again. She licked his lips. It was really unnerving.

"Imagine my pleasure to look through his eyes and find you standing in front of him."

His eyes took on a darker tone; the gaze she gave me through them was heavy. It was full of promise and heat. The look was all bedroom.

"It was a *very* pleasing sight."

This vamped-out bitch was flirting with me, through the body of the male vampire she was possessing. Really? Could my night get any more messed up than this?

Knowing my luck, probably.

"Look, lady, if you wanted to ask me out for a date, you have a fucked-up way of doing it. Or were you just trying to get my attention earlier by sending your vampires to that alley?"

The voice from Gregorios's mouth trilled out a giggle.

"I was told you were a threat to my plans. Looking at you now, I am glad you survived." Gregorios's bottom lip pouted out. "Don't be cross with me."

"Cross? You tried to kill me earlier. Who told you I was a threat to you?"

"An old friend of yours. He knows you quite well. It was his plan that was played earlier. I stole it from his mind."

She cocked Gregorios's head to the side, making his hair fall, a tiny smile on his lips.

"Did you know that you have friends who have plans to kill you if you ever go evil? Does that make you sad?"

She had to be talking about another monster hunter. When you fight evil for a living you know that the worst thing that could go wrong is not that you die. No, the worst thing is that some Big Bad could take control and turn you into a monster. A danger. Someone to be put down. We are a wary bunch, but once you find a fellow monster hunter you can trust to back you up when things get scary, then you trust them to take you out if you ever get turned evil.

She had followed one of my friend's contingency plans for taking me off the game board. Weariness crashed on my shoulders. I wanted to be done with this. I waved my hand to Larson.

"Go touch him and let's get this over with. Stay away from the teeth and the hands."

Larson nodded and took a step over to Gregorios/Appollonia. He still held the cross from earlier. I snapped my fingers to get his attention and took it from him when he looked. However powerful Appollonia may be, she was still a vampire. She could not work through the protection of the cross.

His hand trembled as he reached out to touch Gregorios's chest. I moved close to him, at his back like I was protecting him. Just as his fingers closed in to skim the surface of Gregorios's silk shirt, I lightly brushed my hand on his shoulder, hopefully out of sight of Appollonia. I felt her power stab into him as she gave the location in his mind. It was thin and sharp, like a long needle. A quick, painful jab and it was over.

Larson jumped back like he had touched a hot stove. His back hit my arm and he scrambled away, wiping his face. Crimson smeared across his mouth and chin. Blood ran freely from his nose.

No, his nose was gushing.

Appollonia's smile on Gregorios's face brightened and fangs slid into view. His nostrils flared wide as she inhaled the scent of Larson's blood.

"Ahhhh, intoxicating."

My fingers closed on the heavy red drapes. They were made of a velveteen material. It took only one quick snatch to pull them from the wall. Larson caught it when I tossed it his way and began trying to staunch the flow from his nose. My attention swung back to the vampire chained to the X.

"All right, we'll be on our way to see you. Now, kindly fuck the fuck off."

Appollonia tilted Gregorios's head again. The smile was still there, but it wasn't a pleasant smile anymore.

"We have talked too long. I feel the press of dawn and you will not arrive before then. Come at sunset tonight."

Those cobra eyes locked back on me.

"If you come before the sun has left the sky, my renfield will kill the humans."

I shoved the cross I had taken from Larson into Gregorios's face. Appollonia hissed and threw his head back away from its glow. Steam rose from the skin on Gregorios's face as blisters formed. I leaned in close, locking eyes with the bitch.

"Listen to me. I'll come to you. I'll follow your rules. But…"

Anger pushed my power out from me and into those possessed eyes; something clicked between us and I knew she could feel it. My power pushed down that line and pressed against her.

"If they are not alive and unharmed when I arrive, then all bets are off and I will burn you to the ground and salt the earth behind me."

Anger made my power pulse through that connection.

"Are we clear?"

Appollonia hissed and then burst into laughter that echoed across the room and trailed off as she left. Gregorios lurched against the chains that held him. He hung limp, as if his bones were made of water. Sweat poured from his face and bloody tears ran thick down his cheeks, dodging and darting around the blisters from the cross.

If he wasn't a monster, I would have felt pity for him.

I spoke softly.

"Tell me about Appollonia. Who is she and what do you know about her?"

The 600-year-old vampire in front of me began sobbing. Great, heaving sobs that wracked his body and shook him in his chains. I had never seen something that could break a vampire of his age. He *was* broken, though. Fear rolled off of him like a stench. I snapped my fingers in his face.

"Gregorios, tell me about Appollonia."

He drew in a deep, quivering breath and rolled his eyes up to look at me. They were back to being an almost black–brown. The whites of them painted crimson with burst blood vessels instead of vampire powers.

"Don't you see?"

His voice strained and his eyes danced wildly in their sockets like two drunken sailors.

"We cannot resist her; she takes over and consumes you. She has become to us what we are to you!"

His voice got higher and higher as he strangled out the words.

"I can't, I can't be consumed by her! It would be torment!"

His voice cut off in a gurgle and Gregorios began sobbing again. It was pitiful. Fear of Appollonia and her power had broken him. That fear had destroyed the fragile balance that is a mind held by vampiric power far past when it should have died.

The barrel of the CZ made an impression on his forehead. His eyes crossed focusing on it, but they were glazed over and not seeing anything in this reality.

"Don't worry, I will keep her from consuming you."

He closed those fear-fevered eyes. I took a centering breath—in through my nose, out through my mouth.

I kept my word and pulled the trigger.

TWELVE

MY BRAIN WOULD NOT TURN off.

Inky blackness swirled on the edges of my consciousness. I was tired, exhausted actually, but I couldn't shut my brain down long enough to go under. It had been a long night. A really, long fucking night, and I had another one coming up at sunset. There were things I had to do before then, hours before, but sunset was when everything would go down.

I was in the safest place to be, my room at Polecats. Freshly showered, I lay on my futon on the floor. I took comfort in the way it molded to my body. The low whirr of the fan sent a cool breeze of air over my naked skin. A sheet tangled across my groin, not for modesty but more for comfort. Nothing else blocked the soft air from my body.

My eyes were closed, but that did not matter since the room was pitch-black anyway. It was an interior room with no windows and a towel under the door. The CZ lay on the floor beside the mattress, loaded with one in the chamber.

I really do sleep better with it there.

Rest.

I needed to rest. I needed sleep because I had to rescue Larson's family tonight. I still didn't know for sure why he was even involved. It appeared he really was just bait. Bait and leverage if I wasn't killed. He couldn't rescue his family. He didn't have the strength or the skill, but he wanted to. His anger when I told him we were not going from the brothel to the place in his head threw him into a fit.

I could understand why.

I know the feeling of helplessness when people you love are in danger and there is nothing you can do. I still remember the sounds coming over the phone. I still remember the sounds of my children crying and the wet sounds that ended...

ENOUGH!

I had to derail that train NOW!

I was too tired to think about my family. That was a road I could not go down. If I did, I would be worthless. I would be crippled.

The tears on my face dried in the air from the fan and I pushed my mind away from those memories.

After our argument in the car as to why we were doing what we were doing, I had to have Father Mulcahy put Larson somewhere he could not leave. He had the directions in his head like a messenger pigeon, and if he got out, I knew he would head to Appollonia. I needed him to find her, so he was under lock and key. Kat was working on finding something about her.

Gregorios was broken by Appollonia's possession, so I did not get as much information from him as I should have. I had actually felt a little pity for him. He was a vampire and so I put him down, but I had done it partially as a mercy.

Appollonia was a truly scary bitch if she had me feeling any sympathy for a creature like Gregorios.

And make no mistake about it, he was a monster. Kat had a full report of information about him when we got back. He hadn't seduced any of his kiss. His pleasure was finding a victim, terrorizing them, then drinking from them to enjoy the flavor all their fear gave the blood. If he really enjoyed the flavor, then he would turn them so he could continue in his fun.

This explained why his kiss was all female and why he had them working in a sex trade. His businesses were his hunting grounds, and all of them also filtered drugs to boost his income and victim availability. Being a vampire was enough to get him killed, but Gregorios had been a real piece of shit too.

Thoughts of Appollonia kept my mind racing also. Speaking to her through Gregorios had been bizarre in itself, but the tone of the conversation had me puzzled. The bitch actually flirted with me. I could not wrap my head around that. I mean, I am well aware when I am being flirted with, and Appollonia sounded genuine. Maybe she was trying to throw me off the fact that she had tried to have me killed.

Maybe, but it wouldn't work.

Hell no, it wouldn't.

The change in her tact had me wondering, though. There had to be a way I could turn it to my advantage. I didn't know enough about what was going on to formulate a real battle plan. That's okay, though, I have a hard time planning anyway. As I said, I am more of a "kill 'em all, let God sort it out" kind of guy. But if she really did mean her flirting it might give me even a slim edge tonight.

I have found in my time on this earth that while I do not appeal to every woman, I do appeal to some. Because my appearance is so polarizing, the women who like the way I look *really* like the way I look. There are women in this world who I just trip their trigger.

I'm not handsome.

Definitely not a pretty boy.

What I am, is much bigger than a normal man. At 6 foot 4 inches tall and topping the scales at 320 lbs. in my winter weight, I tower over almost everyone I meet. I keep in shape. I'm not a bodybuilder, but if you are going to kill monsters for a living, you cannot slack on the exercise.

The tattoos also do it for a lot of women. I am covered in tattoos. All kinds of tattoos. Both of my arms are sleeved, including my hands and knuckles. I have tattoos covering my chest, throat, and the back of my head, which I keep shaved. Chicks also really like the shaved head.

To sum up, I am a big, bald, tattooed, scary-looking dude, and that gets some women right in their naughty bits.

Maybe this applied to Appollonia. Yes, she was a bloodsucking, undead, soulless monster. But she had been a human woman once. Maybe she was attracted to guys like me.

If so, maybe it had some possibilities.

From what I could tell, she'd tried to kill me because I am a threat to her plans. I might never find out if that is the case, but now I didn't care. Things had changed. Tonight was going to be about getting Larson's family out alive.

I know vampires, and I didn't think we would be able to get them out unharmed. So alive would have to do.

I had doubts about even accomplishing that much.

Like I said, I know vampires. They are treacherous. They don't lie as bad as demons, but they are still untrustworthy. I had to work on the promise that they were alive because it was all I had. I knew I could count on the promise of their death if we arrived before sunset, but that was my only guarantee.

If Appollonia does not keep her word, though, I would burn her place to the ground with her in it.

And I would use Larson for the match.

THIRTEEN

MY DREAM WAS full of fire and blood and spiderwebs.

Dark and disjointed, I kept seeing Appollonia's eyes and hearing the voices of my family. Deeply unnerving. In the dream there was nothing to strike at, just a deepening dread that threatened to turn my bones into water. Softly, Appollonia's voice called my name and every nerve in my spine froze with fear.

Then she touched me.

My eyes popped opened. It took a second to realize that I had my gun in my hand and a woman pinned to my bed. Blinking away sleep, I looked down at the girl. Blue-black hair wildly framed a small, cute face. Her blue eyes were wide with fear, staring unblinkingly at me above her. Tiny white teeth bit into her full bottom lip, and her pixie chin trembled a little. She looked familiar and I worked to make my freshly awake mind place her.

She was familiar, but I didn't know her.

Who was she?

It took a second because the last time I had seen that face it was covered in thick makeup. It was Tiffany, or Tiff, if I preferred.

Pushing away, I scrambled off the mattress. Standing to put my back against the wall made it so I could see her and the open doorway.

Brightness from the hallway spilled onto the bed, framing Tiff in a box of light like a cage. She did not move and lay looking up at me, eyes still wide. I kept the gun pointing at her. Other than me and her, the room was empty. I didn't know what was going on and I wasn't taking any chances.

"What the hell are you doing here?"

Tiff looked at me. Her lips moved, but her voice didn't work. She swallowed and tried again. Her voice was high pitched with nervousness and her words tumbled out in a rush.

"I came by for the job like you said last night. Kat gave me to the priest to start work. They were both really busy and I don't think they knew what to do with me so when the priest told me to go get paper towels from the storeroom and sent me back here I thought this room was the storeroom and I opened the door"—she took a deep, gulping breath and went right back to her explanation—"and I saw you so came in I didn't mean to do anything I just wanted to thank you for the job and getting me out of that club and I called your name and you moved and then I touched your arm and you grabbed me and threw me down with that gun in your hand"—another great big breath —"and I am sorry, so *sorry* I shouldn't have come in here I wasn't trying to hurt you or scare you."

With that she did move and sit up and put her face in her hands, tears streaming from her eyes.

"I'm really sorry, sorry, sorry. I didn't mean to. I'm sorry."

Her voice got quieter with each "sorry" until it was a tissue-thin whisper.

Shit.

Now I felt like an asshole.

I live a life of monsters and blood and death, and because of that I had almost killed this innocent girl. I stopped pointing the gun at her. With a deep breath I let the tension in my body flow out and my nerves to settle from DEFCON 1 to DEFCON 5. The fan made the air swirl across my body in a soothing manner.

I realized I was standing there naked.

Good going, Deacon. Smooth. Really, really smooth. Walking

around the futon, I went over to the closet and opened the door. Flipping on the light, I set the gun on the small dresser inside that held socks and underwear. Opening the drawers, I took out both. Before you ask, I am a boxer brief guy. Glancing over my shoulder, I saw Tiff wasn't hiding her face anymore. She was watching me. To hell with it, she had seen the full Monty so I just slipped my boxer briefs on and then pulled out some clothes to wear.

I chose my clothes with tonight in mind. Leather pants that laced up the side. They were durable and actually comfortable, as long as it was fall. No way I could wear leather pants in the summer here in the South, I would melt. The pants were real-deal biker wear and made from thick leather designed to protect against road rash. I liked them.

I didn't know what to expect tonight, so I dressed myself to look like a threat. Sometimes you can get an edge in a confrontation just based on your appearance. The intimidation factor. Of course, I was dealing with vampires and who knew what else, so I doubted the edge would do much good, but better to try.

I grabbed a shirt, button up and short sleeve, black with a blue threaded pattern on it. A silver-studded belt went through the loops of the pants, and a matching set of silver-studded bracelets was around my wrists. The shoulder holster for the CZ attached to the belt. I slipped on my socks and boots, then unbuttoned my shirt and applied deodorant and cologne.

A little unscented lotion for the hands and face, a quick comb through the goatee, and I was dressed. I put the CZ in its holster and slipped the Taurus at my back and I was ready to face the day. I still had a scared girl on my bed, but at least I wasn't naked now.

Score one for progress.

Speaking of, I turned to Tiff. She was still on the bed but had moved to the edge of the mattress. She had her feet on the floor, her arms around her legs, and her chin on her knees. The pose actually made her look pretty cute. Adorable, in fact. It was a great improvement over looking afraid for her life.

"I'm sorry. I'm a little jumpy when I wake up."

That was an understatement, to say the least.

She shook her head.

"No, I shouldn't have come in here. It was my fault."

In my head I sighed. I hoped my voice was patient as I spoke, but I can never tell. I usually come off as an asshole when I try not to. It's like I can't help it.

"We can go round and round about whose fault it is, Tiff. It doesn't matter. You shouldn't have woken me up, but you didn't know that I would come to with a gun in my hand."

I moved over until I was standing in front of her.

She looked up at me with her bright blue eyes. They were a bit red and swollen from crying, but she didn't look scared now, not at all. I held out a hand for her to take.

Man, she was pretty.

The skin of her palm was cool and soft. The bones delicate under my fingers. Closing my grip, I pulled her up from the bed. Her head came to my chest.

"I say we call it even and go try to round up some food. I'm starving and I think you should know what we have going on here if you are going to be around."

A nod and a smile on her part and we were off downstairs to find some grub.

FOURTEEN

EVERYBODY HAD GATHERED around the prep table in the kitchen. When it wasn't being used for prep, the employees used it for a table to eat on. Martin, the cook, had the day off with the girls. Polecats was still closed until we got this mess settled. It should be over by tomorrow, but in the meantime, no employees. Well, except for Tiff, I guess. Kat and Father Mulcahy didn't count. They work for the club, but only because it is part of what I do. They were in for the mission. The big mission of killing monsters.

But because the cook was out, the meal was up to me. Father Mulcahy made a mean pot of chili and did fine with spaghetti, but Kat was hopeless in the kitchen. Left to her own, I am sure she would never cook more than a microwave meal.

I actually like to cook. I don't get to often, but I can, and when I do I enjoy it. I used to love Thanksgiving. I would invite both families over and we would have a houseful of guests that I cooked a traditional southern meal for. My kids loved the million dollar pie and red velvet cake.

Now they would never again...

STOP!

I came back to what we were doing with a jolt.

Years after and I still keep doing that.

Focus.

The here. The now.

Breathe.

Relax.

I felt eyes on me and looked over at Tiff.

She stared at me. Looking into her eyes, I knew she caught what was going on in my head. Maybe not the details, but that something had gone wrong. She gave me a soft smile and then looked away. I looked down at my plate and scooped up another forkful of scrambled eggs covered in cheese and salsa. Chewing mechanically, I swallowed and washed it down with a swallow of sweet tea.

Sweet tea is a southern thing. It is the nectar of the gods. You take five tea bags, boil them in a pot, and then let them sit on the stove to steep for an hour. Grab your two-gallon pitcher and put two inches of sugar in the bottom. Pour the tea over it and stir until the sugar is dissolved. Then add cold water from the tap until the pitcher is full.

Viola, southern-style sweet tea.

It goes with every kind of food ever made and can be drank for a snack. Folks from the North don't have sweet tea. They always try to get you to just add sugar to unsweet tea, but it doesn't work that way. It's not the same.

I had whipped up some breakfast for everybody, even though it was mid-afternoon. Breakfast is a good, hearty meal that you can cook pretty quick. Scrambled eggs with cheese, ham heated in the microwave, biscuits from a can, and sweet tea.

I ate and Tiff ate. Father Mulcahy leaned on the doorway and drank coffee. I knew for a fact it was not his first cup; hell, I was pretty sure it was not his first pot. Father Mulcahy does coffee really well, which is a good thing, because he drinks it all day long. He held a saucer that held his coffee cup when he wasn't drinking and also served as an ashtray for his ever-present menthol cigarette. He is the only man I have ever seen that could take a sip of coffee with a cigarette in his mouth.

Kat had eaten already and nibbled on a biscuit slathered with butter and honey. She leaned back in her chair with her feet on the edge of the table. She wore khaki work pants and a Sepultura shirt that was older than she was.

Tiff sat across the table from Kat. She ate eggs with salsa and no ham. When she passed on the ham the explanation given was that she was a vegetarian. Kat asked why she was eating eggs, then, if she didn't eat meat.

Smiling, she replied, "I don't kill animals for food, but I am pro-choice."

That caused Father Mulcahy to suffer a coughing fit. He might've been choking on his coffee or possibly from the cigarette smoke.

Larson was across the table from me. His plate in front of him was as untouched as a nun. He had absolutely no humor at the moment and he looked like shit. Obviously sleep had not come to him. Sitting with his arms crossed, he glared at me through those bloodshot eyes. Dark circles cut under them, making him look almost sinister and slightly mad. My fork crossed the table and tapped lightly on the edge of his plate.

"You should eat something. You'll need your strength tonight."

Larson glared at me some more, but he picked up his fork and scooped up some eggs. I took another bite of mine. They were quite tasty even if they were cooling to a rubbery texture.

Hey, no matter how good of a cook I am, eggs do that.

Larson put his fork down on his plate instead of taking a bite. It made a loud clank as it hit the ceramic. He continued to glare at me as I continued to eat. I took a gulp of sweet tea.

"You got something to say, Larson?"

I was waiting for it. I didn't know how it was going to come, but I knew it was indeed going to come.

His fingers closed on the edge of his plate, jerked, and flung it to the floor. The plate shattered with a loud crash, sending pieces of porcelain, eggs, biscuit, and jelly skittering across the kitchen floor. Tiff jumped, everyone else remained the same. His chair hit the floor as he pushed back from the table and stood, eyes flaming and finger pointing at me.

"Fuck you, Deacon! FUCK YOU! My family has been held hostage by those monsters all day. I know where they are! We should have gone to rescue them! But no, you—"

His finger jabbed and his face turned a mottled purple. He looked like his head would explode he was so angry. Angry and scared.

"YOU LEFT THEM THERE!"

Screaming, he came over the table at me, fingers going for my throat.

He was so out of control it was almost too easy. My arm came around, hand connecting with the side of his head as he got on top of the table. It was a good solid backhand, and it did its job. Larson crumpled over on his side, laying awkwardly. Standing, I pinned him to the table with my hand on the side of his face. He was twisted with one arm underneath him. His head dangled off my side of the table, feet flailing in the air on the other side.

I loomed over him.

Bloodshot eyes rolled up at me.

I know exactly how big I am. I was the only thing he could see. In that moment, trapped under me by my strength, I had become his entire universe. I applied pressure to his neck and knew that it hurt.

So, I leaned in a bit more.

"Listen to me," I growled. "Listen very carefully."

I gave him my best glare. It has been known to make bad guys wet the bed.

"I am your only hope. I am the only hope for your family. Me. No one else. You cannot save them. The police cannot save them. No one on earth can save them except for me. Do you understand?"

He stared at me and I shook him.

"Do you fucking understand that?"

He nodded.

More weight, more pressure, more looming.

"Pay attention. I left your family there because we had *no* choice. The vampires are asleep during the daylight and they are as safe as they can be. There will be a plan. But know this,"—so close our noses almost touched—"it will be *my* plan. I cannot have you do anything more than what I tell you. If you do not listen, then your family has no chance of living until tomorrow."

I let him go and straightened up.

He coughed and rolled over, sliding off the table until he knelt on the floor with his head the only thing left resting on the table. There were tears in his eyes. His voice was weak when he spoke.

"How do you know they are still alive?"

"I don't."

My voice cut into him. He flinched. On his knees, in the floor, he flinched so hard it looked like he'd been slapped by an invisible hand.

"We have to act as if they are alive and we can save them. But, until we get there we will not know. I can promise you that if they are not, then we will kill every motherfucker who touched them tonight."

Picking up my plate, I carried it over to the sink.

"We need your knowledge to make our plan. Get your shit together for your family and come to the conference room."

I stopped at the door now and turned to look at him.

There was one last thing.

"And clean up your fucking mess before you come."

FIFTEEN

IT WAS CRUNCH TIME.

We were going up against the scariest fucking vampire I had ever heard of.

We had innocents held hostage by the monsters.

They knew we were coming.

We had no advantage.

It was a crap situation and I'd had to remind Larson who was in charge of things. If he didn't get it after the scene in the kitchen, then he never would. If that was the case, I would use him to get to Appollonia and once that was done, I would tie him up and stuff him in the trunk of the car until it was all over.

The chair I always picked in the conference room molded to my back. Feet up on the table, I leaned back into it, finding the sweet spot that made it *my* chair. Everybody would be in shortly and we would come up with the best plan we could.

Would Larson's family survive?

I didn't know. I didn't even know if they were still alive at the moment. That couldn't come close to being my concern. I could only pray they were. I had never met them, and so far Larson had almost been more trouble than he was worth, but they were human.

Since my family was taken from me, I've worked to save any humans I can from the monsters. If you are human, I will put my life between you and the monsters. One day that mission will end and send me to where my family is. I know this, and it is fine by me. I can't take myself there, though; it has to happen when it happens. One day my ticket will be punched.

Until then I take out every monster I can.

I said a prayer of safety for Larson's family. Yes, I pray. For all the blood I shed, I do pray. I firmly believe in God, I'm a good Catholic.

Well, I try to be a good Catholic.

I ain't never going to get sainthood, but I keep the sacraments as best I can. Father Mulcahy would kick my ass otherwise.

If you had seen a demon face-to-face, you would believe too. I've watched crosses turn away vampires, I've seen holy water drive away demons, and I have rescued an Angel of the Lord. Hell yes, I believe. So, I prayed for their safety and their lives. I don't pray nearly often enough. Truthfully, I pretty much rely on Father Mulcahy to cover that department.

Prayer doesn't result in thunder and lightning. There haven't been any burning bushes. Sometimes there is nothing at all. But occasionally, sometimes, I get this *feeling*, kind of like a weightless weight, and it causes a shiver down my spine. I believe this is an acknowledgment of my prayer. Not an answer, just an acknowledgment.

It's enough because it has to be. That's the deal.

The prayer was short. As I finished I felt eyes on me. Looking up, I found Tiff leaning in the doorway. I didn't say anything, just looked at her. She was dressed normally in a pair of jeans and a blue and black sweater that matched her hair color. Her hair wasn't straightened today and had nice wavy locks that framed her face.

The heavy makeup was gone and in its place were freckles dusting her cheeks and nose. Her eyes were still big and blue even without the mascara frame around them. The jeans and sweater fit well. She was small and built like a gymnast. There was something that felt almost delicate about Tiff. Something that made me feel like protecting her but not because she seemed helpless. The opposite, in fact, I believed she would be incredibly capable at any task she put her hand to. She just had that posture that read as ability.

She did not waver as she stared at me.

In her eyes I saw care. And concern.

Care, concern...and something else.

There was a heat in her eyes. She did a long, slow blink at me and a smile danced at the corners of her mouth.

Pushing off the door frame, she walked into the room.

"I am not sure I know all that is going on around here. I know something happened last night at the club. I don't know exactly what except I'd list it as weird. You promised me a reason why I had to leave my job, and all I have gotten so far is a really tasty omelet."

I had promised to tell her why she was here. Truthfully, I didn't completely know. Getting her out of Helletog was a no-brainer, but telling her to come here for a job wasn't a well-thought-out plan. Still, I could at least tell her why she had to leave her job, especially since she had seen the confrontation with Larson.

Should I break it to her gently? Nah. Not really my style.

"The club you worked for was owned by a vampire. I had gone there to kill him and I didn't want to leave you behind."

See, that was simple enough. Rip the bandage right off, won't sting a bit.

I watched her process what I said, seeing the concepts spin in her mind until realization dawned on her face.

"Gregorios was a vampire? A real vampire? As in 'I vant to suck your blood' vampire?"

I nodded to her question. Her head shook, sending those big locks of hair sweeping across her face. Sitting in the chair closest to me, she leaned forward.

That was one really well-fitting sweater she had on.

I was listening as she continued, I promise.

"I mean, I knew he was Goth, it was a Goth club, but I met him during the day. Don't vampires explode in the sunlight?"

"Not so much explode as they burn up like a human-sized birthday candle. And during the day you met his renfield, and that is a whole other subject. But Gregorios's renfield looked a lot like him."

Greggie had not survived his master's demise. Father Mulcahy went to check while we headed to the jack shack earlier. Greggie had putrefied, then petrified, then turned to dust. He had obviously lived far longer than a mortal was supposed to. Both the bouncers were gone when Father Mulcahy got there.

Tiff's lips pursed and blew a puff of air to move the hair that had slid down toward her eyes. She sat in shock, thinking about what I had said. It was a lot to take in. Undead, bloodsucking creatures of the night are always a shock the first time you realize they actually exist.

After a long moment, her big eyes turned up to look at me again.

"So, if my boss was a vampire, then why didn't he try to bite me?"

I thought about my answer for a moment. "Oh, I am sure he would have gotten to it soon. You are pretty bite-able."

A blush crawled up her cheeks and came to stay for a minute. It made me grin.

"Why, Mr. Chalk, are you flirting with me?" The smile crossed her face, cheeks still glowing pink.

"I could be, darlin', I very well could be."

My smile matched hers. Yep, I could be indeed.

It wouldn't be the weirdest thing to happen in the past twenty-four hours.

SIXTEEN

THE HIGHWAY STRETCHED BEFORE US. Sunset was running away and we were chasing it to a place that was in Larson's head. I could feel the night coming on like a pressure building in the atmosphere. The sun barely crested the pine trees along the asphalt, peeking out like a child playing hide-and-seek. Larson's family was counting on us to beat that sunset. The vampires were out of commission as long as the smallest sliver of sun remained above the horizon.

So far, the directions had led to Interstate 75 northbound. Highway 75 is one of those huge stretches of road that you can travel from Detroit all the way to Miami. It cuts straight through the middle of Georgia and is a well-maintained piece of roadwork. After driving for about two hours, we were not far from the Tennessee border, in the no man's land of small towns and middle-of-nowhere's. The Comet streaked up the road like its namesake, eating the miles in a rumble of engine and whine of tire tread.

My compass and traveling companion sat up against the seatbelt. His head leaned like a golden retriever. He was paying attention to the directions Appollonia had put in his head. Sweat oiled his face, and the veins in his temples stood out like wires under his skin. Traveling had activated the power Appollonia had sunk into his brain earlier. Since getting into the car the strain of those vampiric powers had shown more and more in Larson.

Plus, he hadn't slept and really hadn't eaten, so they were doing a real number on his system.

The feedback from that psychic implant had my own angel-laced blood a humming like I'd drank three coffees too many.

We had researched Appollonia, but Kat had found very little information on her. She was old, very old, but not much other than that. No history or rumors about her, no picture either. So old and powerful was about all we knew.

Oh yeah, we knew one more thing: She was scary as hell.

In our research only three other vampires had ever shown the ability to possess another bloodsucker. Three. In all of history.

"Turn off here."

I took the next exit. The Comet complained its annoyance at slowing down with a loud rumble of pipes. The end of the ramp came and I followed Larson's finger point. The road curved and swayed like a drunk uncle, asphalt ribboning between hills and dips.

"We're getting close. I can feel it."

His eyes turned back to me. He had some color back in his face, especially on the left side where my backhand earlier caused a bruise to blossom along his cheek. His left eye was swollen and red. I really hadn't meant to hit him that hard. Maybe it looked worse because of his pale skin. Yeah, that was it. At least he could still see out of both eyes.

I turned down the stereo. During the trip we had been listening to Son Seals and were on his *Lettin' Go* album. Chicago blues, deep and true. It was Son's last studio album before his death. Recorded after he had survived being shot in the mouth by his wife and having his leg amputated because of diabetes complications, it was a powerful record. Every song vibrating with the power of Son's charisma in spite of his hardships. Larson wasn't very talkative once we hit the highway, so music it was. I could see in his eyes he had something to say now.

"Do you really think your plan is going to work?" he asked. "It seems pretty unplanned to me."

Truth was, the plan was not really a plan. It was a string of ideas that should work. But really, it was the best we could come up with considering how little information we had to go on.

"It'll work."

What other answer could I give? No, it will fail spectacularly, and your family will die, but don't worry, when it fails we won't be far behind them? Yeah, I don't think so.

Besides, confidence will carry you when ability fails.

Sometimes anyway.

"Do you really think they will let you keep your weapons?"

I couldn't look at him, I was still flying down the road and it was getting curvier as we went. Darkness filled the area around the car, cut by the headlights. The sun was still up, but on the road we were in the shadow of the mountains. Out in the country there are no streetlights.

I felt it the second we crossed the Tennessee line. Tennessee has no state taxes and their roadwork is not the priority it is in Georgia. The road changed from smooth and even into something more like an alligator's skin.

"I doubt they will let me hold on to the guns, but who knows about the rest. Vampires are strange. I don't know why, since they used to be humans, but their brains don't work like humans do. If they are old enough, they won't even recognize the other stuff. Since we don't know what we are walking into, it won't hurt to try."

Larson's fist slammed into the dash and he convulsed like a live wire had switched on in his brain.

Spine bowed and teeth clenched, he growled. "Turn here!"

My eyes began searching the side he was pointing at. That's the only way I saw the turnoff. It yawned out in the midst of the grass that stood sentinel at the road's edge—a dirt road, narrow and red that cut back into the weeds and woods. Hitting the brakes, my fingers pulled the welded chain-link steering wheel in a hard right. The Comet slid onto the road, tires chewing the dirt like a pit bull on a bone.

A tap on the gas to goose the engine pulled the car straight and onto the crooked road.

Red dust billowed up around the car, wafting across the headlights and powdering the windshield. Driving on a back-country dirt road is an experience unto itself. The dirt is a reddish orange and made of clay. The red comes from a combination of Georgia and Tennessee's high heat and heavy rainfall that leaches out most minerals in the soil, leaving behind high doses of iron oxide. It's really good for growing pine trees, some shitty crabgrass, and kudzu, but not much else. On an unpaved road the red clay does two things.

First, rainfall washes away the soil unevenly, making ruts and gullies in the road. This makes driving down them quite the adventure. Especially if you are into bronco riding.

Blindfolded.

With your hands tied.

The second thing is the dust. Red clay turns into a powder when it's dry. This makes a huge dust cloud that can make it damn near impossible to see. You drive by feel for the most part. If the road is wet, you don't get the dust, but you exchange it for a mud that is as slick as oil.

I brought the Comet's speed down some so that I wouldn't damage anything on the bumpy road. The car is a good, solid hunk of American Detroit iron, but it ain't invulnerable. I really didn't want to get where we were going and not be able to leave.

As the dirt road went farther, the pine trees continued to thicken along its side, completely blocking the sun. I knew it was still up but couldn't see it at all. As the car straightened on the road, a peeling white sign loomed in the tall grass on the roadside: SHADOW WOODS MOBILE HOME VILLAGE. TRAILERS FOR RENT.

A smaller sign underneath swung like a hanged man from a single rusty nail: SHADOW WOODS BAPTIST CHURCH.

Larson slumped in his seat.

If he hadn't been wearing his seatbelt he would have fallen to the floor. The road spewed us out into a clearing where all the trees had been cut away. I put on the brakes and the cloud of red dust shot past the car.

Hills rose in the clearing, bare of vegetation. It was a dead place. No trees. Not even kudzu, which could grow in hell. Trailers thirty years past their prime leaned and sagged, scattered on the hills like rice thrown at a wedding. The trailers were mostly single-wide. Their paint schemes were straight from the seventies and faded from decades of the southern sun.

Here and there were cousins of the Comet, square-bodied cars and step-sided trucks abandoned and hopeless. Stripped of parts, what was left of the cars had been smashed by someone who just didn't care. Trash abounded, faded beer cans and cardboard boxes mostly. The road we were on was a ribbon cutting back and forth among the trailers. It was a big, dirt bowl of death.

It was a trailer park from Hades.

His finger touching the window, Larson pointed to the crest of the tallest hill. The road crept over it. The voice he used was hushed. "There. Over that hill. That's where we are going."

The sun couldn't be seen on the other side of that hill, but I felt it as it slipped below the horizon. The slow leeching of protection until it just vanished.

It felt like a door that was open had shut with a muffled push.

In its wake something filled the trailer park. It wasn't life. No, what spilled into that place had nothing to do with life. Inside, my head hummed with a buzzing of power. Buzzing like zombie flies over a bloated corpse.

One by one, the doors on the dilapidated trailers popped open. Stumbling out of them were vampires. Lots of damn vampires. Ten and twenty to a trailer. They poured out of every place you could have hidden a vampire from the sun.

But they were off, way off, not right.

Not one of them looked at the Comet or the two humans inside of it, and none of them moved with the unnatural grace that all vampires seem to come stock with. Each step fell heavy as if they were marching to a drumbeat we could not hear. Their arms hung limply at their sides as they moved almost in one mind and headed toward our destination over the hill. We watched as they formed a mass and marched out of sight in lockstep.

    I had a very bad feeling about this.

SEVENTEEN

THE NOSE of the Comet topped over the crest of the hill several feet behind the stragglers in the vampire crowd. Just below it sat what used to be the Shadow Woods Baptist Church. It looked like most country churches in the South. Made of red brick with a sharply sloped roof, it sat forlorn and misused. The stained glass sides were all broken out and replaced with plywood to block the sun. The cross on the steeple had been taken and turned upside down. Cobwebs draped the church building and fluttered in the breeze.

Vampires cannot be on holy ground. Churches are consecrated buildings and vampires generally steer clear. Being in a church won't kill them, but it is so uncomfortable they will normally not even be on the property.

This church had been desecrated, so it was fair game for them. It wasn't just the cross being upside-down either; you could feel the desecration in your bones. A taint of evil hung in the very air around it, almost shimmering in the twilight. This church had been used for blasphemous purposes. Evil had been done here with determination.

I hoped that the stain of evil wasn't so powerful that it messed up what little plan we had. Either way, we had no choice, full steam ahead, and damn the torpedoes.

The vampires filed inside the building, shuffling up concrete steps to the double doors. We had waited and watched until the roads had cleared of them. They moved in unison, more like zombies with their hive mind than vampires who tend to act more like rabid packs of rodents in large groups. Lockstep, they entered the church, closing the door behind them.

Gravel crunched under the tires as I pulled in front of the steps and turned the car so that the nose faced out away from the church. If we made it out of this, I wanted it easy to get the hell out of there. Turning to Larson, I tapped him on the shoulder. He was facing out the window, attention locked on the church. With the touch of my finger he jerked toward me, eyes wild in their sockets. I pointed to the glove compartment. He nodded and opened it to get the blessed crucifix I'd put in there earlier.

He slipped it over his head and under his shirt. Instantly, his face relaxed. Not by much, but some. He didn't look as panicked now. Leaning into the Comet's upholstery, he closed his eyes.

"Remember, when we get in here, you listen to me. I have no idea what we are walking into, but if I tell you to do something, you listen to me and you do it. This part we are playing by ear."

He nodded, still keeping his eyes closed. This part was going to be hard.

"Look, Larson, we don't know what we might find in here. If your family is gone, then we will make these bastards pay."

His lids snapped open and the look in his eyes was harsh. He nodded once up and down.

"I know," was all he said.

The warning was the best I could do for him until we got inside. Stepping out of the car and into the chill night air, I grabbed my coat and flung it around me, slipping my arms down the sleeves. It was heavy on my shoulders. Larson was still dressed in his T-shirt, but he also put on his coat. His spine was straight and the big trench coat didn't seem so silly now. Larson squared his shoulders and we walked up the short stairs without a backward glance.

Swinging the double doors of the church open, we entered a

vestibule. It was dark, the interior lit by lanterns. Most vampires shun open flame. The most they will have around them are candles and sometimes a fire in a fireplace; but vampires, especially older, drier vampires, are actually fairly combustible, so they like to keep fire pretty far away from themselves.

Plus, they could see in the dark, so they really had no need for light at all.

To the right, the vestibule ended in a stairwell that went up, I assumed to the steeple since there really wasn't enough building for a second story. To the left were stairs going down to either the basement or what used to be Sunday school rooms. This was only a guess based on a childhood of going to little country churches just like this one whenever we would visit my dad's Protestant relatives.

Well, except for the desecration part.

Directly in front of us was another set of double doors for what would be the sanctuary. Light spilled from under the doors. The walls were bare of ornament except painted symbols of occultism—signs, symbols, and sigils. I recognized some, others I didn't. Not that it mattered, it was just more blasphemous crap. Spiderwebs hung from every corner. Huge, thick spiderwebs that covered big areas.

The spiderwebs were not surprising considering what met us at the sanctuary doors.

She stood almost as tall as I did. Slender as a razor, she was all arm and leg in a brilliant crimson dress. The line of her torso was broken only by the swell of small breasts, the rest of her midsection a flat plane. Long black and gray hair flowed from her head and around her shoulders in a cascade. Her head was elongated, bulbous. Two large eyes glistened red, set in deep hollows. Above them were three more sets of matching eyes that progressively got smaller as they neared her hairline. Her nose was nonexistent, just a small bump with two pinholes for nostrils. Full red human lips that would make a pinup jealous surrounded a mouthful of tiny sharp teeth. Tiny, coarse gray hairs covered her entire body.

Were-spiders are freaking creepy.

One hand rose up, composed of reed-thin fingers that had five knuckles instead of three like a normal hand. Between each finger were tiny webs. Her voice almost sounded normal, a nice, silky alto. But her inhuman larynx gave it a metallic vibrato, making her sound almost like a machine.

"I have to search you for weapons," she said. "Don't fight me. Just stand with your arms out and be still."

I spread my arms and nodded for Larson to follow suit. The Were-spider stepped between the two of us. Her hair moved and from her back unfolded two more sets of spider arms. They were long, spindly, and also covered in gray hair. Waving in the air, they began to descend toward us. Her human arms extended toward the ceiling and two large spiders slid down slender ropes of silk and dropped onto her hands. Perching delicately, they stood on her palms.

Both were shiny black, their carapaces glistening as if wet, with long legs and bulbous bodies. I was sure if you turned them over there would be a red hourglass mark on their bellies. Black widows are normally the size of a pea and had enough venom to make a man my size sick for days. These were as big as small kittens, and I was sure they came stock from the factory with enough venom to put down an elephant.

I hoped I didn't know what she was planning to do with those two spiders.

Her arms extended toward me and Larson, spiders twittering on her palms.

No, c'mon, surely not.

With a flurry of legs, both spiders launched off her palms. The one hit me in the chest like a baseball, falling then catching itself and hanging on to my shirt with its pointed legs. Grinding my teeth together, I managed to stay still as it crawled across my chest and under my coat. I could feel each of its legs as it moved pricking along my skin through my shirt.

Generally speaking, I don't mind spiders. In the garden they are great and even around the house, but a venomous spider the size of a kitten actually crawling on my body where I could not see had a very high freak factor. If it bit me, I would die, painfully and pointlessly. I would see to it that the spider died with me, but that was absolutely no consolation. Closing my eyes, I pushed breath through my nose to calm myself.

"Deacon..."

Hoarse and brittle, Larson's voice sounded like glass cracking under pressure.

Shit.

I'm a badass monster killer, I've seen some shit, and these spiders had me fucked up. Larson was a plain old human who was working on almost no sleep and the stress of his family's safety sitting on his shoulders. These things had to be pushing him into the red zone.

Damn it. He could NOT freak out now; if he did, he was as good as dead.

"Be cool, man. Just relax. This will be over in a minute."

I tried to send calming thoughts to him.

The spider woman laughed.

"Yes, be still. My pets will finish their job soon enough."

It should be true; I sincerely hoped it was. My spider had made a few trips around my chest, spiraling around my body and moving toward my legs. It paused at both guns and my cross under my shirt.

Relief washed over me when it made the transition to my lower body. I couldn't feel it walking through the leather pants and I was pretty sure the thick leather would stop its fangs from penetrating.

I also hoped they were thick enough to keep it from finding the knife tucked into my boot under the leg of the pants. The knife wasn't very big, only about nine inches long, but it had silver wire hammered into the blade. Nine inches is enough blade to hit a heart from under a ribcage if you pushed real hard. I was going to lose weapons in this, and it would be better to have than nothing. The spider had not gone into my coat pockets, so if things went well, part of my plan was still in play.

I began talking to her to give Larson something to concentrate on besides the gigantic, deadly spider crawling around his body.

"So what's your name, darlin'? And what is a lady like yourself doing in a place like this?"

I used a cordial, almost flirty tone. It couldn't hurt, and she was a Were, which means she was a human woman at least part of the time.

"My name is Charlotte." Her full lips curled up into a smile. Those alien hands flourished out to the side, like a hostess on a game show. "Welcome to my web."

Humor was not what I expected in the situation. I cocked one eyebrow up.

"I must be some pig, then."

She giggled.

It was weird to say the least. Were-spiders are very alien looking to begin with. When they do things that remind you they are human, it just adds to the creepy. To see this creature with its odd-knuckled hand covering its thick red lips in a girlish manner was...disturbing.

The giggling itself was a good sign, though.

"So, why are you in with the bloodsuckers, Charlotte?"

Before she could open her mouth to answer I felt a push in the air. It ripped up from behind her and swirled around to brush into me. Her head jerked violently side to side, making black hair flail wildly around her shoulders. Her legs gave out and her body fell toward the floor like a sack of cement. The two sets of spider legs protruding from her back caught her before she hit the ground. They held her suspended in the air, the rest of her body curled in on herself. Convulsions caused her spider legs to sway side to side. I stood still against my first instinct to help her.

The gigantic black widow still on my thigh made sure of that.

Apparently Appollonia was listening and didn't seem to want me to know Charlotte's answer.

Dumbass vampire. Her action revealed two things: one, her familiar animal was spiders; and two, she, like most vampires, was forcing her familiar to act against their will. Charlotte did not want to help the vampire, she had no choice. It was good information to know for the future. I hate killing the wrong people.

Charlotte was a victim. It meant I had a chance to free her of the vampire's influence instead of killing her outright. The Were-spider in question slowly unfurled from her position and stood on shaky legs. Tremors ran up and down her limbs, rippling the gray furred skin. Odd-knuckled fingers fluttered at her hair to put it in place as she composed herself.

Larson shuddered and gave a long exhale beside me. Looking over, I saw the spider had crawled off of my leg and was now climbing the lady's dress along with the one that had searched Larson. Her face turned to me, red eyes glistening.

"You will have to remove your guns, both of them." Her voice was clipped, back to being all business.

I knew it was coming, I was even prepared for it, but I really hate giving up my guns.

Using both hands, I pulled out the guns. For just a moment I thought about pushing past Charlotte and storming into the sanctuary, guns blazing. I didn't know what lay on the other side of those doors, but I was absolutely positive that I didn't want to go in there without my guns. But trying to get past Charlotte would probably mean I'd have to kill her.

Dammit.

Turning the guns handle first, I handed them toward her. Two of the spider legs descended and the sticky pads on them grabbed the guns and took them away. Charlotte dipped her head in thanks.

"Now you have to take off your crosses." Her head cocked to the side. "Please."

The cross came out of my shirt. I pulled it over my head and held it out to Charlotte.

I motioned that she should put it on. She took a horrified step back, waving her hands frantically back and forth. She turned to a table behind her and picked up a glass jar. The liquid inside was a slight amber color. Very carefully, she removed the lid of the jar, releasing a sharp, chemical smell that stung the inside of my nostrils.

"You have to put your crosses in this solution. Don't let it splash you."

Well, shit.

Larson dropped his cross into the jar while I debated with myself. As much as I hated giving up my guns, I really, really didn't want to sacrifice the cross. It was my last line of defense. Larson's rosary quickly dissolved, swirling darkness into the liquid. Acid. To Charlotte's credit, she did not pressure me, just stood watching me with eight red eyes and a jar of acid in her hands.

A shrill scream from the other side of the sanctuary doors made my decision for me.

I dropped the cross and put my boot forward, stepping toward the doors without watching the crucifix pull apart like taffy as it dissolved.

Now that I was disarmed, I was going in that damn room. Charlotte stepped aside before I could shove her out of the way. My hands closed on the handles to the double doors. They were cold and hard under my palms. Leaning my considerable weight back, I yanked on them with a sharp tug. The wooden doors parted toward me with no resistance and hit the walls on either side with a loud *BANG!*

With that abrupt introduction, Larson and I entered the scene in the sanctuary.

It was almost too much to take in.

The sanctuary was like most country churches, a big rectangle with a steeply pitched ceiling. Light filled the room from lanterns and hurricane candles hanging on the wall, and set on every surface. Pews in rows on each side of a center aisle were packed shoulder-to-shoulder with vampires. Damn, the room was filled to capacity with vampires. Probably around five or six hundred of the bloodsuckers. They did not turn to us, but instead stared straight ahead at the stage in front of them.

A deep charnel smell washed over me, the smell of rusting iron and rotting meat. Like a slaughterhouse in the summer heat. Gorge rose in my throat and I swallowed hard, forcing it down. The stage up front was where the pulpit would be in a normal, Protestant church. It had been tossed aside. The altars, low benches in front of the stage, one on each side, had been covered with what appeared to be roses and body parts, tied together and glued in place with spiderwebs.

There were ten other Were-spiders in various positions hanging from huge webbed areas along the roof and walls. I could tell by the feel of their lycanthropy that radiated down upon us some were the same as Charlotte, and some were other kinds of spiders. One appeared to be a black widow Were-spider. Hopefully, they were like Charlotte and serving Appollonia against their will, but my luck would be that most of them gladly served the vampire. There were benefits to a vampire and familiar relationship, just like there were for vampires and renfields, so there was a chance some of them would be a problem even if I had a chance to break their connection with Appolonia.

The half of a legion of vampires was really bad news; the Were-spiders were icing on the cake. Even if they all were serving Appollonia against their will, if she ordered them to attack, they would.

Speaking of the vampire in question, she stood center stage and she wasn't alone.

Her back was to us as we entered. The long strands of a cat-o'-nine-tails whipped out from a long slender arm as she scourged a man chained to the front of the baptismal. I couldn't see much of him. He was kneeling and what was left of his back was toward us. She had whipped him until his skin hung in literal ribbons. Blood wasn't even running. She had been at it long enough that it had congealed and sat like jelly on his flesh. Even in the low lantern light I could see the glisten of ribs. The air held the scent of iron over the smell of snakes.

Blood and vampires, they go together.

To the left of the stage stood two women, I assumed they were Larson's mother and sister. They looked like him, with pale skin and thick red hair. Torn clothes didn't cover up the bruises blossoming on their pale skin.

His mother was still screaming. It was her screams that had brought me into the sanctuary. The reason she was screaming, besides the horror that she was on stage with, was the man twisting her hair in his hands.

He was large and muscular, easily my size. Blond hair flowed from his head down around his shoulders, framing a face made of angles. All corners and edges, it was a face that looked angry all the time. A patchwork cloak of tanned skins and pants made of brown strips of leather that tucked into calf high boots were his only clothing.

He looked like a hunter of animals. A short sword was strapped to his left side. It had a black knobby handle made of onyx or some similar dark material. One hand was knotted full of red hair and his other lay along her jaw, caressing her face.

Another scream tore out into the air, hoarse and filled with rage. Larson's coat slapped into my arm as he ran past me to the stage.

"Quit touching her, you bastard!"

Larson slid in a huge puddle of blood surrounding the altars. It spread out from the altars all across the front to the first pews. His arms windmilling to try and keep on his feet, Larson fell heavily. Blood, thick and slimy, congealing, splashed up over him. The man holding his mother looked down at him, laughing. Larson had gained his attention.

He had also gained the attention of Appollonia.

She turned away from her victim on the stage with a slow movement of her head. As she turned to face us, so did all the vampires in their pews. In unison, their necks moved and every vampire eye fell on me.

Creepy again.

Stepping to the front of the stage, she stood proud and haughty. Tiny, she was all of five foot tall. Long, thick locks of hair fell to her hips in big waves.

Other than being covered in bloody splatter from whipping the man chained behind her, she was completely naked.

Long ago she had started life with a darker skin tone, but centuries without sunlight had paled her to a stained ivory. Fine muscles traced along legs that rose to a full swell of hips. Her ribcage flared out from her narrow waist. Muscled shoulders became muscled arms and a slender neck. Her face was dark with drying blood splatter.

The gore covered, but did not hide, the delicacy of her features. Thick, full lips parted in a smile to reveal white teeth, complete with small fangs. Large eyes blazed out of the blood mask and sat between a strong nose and thick, full eyebrows.

In her right hand she held the cat-o'-nine-tails. It dangled to the floor of the stage. Dark with congealed blood, each of its lashes were thick as a finger and glistened with interwoven bits of metal, bone, and glass. Strips of flesh clung to the evil device. This was not a bondage toy, some light flogger to bring a blush to a playmate's bottom. No, this was the real thing. An awful, terrible instrument of punishment. No wonder the chained man looked like he had been filleted.

I did not even know how he was alive still.

In her left hand she held a lance. It had a thick wooden handle that was wrapped in leather and had been cut down to a shorter length, maybe four foot long overall. The head of the lance was almost a foot long, a wavy leaf shape in a dull iron color with a gold center section. Something was inscribed on the blade, but I couldn't tell what it was.

Appollonia stood on the edge of the stage looking like a dark goddess. Punishment personified. A blood-kissed Fury that radiated death and lust.

I did not want to go near that stage.

Everything in me screamed to turn and leave. It was a primal reaction, deep in the lizard part of my brain.

Good thing I have made a life of ignoring that.

But Larson was not getting up. He kept slipping on the blood on the hardwood floor because his boots sucked. It was almost like a comedy act. The Three Stooges meets *The Texas Chainsaw Massacre.*

Time for me to step up, be the big damn hero.

Or the big damn martyr.

The big damn something.

Slowly, carefully, I walked to where Larson was. He had stopped trying to get up and simply lay on his back, looking up at the stage. Keeping my eyes on Appollonia, I reached down and grabbed the sleeve of his duster, pulling him to his feet. When I took my hand from his arm it was covered in blood. The floor was sticky with it, like a ghetto porn theater.

If that theater was in hell.

How were this many vampires sitting so calmly when there was this much blood around them? There was blood splattered all around the stage, blood covering the blasphemed altars, and a twenty-foot pool of blood in front of the stage that was almost an inch deep. There was so much blood that the air smelled like iron.

Vampires are a lot like sharks. Blood drives them into a feeding frenzy. They should be attacking each other to try and get to the blood. They had all just risen for the night and their hunger should be at its peak. Instead, they sat, stone-still as only the dead can, and watched unblinking.

If this was the level of power Appollonia had, then we were dead.

There was no way to win against something that powerful, especially without a cross or a gun. This realization wanted to settle down and gnaw at my bones. It wanted to make me give up, to quit, to lay down and die.

But I have a secret.

I don't give a damn if I die. It's fine with me. That means I get to go be with my family. If today was the day I cashed in my ticket, then so be it. Now my only concerns were to try to save Larson and his family, and to take as many of these vampiric bastards with me as I could.

I had to stop myself from putting my hands in the pockets of my jacket.

It wasn't time for that.

Not yet.

Appollonia stared down at us calmly from the edge of the stage. Everything had gone silent as she appraised me. It was a cool look that went from the top of my head to the bottom of my feet. The look was full of dark promise, heavy with an arrogant lust. She stood in naked glory with eyes just for me.

Women have looked at me like that once or twice but never in church.

If this still counted as such, the woman being a vampire and the church being a blasphemed charnel house.

When it came, her voice matched her eyes and rolled out with a soft, sensual purr.

"You should join me here, Deacon." Thick hair swayed as she motioned with her head. "Come closer so that I may know you better."

My head shook from side to side.

"No way in hell am I coming up there with things the way they are." I pointed at the man who still had his hand on Larson's mother's face.

"Tell your boy there to back off."

Amusement crossed her eyes. Leaning back and thrusting her hips forward, she said, "Do you not find me glorious? Surely you are drawn to me."

This was a prickly situation. She was an ancient, powerful vampire. In my experience, the older a vampire gets, the more unhinged they are. Appollonia was obviously used to men and women, definitely other vampires, slavishly lusting after her.

I could see it. She was powerful, beautiful, and glorious, to use her word; but I knew the truth behind the lie.

She was a bloodsucking, homicidal beast, regardless of what package she was in.

Like most situations that called for diplomacy, I chose to go with the truth.

"Don't get me wrong, you're hot, but the blood thing is a little much. I know it works for you vampires, but not so much for the rest of us non-blood drinkers. Gross is not sexy for me."

For the first time since she turned around, Appollonia let her gaze move from me to something else. She examined her arms and torso. From an unspoken command, two Were-spiders dropped from the ceiling to stand behind her. They had a robe made of a thick, silky material, spiderwebs, that they put over her shoulders. As they stepped back, she shook out her long mane of midnight hair. Thousands of tiny black specks moved from her hair and the robe to crawl over her body. It took only a moment, but the tiny spiders cleaned her of the blood and then retreated back to the robe and her hair.

She handed the cat-o'-nine-tails to one of the Were-spiders but held on to the lance.

"Is that more to your liking, Deacon Chalk?"

"Sure." I shrugged. "But I am still not coming up there until we get some things worked out first."

I stepped up to the edge of the stage, just below where she stood. The robe of webs hung loosely from her shoulders, framing her body more than covering it.

"If you want me, then you need to allow all the humans here to leave with no further harm." I pointed at Larson's family, "Not just them but any human you have here."

Larson's mother and sister shrieked as the man with them stepped forward. He now had both of them by the hair, dragging them with him. Muscles stood out with tension as he dragged them across the carpet. Rug burn blossomed ugly on their knees as they struggled. The fighting ended as he shook them violently, still using their hair to control them. They both slumped in his grip, whimpering and crying. His face was a contorted mask of rage.

My hands itched, wishing I had my guns.

"You do as you are told or these two will pay the price for your insolence!"

Muscle corded in his arms as he shook both women again. Tears streamed from their eyes and they howled in pain. Larson jumped forward and I grabbed him. It took both hands to hold him in place next to me.

I didn't even look at the man, my eyes stayed pinned to Appollonia. She was the power. He was her renfield. He would do what she said. Throat tight with the strain of control, my voice sounded mostly calm when I addressed her.

"Appollonia, you tell your slave there to let them go. If he does one more thing to hurt them, I am going to break every bone in his arms. I will leave him crippled and useless."

Threats are better if you are specific with them.

Pointing at the man, I said, "If you don't reign him in, I will. I don't respond well to threats. They never make me do what the person wants and only piss me off."

Appollonia looked at me with heavy lids. She simply stepped back and gestured toward the man. It was an invitation to reign him in myself. Good, I was feeling like hitting somebody right then.

One quick hop put me up on the platform. Once I was on the stage, I kept moving, striding to the man. I could feel the smile on my face. A sharp shove pushed Larson's mother and sister away from him. They scrambled away, off the stage and into Larson's arms.

The man flashed teeth, his smile matching mine. A big hand moved to the hilt of the dagger on his hip. Slowly, he drew it out and flipped it into an upside-down position.

A knife fighter's position.

Great.

Not only did he have a weapon, but it looked like he knew what to do with it. In a knife fight, you are going to get cut, especially if you don't have a knife. I had one still in my boot, but I would be stabbed before I got it out. I looked around for something to pick up as I kept moving forward.

Appollonia's voice called over my shoulder, power pulsing in every word.

"Matthias, I want him alive. Drop your knife. You will fight skin-to-skin."

I saw the anger flash in his eyes, burning like a brush fire. His hand unfurled around the knife and it fell away to the stage. My smile widened, becoming even more sadistic.

Now we would see how things went.

Matthias lifted his hands up, holding them loosely like a boxer. We circled a step or two around each other. In a one-on-one fight, if you don't get the drop on someone, it's always risky to make the first move. You have to open your defense to strike and you don't know how good the other guy is.

This is why in a lot of fights you have name-calling. You are trying to goad the other guy into breaking defensive posture and making the first move. This is why there is a saying that if two masters ever fight, there is no fight, because neither would make the first move.

I was not going to dance with Matthias, so I just stopped moving. I stood with my arms to my side and my feet planted. It was something

I learned in Kenpo. You never know when someone is going to jump you, so you learn to defend from natural positions. When I would compete in tournaments I found that standing still and not in a fighter's stance drove my opponent to make the first move. I don't know why, but it seemed to infuriate them, like I wasn't taking their threat seriously. Later, as a bouncer, I found that it worked in the real world too.

Matthias was already pissed. Appollonia had made him drop his knife when he did not want to, my tactic drove him over the edge. Those hands clenched and unclenched, and his face mottled purple with rage. Stepping forward, he threw a big hand toward my face. My elbow came up to block it and his knuckles skimmed across the leather of my coat, not hurting me at all. It was a big punch and could have done serious damage if it landed. But big punches are easy to see. I brought my hand down from blocking his punch to grab his arm.

A sharp pain jabbed into my ribs, shoving my breath out of its way to filling my chest.

He had slipped his other hand inside as I blocked his punch and hit me between my ribs and hip. His fingers felt like steel rods driving into my spleen. My diaphragm spasmed like an epileptic in a disco.

Our faces were close and I saw smug satisfaction in his smile.

He knew he had hurt me. And it did hurt. Like a charley horse in my diaphragm, it doubled me over and made me stumble backward a step.

As I moved back, my foot kicked out. A short, sharp snap, the edge of my boot connecting with his shinbone. It wasn't flashy, but it was a good solid kick. The satisfaction left his eyes as the pain flared in his leg. Getting kicked in the shin is no joke.

Hopefully I broke something.

We both pulled away and I tried to suck air in. I was hurt a lot worse than he was for the moment, but I would get my breath back in a second, that kick was good enough that, barring some mutant healing ability, he would have trouble putting weight on that leg for the duration of the fight.

As the oxygen pulled into my lungs, I felt my brain slip into that animal part that we all have. When you fight, thinking goes out the window and training takes over. That's why fighters train all the time. You can't pull it from your bag of tricks if you never put it in there.

It took only a second and my air was back, flowing into my lungs, but I stayed slightly crouched, acting more hurt than I was. He moved toward me and I leaned out. He took the bait and his boot flew in the air toward my ribs. Up came my knee to hit his shin and push the kick away. His shinbone connected solidly with the thick part of my tibia. Another injury to his shin.

With fluid grace he used the momentum of the push to move into a spinning heel kick. This time his boot flew toward my head. Standing tall and reaching up, I threw my arm over his leg, using my coat to capture it and absorb the blow. I clamped my arm down and held his leg. My forearm locked around his knee, putting his back to me. His cloak whipped around me and I grabbed a handful of it.

His leg slipped out of my grip as he tucked his head down and rolled toward the floor, but I held on to the cloak. I had that tightly in my fist. Using both hands, I yanked on it, pulling it tight around his neck. He wasn't a vampire, he needed to breath. I pulled harder as he scrambled on the floor and I almost fell on my ass when the cloak came away in my hands.

The leather it was made of was soft and thin, like lambskin. My mind blinked, stuttering as I understood what it was made of.

This was human skin in my hands.

Revulsion rose up inside my gut and I threw it as far from me as I could. Matthias slammed into me and pushed me toward the edge of the stage, his shoulder in my stomach. If he drove me off the stage with his weight on top of me, I would be at his mercy.

I did not want to be at his mercy.

My legs shot out from under me as I threw all my weight onto his back. The angle was right and my weight crushed him to the stage. I felt the satisfying crunch of his nose as it broke from the impact of being driven into the stage. Air whooshed from his lungs. Sitting up and leaning back put my ass on his skull, grinding it into the stage even more. My knees went on his arms, pinning him facedown on the stage. I brought both hands down with as much force as I could muster.

My fists battered into his kidneys and lower back with dull thuds. In my head I saw him hurting Larson's mother and sister. This drove my fists even harder. I felt his lower ribs crack and give, feeling like a broken wicker basket under my hands.

I stopped beating on him.

Matthias moaned under me, a wet, thick sound. My limbs were leaden even though so much adrenaline coursed through my bloodstream I had the shakes. Crawling off his back, I rolled him over. It felt as if he weighed a thousand pounds. His arms fell akimbo limply.

That handsome angular face was a red mess. Blood and mucus poured from his flattened nose, running over upper teeth that were ruined and broken. He would never be pretty again.

Good. Fuck him.

Getting to my feet, I stood looking down at him.

I stared at the man who had hurt Larson's mother and sister. God only knew what he had done while Appollonia slept. He wasn't a vampire and would not have needed to sleep during daylight. The cloak of human skin I had pulled off his shoulders rolled through my mind. This was one evil bastard. Evil in his own right, no matter how human he might be, he was a monster.

Putting my boot on his upper arm, I stepped down, applying my weight. The crack of the bone sang out in the silent sanctuary. Only Larson's mother had a reaction, hiding her face in her son's coat. His sister stabbed eyes of hate at the man under my foot. For her, what I was doing was personal, but for me, there was no sense of satisfaction or revenge in that break.

It was business.

I had a threat to back up.

He had been warned to stop hurting Larson's family and he had chosen to push that one last inch. Plus, in a roomful of monsters, I had to back up my threat if I wanted any chance of getting the humans out alive. After stepping on the other arm, I knelt down and took his wrist in one hand. It was thick and warm. My other hand clamped down on

Matthias's elbow. Pain flared in my side from the fight as I twisted my hands in opposite directions.

The spiral fracture of his forearm sounded like fiberglass twisting together. It took a few minutes, but I finished on Matthias's arms and stood again. His arms lay to his sides like mangled chicken wings. He had been out the whole time, but now he would never harm anyone again.

Ever.

My adrenaline rush had fled from me. In its place was the ache in my side from where Matthias had gotten me. Weariness settled in and I was sweating lightly all over. Turning back to Appollonia, I wiped my head. Moisture covered my palm. Flicking it away, I dried my hand on my shirt.

Imperiously, Appollonia pointed at Matthias's mangled body and then waved her hand away in dismissal. Two Were-spiders crawled down from the rafters. They were mostly changed and had an upper body that was a half-human, half-spider hybrid, but from the waist down they were gigantic spider bodies, complete with long, furry legs and a bulbous abdomen. Like centaurs if centaurs were spiders. Quickly they scooped him up and scurried away.

Appollonia's voice was a purr, rolling from deep in her chest. "That was most"—a blood-red tongue slithered over her lips —"impressive."

Her dainty hands skimmed along Appollonia's body. Taloned fingers caressed her breasts and scratched up her thighs. The heat in her eyes now blazed in an inferno.

There are women in the world for whom violence just works.

Firestarters, usually they have a boyfriend or a husband they are constantly cheating on just to get him to fight over her. Maybe Appollonia was one of those women before she died. Now, after the fight with her renfield, she was acting like she was in heat. Maybe her whipping of the man earlier had warmed her up, like foreplay. Vampires get like that. Their whole nature is predatory, seductive, blood-thirsty. Just my luck to be the object of affection for an insanely powerful, sadistic, vampire hell-bitch.

I sighed wearily. I couldn't help it.

"Glad you liked the show. Now tell me what I have to do to get the humans safe."

Hips swaying, panther grace stalking, she moved toward me. Stopping about a foot away, she ran her free hand through her hair, dislodging tiny spiders, and waved the lance in front of me, indicating my crotch.

"We can talk after you have shown me your magnificence."

I firmly shook my head on her implication. "Thanks for the vote of confidence, but no deal, lady; if you want to talk about a peep show, then you have to cut the humans loose."

Her head tilted back and she looked up at me with her big golden brown eyes. They were like pools of dark honey. Thick lashes fluttered up and down in a long, slow blink.

"But, Deacon, I am not threatening, I am requesting. I am interested in seeing your flesh naked." The look she gave was meant to be seductive, but a lion does not seduce a gazelle. "If you are not going to cooperate, then I will not either. Look at my people." Gesturing with the lance, she indicated the sanctuary full of vampires who were still watching us with serene expressions, still as statues. "If we cannot come to an agreement, then I will turn your friends over to them. It is only my will that keeps them in check. You know very well what we are like."

It wasn't an outright threat, it was the implication. If that many vampires fell on us, then we would all be torn limb from limb. They would fight over us so much that they would not drink our blood from our veins, they would lick it from our shredded bodies. They were so still it was easy to forget they were even there, but that would be a very bad thing to do.

Terminally bad, dammit.

I shrugged out of my coat, controlling it to the floor so it would not thud against the wood. My fingers were slow as they undid my shoulder harness and the buttons on my shirt. I let both fall to the stage and stood shirtless before Appollonia.

No way in hell was I taking my pants off for her. Besides, I had lost two surprises in my coat, taking off my pants meant I would lose the only weapon I had left, which was the knife in my boot.

Facing her, I watched her expression. Appollonia's mouth was open, dainty fangs glistening in the low light of the sanctuary. If she had needed breath, it looked like she would have been holding it. I have undressed in front of women who were attracted to me before. It was always the same the first time if they had never seen someone with as many tattoos as I have before. Appollonia's face was slack with lust. Her mouth soft and open with want.

My arms are sleeved with tattoos from the knuckles of my fingers all the way up and spilling across my chest and shoulders. Ink covers all the skin on my arms and on my chest from the bottom of my sternum to my jawline. Black letters cross the top of my stomach. My tattoos are a combination of styles and colors that flow across my skin. Combine the tattoos with my sheer size and it's actually very impressive to see it all when I take off my shirt.

Appollonia stepped forward, reaching for me. My hand went up, stopping her in her tracks.

"We had a deal. Humans safe, then we can talk."

The smile that slid over her face was very human-like. "I would not be satisfied with merely talking, Deacon."

Now was the time for negotiations. Careful negotiations to get the others safely out of the way. Vampires are strange creatures. Evil to the core, but occasionally you could negotiate with them. Phrase things correctly and their vampiric nature had to stick to their word. It's similar to the demon thing. It's all about the deal.

You cannot reason with a vampire or a demon, but you can deal with them sometimes.

"I want the humans safe."

"You have my word."

I shook my head. "Not good enough. You cannot promise their safety while they are here in harm's way."

Her chest thrust out, spiderweb robe slipping to the side and revealing her breasts. The lance swung as she gestured. "My will is law. They are safe as long as I will it to be so."

"I want them physically away from these vampires. Outside in the open air, free to walk away from this place unharmed."

Her eyebrow arched. "And what would I get if they were to be taken from harm's way?"

Here we go. "What would you want?"

Her tongue slid across her lips, leaving a glossy trail of moisture behind. "I want to touch you. To run my hands over your skin." Her voice was breathy, thick with lust. "I want to *explore* you."

Careful.

Careful.

I looked over to Larson. He had his arms around his mother and sister, hiding them in his coat as much as he could. His eyes were pinned on me. I don't know if he knew how deep in the hole we were, but those eyes were looking to me to dig us out.

Both his mother and sister peered out from under his embrace. Their faces were puffy and red, tears streaking down their cheeks. They were frightened. The sister was scared, her lips trembled as she stared at me and the vampire on the stage. Larson's mother was so frightened she was almost crazed. White showed all around her eyes and they darted wild like caged animals. She was so terrified she was almost broken.

Son of a bitch.

"You allow the humans to walk away from here. Let them leave the building and walk away free and unharmed, and you can touch me."

The last fucking thing I wanted was her hands on me, but I would not let anyone hurt those two women again if I could help it.

"Done."

Appollonia snapped her fingers and two other Were-spiders dropped from the ceiling. As they descended, they shifted from the form of gigantic spiders into the graceful form of half man, half spider. Politely, they gestured and guided Larson and his family down the center aisle away from the stage. Larson looked at me in question. I nodded that it was okay and waved him on. They needed to go, to get out of the roomful of vampires, to be away from the danger. It didn't matter what happened to me as long as they got out. The doors to the sanctuary shut behind them and I had to assume they were going to be taken all the way outside.

The smile on Appollonia's face would have made a hungry tiger jealous. She took another step to me, her arm extending toward me. I stepped back out of her reach.

Her full lips turned down into a frown and a crease appeared between her eyebrows. Poisoned honey-colored eyes flashed killing daggers.

"Do not mock me, Deacon Chalk. We have an agreement."

I waggled my finger at her and pointed to the man slumped in chains at the back of the stage. The red ruin of flesh that had been his back was turning into something that looked like spoiled meat. The skin had been flayed away in large sections. Raw muscle had been frayed and torn. In places the bone of his ribs and spine glistened in the one gigantic wound his back had become.

"There is still a human who needs to be set free."

Appollonia's laughter pealed throughout the sanctuary. It grated along my nerves like ground glass.

"He is not human. He has not been human for a very long time."

Even though I did not understand her remark, I wasn't letting it slide. If she had that much wrath for anyone, then the safe bet was that they were her enemy and could be a potential ally for me. Plus, I just could not leave someone in that condition if I could stop it.

"He looks human to me. I can definitely tell he isn't a vampire. If he isn't human, then what is he?"

"He is cursed."

Cursed?

"Doesn't matter. Cursed or not, he *is* human, and if you do not take him out of here and into safety, then we have no deal and you are a liar."

Spiders crawled down her arms and shoulders as she shook her head side to side. Her voice dropped a full octave into a growl. Vampiric anger rolled off her, slapping into my skin like tiny whip cracks.

"I will not give him up. He was not in our agreement."

"He was on my part and that's all that matters."

Standing tall, I ran my hands over my chest and stomach, trailing them down to hook my thumbs in the belt of my leather pants. My splayed fingers framed my groin. Tensing my arms brought the muscle to definition. I was putting myself on display.

"If you want to touch me, then you have to honor the agreement. Otherwise, you can fuck off and forget it."

I was gambling, rolling the dice as hard as I could.

She weighed out my words. In her eyes she was deciding if she wanted me enough to give me what I demanded. Watching carefully, the tension built along my spine. If she chose to call off the deal, I was going for my coat.

After a few moments her hand motioned to Charlotte. The Werespider came forward, small, tightly controlled steps carrying her swiftly down the aisle.

"He cannot be set free, but I will have him unchained and taken to safety. If I do this, then there is no limitation on my touching you. You will be mine to explore at my leisure."

She was evil.

She was a vicious creature who stole lives.

But I was pretty sure she wanted my body and not my blood. Still, to be careful,

"If he is included in our agreement, there is no limit to you alone touching me."

Again, careful, I did not want her to pull some mystical vampire crap about all the vampires and Were-spiders in her control being extensions of herself.

"Enough banter. Agreed."

She nodded at Charlotte.

Charlotte produced a key and unlocked the shackles holding the man upright. Her four spider arms caught him as he slumped bonelessly to the floor. Lifting him as if he were weightless, she was careful to avoid his injuries as much as possible. His back was such a large wound she couldn't help but touch it somewhat, which brought a moan of pain from his lips. Charlotte carried him past us and I got a good look at him.

He was almost as tall as I. Thinner. Not in a scrawny way, but rangy, sinewy. His limbs were long and straight, the muscles stretching along his frame. Blue ink traced out Celtic tattoos across his chest and biceps. I recognized the designs. I had some that were similar tattooed on myself.

Thick, tawny hair surrounded his face, one thin braid of it hanging along his cheek. The rest was lank and limp. Fierce eyes shone out from sunken hollows. They were a crystalline gray shining fever bright. His features were full and very European. A thick nose sat above heavy lips and a strong chin. Those fever eyes stared at me as they passed. A shaking hand fell out and touched my arm.

Charlotte stopped.

"Thank you." His voice was deep, but it rasped weak and soft, as if his throat had no moisture at all. I nodded sharply up and down at him. His hand fell away and those eyes closed. His face turned into Charlotte's breast like a hurt child would do for comfort.

I turned back to face Appollonia as he was carried away down the aisle. The moment the door shut behind Charlotte, her lips parted in a smile pinpricked by dainty fangs.

Time to pay up.

Hips swaying like the pendulum of a clock, she closed the distance between us. As she moved, she shrugged out of the webbing robe. It fell behind her in a gossamer drift. I did not move as she stepped in front of me. She was very close, so close that her nipples brushed the tattoo on my stomach. I felt them harden as they grazed my skin. The top of her head was even with my collar bones. Taloned fingers trailed across my chest and up my neck until they stroked my beard. This close she smelled hot, the sticky heat of clandestine lust. Sex and vampire and blood.

"Put your hands on me." Her breasts pressed harder against my skin. "Caress me."

I shook my head.

"That wasn't our deal."

The skin on her tiny forehead creased, then smoothed as that evil smile came back.

"I am so glad you reminded me of our agreement."

Her hand slid along my cheek and cupped the back of my head. I felt her nails scrape along the scabs from the vampire at Gregorios's jack shack earlier. The pain of the wounds being opened prickled along my scalp.

"I get to explore you."

Pressure on my head pulled me toward her as her mouth opened wide. I bent down. Strong as I am, I'm no match for a vampire, even one as tiny as her. Our mouths met and she kissed me. Soft, full lips pressed into mine and her wet tongue slid into my mouth, exploring eagerly. Her mouth was cool and moist and carrion sweet. The kiss tasted like blood, all iron and copper. Her eyes were shut as she gave herself over to the kiss. Mine were not. I grabbed her arm and pushed it away.

Pulling back, her eyes flew open, anger flaring in them.

"Watch the spear, lady."

The lance in her other hand was waving by my head as she was caught up in the kiss and I did not want to lose an ear. She nodded and moved it away from us, but still she held it.

"Why don't you return my kiss? You must desire me as I desire you."

"Look, you're hot and all, but our agreement said nothing about me returning the favor. You do what you have to do, but I do not have to help you get there."

I was willing to take her 'exploring,' but that was all. Yes, she was beautiful and sexy, but she was a vampire. I would not forget that she was an evil, bloodsucking, undead creature of the night no matter how hot she was.

"Our *agreement*."

The heat in her voice flared. Lust and anger mixed into a deadly cocktail. A Molotov one.

"Our agreement you cling to so closely said that I could explore you fully and at my leisure. I will have you, mind and body, before the night is over. You will desire me. Your lust for me will overwhelm you."

Since the transfusion by the angel I rescued years back, I have been pretty much immune to vampire powers. I hadn't met a vampire yet who could roll me with their abilities.

"Go ahead. Give it your best shot, sister."

Her hand was still behind my head and she pulled me down and kissed me again. This time her lips were bruising hard on mine. Her carrion tongue thrust into my mouth like a knife in a killers hand. The arm with the lance circled around my body and pulled me to her. Cool skin pressed against me.

Vampires are not cold, they are cold-blooded. Like lizards, they take on the temperature of their surroundings. The skin that touched me was smooth as silk. Lush breasts pressed against me, full and firm. I felt her sex slide along my leather-clad thigh.

Inside my mind the pressure of her vampire powers trying to reach inside rubbed like velvet on the inside of my skull. It was a warm, wet feeling against my brain. The slick feeling of something trying to worm its way in.

Her hand slid from my neck, caressed down my chest and stomach until her fingers found the top of my pants. Turning, they slipped inside to surround me. Her grip was firm and insistent. Regardless of what she expected, though, she found nobody was home.

The arm around me pulled, pressing us together crotch-to-collarbone. Her arm was trapped between us. Her hand stayed inside my pants gripping me firmly. Power washed over me as her mouth worked insistently on mine.

Her hand stroked me up and then down.

That power trickled into my mind.

I felt the tear.

The small crack in the dam.

My eyelids grew heavy and fluttered closed against my will. I hardened in her hand as wet, slick power broke through and washed me away.

Thick, silken hair filled my hands and I pulled the mouth I was kissing closer. I ate at that mouth with a hunger that raged from my crotch to my throat. There was no breath, no hesitation, only need.

Familiar skin brushed against mine.

God, I hadn't touched her in so long. I missed her so much. Her touch, her taste, her smell.

Need pushed me against her, my hardness trapped in her hand. My fingers came down and cupped my wife's breast. Leaning back slightly, she gave me room to flick my thumb across her nipple. Her mouth pulled back to let her gasp in pleasure.

I was complete, healed, once again. My love in my arms touching me, holding me.

My wife tightened her grip on the base of me, squeezing so slightly. Her tiny, soft hand stroked me. Mine was full of her breast and the one in her hair pulled her mouth back to mine.

My wife, my wife, oh God how I missed this, how I missed her. My heart had been so empty with her gone.

Finally, I was whole, reunited with my wife.

Lust for my wife coursed through me, burning away the ache in my heart.

I was healed by my love for...

my...

wife.

My hand tightened around the hair in it and yanked her head back, pulling her mouth from mine. The illusion shredded as I stared down at the face of Appollonia, her eyes half closed in lust, mouth slack with need. Anger filled me in a spontaneous combustion. My fist swung back as far as it could on the end of my arm and then slammed down into her face. My knuckles crashed, covered her entire eye socket.

"NEVER, EVER USE MY WIFE'S MEMORY AGAIN! STAY THE FUCK OUT OF MY HEAD!"

My fist drove her away from me and to the floor of the stage. The hair in my hand tore out of her scalp by the roots. Sprawled on the floor, her eyes had gone wide with shock.

The lance fell from her grip, clattering loudly on the wooden stage.

The power of her tore from my mind, ripping like tendrils from my brainstem. Pain consumed my anger. Sharp, stabbing pain, the inside of my brain being rubbed with a cheese grater. Nausea closed under my sternum like a physical blow. What was left of my dinner spewed out onto the stage in a rush. My stomach emptied itself like a purse. Sweet oxygen was driven from my lungs in the spasms of my diaphragm, and I couldn't breathe.

I felt like I had been turned inside out.

Hissing filled the air as the vampires in the pews all began to move. They shook themselves as if coming awake after a long sleep. Appollonia's head jerked to look at them, fear naked on her face. She scrambled, faster than you could follow with human eyes, and snatched the lance from the floor. The moment her hand closed around the haft of it, the vampires in the room all silenced as if a switch had been thrown.

Spots of black crowded the edge of my vision as her power lashed back at me. It was the metaphysical version of the cat-o'-nine-tails. That vampiric power scourged my mind.

She rose to her feet as if she were pulled up by strings. With her vampire speed I didn't even have time to try and move as she swung the lance, smashing it across my temple.

White pain light blasted my eyesight into smithereens.

I didn't have time to feel myself hit the floor either.

EIGHTEEN

BEING KNOCKED unconscious is nothing like falling asleep. The thing about being knocked unconscious is that you never remember being out of it. One moment you are awake, then BAM! The next moment you are coming to and you have no idea where you are.

I woke up sharply, but the entire world was covered with a haze, almost like a fog. Black specks clustered in my vision to form a tunnel, and everything in that tunnel seemed far, far away. Confusion wrapped around me like a blanket. I was disorientated and my hearing was off too. The static *whoosh* of my blood pulsing filled my ears and I could hear nothing else.

Slowly, my vision began to clear and the whoosh lowered in volume. Problem was, the blurry vision and head whoosh were replaced by a grinding ache in my skull.

Rats were gnawing their way through the bone in my head—that was the only explanation.

The pain made a migraine feel like an orgasm.

Even through all this I tried not to move or change my breathing. When you wake up from being knocked out, sometimes you do not want the people who have you to know you are awake.

Dust skittered across the surface of the floor like insects. My face was pressed to the wood. As I became clearer in my mind I tried to ignore the pain in my skull to feel my body and see if anything was broken.

I didn't have the sharp, sickening pain of a broken bone anywhere. I thought I was good, but I wouldn't really know until I tried to move. My body ached, especially around my head. The pain inside my skull was a combination of trauma from Appollonia knocking me unconscious and fighting off her invasion of my mind. Vampire powers are a bitch. They crawl in your brain and if you fight them, then it feels like your brain has been dropped into an iron skillet and fried like an egg, like you have third-degree burns inside your skull.

"I know you are awake. Sit up if you are able; it is just the two of us."

The voice came from behind me, deeply masculine with a thicker accent. Not a lilt like Irish, more guttural like Scottish, but something a lot older. I couldn't see who it was. The skin on my face pulled, stuck to the floor with dried blood as I rolled over. Movement made the ache in my skull worse and the black spots came back to the edge of my vision. Slowly, I made my way up to a sitting position, putting my back to a wall.

When the wave of pain passed, I slowly opened my eyes.

The room was dimly lit by a small lamp, a kerosene hurricane lamp. It had been a children's Sunday school room when this had been a church. All the furniture was miniature—low, round tables with small, square chairs. The pictures on the wall were from Bible stories, cartoon versions of Noah's ark, David and Goliath, Moses and the Red Sea. The vampires had defiled these also. They were smeared with what looked to be dried shit and blood. Symbols of evil had been painted over them and some bloodsucker had fancied themselves an artist, drawing in absurd genitalia on all the figures, men, women, and animal. The room was a mess, the blasphemy somehow worse with it being a children's room.

Evil always hits harder when juxtaposed with innocence.

The other person in the room was the man who had been flogged. He sat across from me, arms on his knees. The same spiderweb silk that Appollonia's robe had been made of wrapped his chest. Tattered slacks covered his waist and legs. The exposed skin was filthy with dried blood and had a waxy pallor. Fierce eyes watched me, waiting for me to speak.

Softly, my fingers touched my face. Damn it hurt. The skin around my eye and cheek was puffy, soft and tender like overripe fruit. Gingerly, I rubbed my hand over the surface and the copper powder of dried blood drifted down. I worked my jaw up and down to see if it was broken. It wasn't, but my molars on the top felt off. Pushing up with my thumb confirmed that they were a little loose. Pressure straight up helped adjust them back in their sockets. As long as nobody caught me in the jaw on that side, I should be able to keep those teeth.

Man, she had really nailed me a good one.

The man adjusted, pushing his leg out from him to a more comfortable sitting position.

"How is your head?"

"I'll live."

And I would.

Never mind the fact that speaking aloud was like shaving the inside of my skull, this injury would not be the thing that killed me. In fact, if I made it out of this alive, it wouldn't even leave a mark, thanks to my being more than human. Didn't make it hurt any less right now, but the thought was comforting in a small way.

"Speaking of, you look pretty good for someone with their back torn off like you had earlier."

He shrugged.

"It still hurts a great deal, but I am used to that by now."

Long fingers waved to indicate the silk wrapped around his midsection.

"If it were not for this bandage woven by the spider-folk, I must admit I would be unable to move still. It holds in my viscera and supports my muscles as they heal."

"What's your name?"

"I am called Longinus."

I waved to him. I would have extended my hand to shake, but I wasn't quite up to moving that much, although the pain receded in small waves as the minutes passed.

"Deacon Chalk. Pleased to meet you."

A sneeze tickled the back of my throat and I swallowed it away. If I did sneeze, I was sure it would make my head explode. I would definitely pass out again. Consciousness was something I planned on holding on to.

Longinus stared at me for a moment and then muttered something under his breath. It was in a guttural language I couldn't understand.

"What was that again?"

He shook his head.

"Sorry, I slipped back to my native tongue."

Long fingers pushed his hair away from his face.

"I have heard of you. Thank you once again for speaking on my behalf. It has been a long time since anyone has shown me mercy."

I nodded. More to test how my pain was receding than anything else.

"Don't mention it."

Adjusting my position made me realize for the first time that I was still shirtless. At least I wasn't naked. Hurrah for good news.

"So how long have you been Appollonia's prisoner, and what did you do to deserve it?"

"It has been almost a half of a year since I tried to kill her and she took me captive."

A shudder chased itself through his form.

"It has seemed like an eternity. She is fond of her cat-o'-nine. She brings me to the end of my endurance, lets me heal, and then starts again."

I pulled up my pants leg and found that my knife was still there. I slid it from its sheath. The blade was blackened, but the silver wire hammered into it glimmered in the dim light. I wished I still had the phosphorus grenades that were in my jacket pockets upstairs. They had been plan C. If I couldn't kill Appollonia or save Larson's family, I would have pulled them out and burned this place to the ground.

If Larson's family was dead when we got here, I would have let him do it.

Ah well, that plan had all gone to hell.

"That sounds like a crappy way to spend a Saturday."

I pushed up to try and stand and my brain rebelled. Nah, it didn't rebel, it threw a fucking bloody coup. Pain roared back inside my skull and my vision swam in black spots.

Okay, okay, I'll sit here for a few more minutes. When I could open my eyes, I found Longinus watching me.

"Tell me how she got the drop on you?"

"When I attacked I was unaware she could control other vampires. Before I could deal the deathblow, one of her minions put me down."

"So, what are you? No normal human can take the damage you have on your back and live, much less go through it for six months. Queen Hell-bitch said something about you being cursed?"

A sharp laugh, like a cough escaped his lips.

"I am human. I am under a curse to walk the earth until Judgment. I can take Appollonia's abuse forever and still live on."

Wait.

I had heard this story.

My brain worked against the ache to find the memory. I had read about a Longinus before.

"Are you telling me you are the Wandering Jew? Longinus who pierced the side of Christ at the crucifixion and was cursed by God with immortality?"

"I am not Hebrew. I am from the Isle of Albion, England today, but I am the Longinus you speak of."

Setting the knife aside, I pulled my hands up to my temples and began massaging them. The ache kept easing up little by little. It was getting better, but slowly.

"Why don't you tell me about it?"

"It is a long story."

My fingers kept moving in small circles.

"Trust me, we have a few minutes before I'll be able to blow this Popsicle stand." Pain from my eye throbbed as I rubbed too briskly near where I had been cracked across the face. "Go ahead, I would like to hear it."

Longinus sat up straighter crossing his legs. He gave his own wince of pain. It took a moment for him to settle in, but then he leaned forward, placed his elbows on his knees, and began to speak.

"I was born over two thousand years ago in what is now called Scotland. When I was fifteen years old I left my homeland and traveled to join the Roman army."

Pride swelled his voice, making it fuller.

"With the army, I traveled the world. Exotic locations became my home. I was young, strong, and a part of the greatest army to ever exist. I swaggered the streets of wherever we were full of confidence. I gladly took part in all the pleasures being a Roman soldier afforded me."

His voice lowered, shrinking into quiet. Shame bowed his shoulders, causing him to tremble.

"Drunkenness, sexual perversion, worshipping idols, blood rituals, I enjoyed them all."

A desperate sense of sorrow rolled off of him. I kept quiet, not wanting to interrupt.

"I was so arrogant. So damn stupid when I was sent to Jerusalem where I continued my hedonistic ways. I was hungover the day they brought Christ to us at the Hill of the Skull for crucifixion."

His eyes turned to me, looking for comprehension.

"Understand that, to me, He was simply a political upriser being put to death. This was nothing uncommon. I had heard of Him, but had never seen Him or heard Him speak."

I stood watching his agony and worried about my own throbbing skull. Eyes closed with the pain of the memory, he paused. I watched him carefully, waiting for the rest of the story. Long minutes passed. When his mouth opened again, his eyes stayed closed. His voice was soft and controlled.

"We hung Him on the cross, as was our job. A crowd had gathered and we stood to keep them at bay. They surged in the hot sun, like hounds in a pit, surly and belligerent. They called for the Christ to answer them, to respond in any way, but he simply hung there, pinned betwixt heaven and earth. After hanging for hours He began to die. The sky overhead darkened and the sun went away. My commander became frightened and ordered me to make sure Christ was indeed dead."

Longinus swallowed a deep breath, eyes still shut against the memory, but he kept going. The next words were so bitter I could almost taste them.

"I took my lance and shoved it between His ribs into His heart. He had already died, so blood and water poured down my lance splashing onto my hand."

Agony stamped on his face and his eyes flew open, he moved to his knees. Fiercely, he leaned in and gestured, eyes flashing, fist clenched.

"I took His blood and put it to my mouth, as I had done to many others in my sin. My arrogance! I actually thought to myself, 'So this is what the blood of a god tastes like.'"

Thick hair stuck to his cheeks with the tears that streamed freely. His body collapsed forward. His head hung in shame.

"The ground shook and heaved and I felt the voice of God Almighty like thunder in my bones. He cursed me. The Curse of God seared into my soul, writ on the bones of my body, sealed into my flesh. For my arrogance and blasphemy, He cursed me to live in the darkness, survive on blood alone, and to only know death at the point of my own spear."

Longinus was almost prone on the floor. Silence filled the room. I didn't know what to say. Even for me it isn't every day you are confronted with a living myth. I thought about all that he had said. The implications of it all.

Softly, I asked the question that was forefront in my mind.

"Are you a vampire, then? With the blood, the sunlight, and the immortal thing, it sounds like it."

Raising his hand, he wiped the tears from his cheeks.

"No, I am not undead I am immortal. I am still human. I can be in the sun, but it causes me agony. I do need blood, but I am not a vampire. *They* are my second great sin."

"What the hell do you mean by that?"

He pushed himself back upright. The movement brought a grunt of pain from him.

"One night, after a hundred years of wandering, I attacked a criminal outside of an inn. He fought back and injured me, but I managed to overcome him and take my fill of his blood. I felt him die, but our blood had mixed in the fighting and he resurrected."

Guilt burned in his eyes, pulling the skin around them tight.

"When he came back to life he was like me. He ran away, but it put the thought in my mind that I could make another like myself. I did it again, attacking someone, mixing our blood, and killing them. Each time they came back like me, but evil, twisted. It did not matter if I chose a criminal or a saint. I abandoned trying after only a few attempts, but Pandora's box had been opened."

I could see his shame, but he still faced me. "I created the first vampires and began the undead blight of humanity."

"Let me get this straight," I looked him in the eye. "You made another of you, but different. You bit someone, then they bit two friends, and they bit two friends, and so on and so on until you have today's vampires? Is that what I hear you saying?"

Longinus nodded.

"Well, you really shit the bed on that one, didn't you?"

His mouth tightened into a grimace.

"That is why I walk the earth, hunting vampires and destroying them. If I can atone for my sin, my hope is that God will lift my Curse and I can be at peace."

I got that. I could understand that. It was similar to my reason for hunting monsters. It wasn't seeking redemption for me. Then again, maybe it was in a way. If I had been there that night, my family may still be alive, and if not, then I would have at least gone with them.

Something occurred to me about Longinus's story, something horrifying.

"So is it the Spear of Destiny that crazy dead bitch has?"

A nod was his answer.

That explained a lot. It explained why she was so damn powerful and why when I knocked it out of her hand earlier the other vamps started moving.

The Spear of Destiny has been a legendary relic, second only to the Holy Grail. According to the legend, the bearer of the Spear was to gain power and ability beyond measure. I would have called bullshit on the very idea, but here I was faced with living, breathing proof that the legend was true.

"Is the Spear how she can control so many vampires, or was she this powerful when you went up against her?"

"It is the Spear's doing," he said. "When I first faced her, she controlled only a few. Now, she travels the country gathering vampires in her thrall, forming an army to enslave the human race. The Spear extends her power and evil almost infinitely."

This was bad. This was really, really, incredibly bad. The only thing that keeps vampires from taking over is the very fact that they cannot get along and work together. Appollonia controlling them all would make it not just possible, but a foregone conclusion.

"We need to get that Spear back and kill her dead."

Pushing against the wall, I stood up. No nausea or black spots. My head still ached to high heaven, and my vision was a bit blurry in my swollen eye, but I could move and function. I looked down at Longinus and held out my hand.

"You coming?"

He stared at me for a moment and then looked at my outstretched hand. Nodding once, he reached out and took it. The palm of his hand slid past mine until his fingers closed around my wrist. The grip was light and shaky. Pulling up as he stood, I helped him to his feet. It took a lot of effort, but at the end he was upright even if he did sway a bit side to side. We waited a moment while deep, rasping breaths pulled air into his lungs. I didn't mind. The work of helping him had brought back the pain in my head, so I didn't mind waiting. My vision was still relatively clear, though.

The knife was bare in my hand when the door to the room began to open. Turning away, I slid the blade into the laces on the sides of my leather pants. If no one was looking closely, then they would not see it in the dim light. Charlotte stepped into the room followed by a vampire.

"Appollonia has sent me to fetch both of you."

Well, well, let's see where the night goes from here.

NINETEEN

WE FOLLOWED Charlotte into the hallway. Longinus managed to walk unassisted. Considering the damage I had seen on his back, I was surprised he could even move, but with the spiderweb bandage he didn't even need anyone's help. Pain haunted his eyes with each step and he moved as slow as Christmas, but he moved on his own. I was glad because it kept my hands free. Longinus was directly behind Charlotte, I was behind him, and bringing up the rear was a vampire who walked with the jingle of spurs.

The vampire in question was not as tall as I and thin as a whip. A battered black cowboy hat sat on top of salt and pepper hair that hung shaggy over the collar of a western-style shirt. A beautiful chrome Colt .45 revolver slung low over his narrow hips in a cowboy-styled, tooled leather gunbelt.

Western Jim's undead eyes stared blankly at the back of my skull.

There was nobody home in those eyes. If a vampire isn't in full-on predator mode where their fangs distend, they actually look pretty normal. When they are newly turned, they still have the habits of humanity that carry over, and as they age they learn to camouflage themselves to get next to their prey. This vampire was almost like a zombie. No recognition in his eyes, no illusion of life. He walked behind me stiffly, just following orders. This is what Appollonia did to the bloodsuckers she controlled.

I didn't know if she had sent Western Jim to make a point to me, but his presence answered a lot of my questions. I had to assume that he had gone up against Appollonia and lost out just like Longinus had. Once turned, she had likely used his knowledge of me to set the trap that started all of this.

He probably had a file on me and a plan to take me out if I ever was taken over by some ghoulie.

I know I had one on him.

It's a sign of mutual respect. Thankfully, I was the only monster hunter between here and Texas.

I could see that he would have known me well enough to use a girl who looked like my daughter to distract me, then to set me up where I would have to not only keep myself alive, but watch out for Larson's ass too. It made sense now. It didn't work, because he had either underestimated me or Larson, or he had left me the wiggle room to survive so I could stop this, or Appollonia was crap at translating his plans into action. At the end of the day, it didn't really matter. Now I would find a way to lay my friend to rest before this was over.

The hallway itself wasn't very long. One incandescent bulb glared its yellow light from a broken fixture in the ceiling. The shadows it cast were deep and black. There were other closed doors along the hallway and stairs leading up on one end. Charlotte was leading us to those stairs.

"Charlotte?"

The spider lady spun on one foot, turning to me. The movement was graceful, like a ballerina. Unblinking eyes looked at me from a head on a tilted neck. She arched all the eyebrows on all the eyes on the left side of her face in question to me.

"Are there any other people in these rooms?"

Full lips made a sad smile and she shook her head.

"No, Appollonia has taken no prisoners besides you and Longinus. Any others are used for food and then turned for her army."

No innocent bystanders made the rescue plan simpler.

I know she was on the side of the monsters, but I trusted Charlotte. More I trusted that she was not working for Appollonia willingly and would help us if she could. Her head tilted and that long-fingered arm reached out to softly touch my shoulder.

"Thank you for what you did with Matthias."

Her voice was low, almost a whisper.

"He was in control when Appollonia would sleep. He was"—a shudder passed through her shoulders, vibrating the furry fingers touching me—"he was a perverse man. I am glad he will be of no use to her now."

I had held that cloak of human skin in my hands. I could only imagine what kind of evil he would be if he were in complete control. If I had known the implications, I would have threatened to cut his manhood off.

The nod I gave her was short.

Turning back, she began walking to the stairs. Her red dress was cut low in the back to allow the four spider legs room to curl together. There was a patch of webbing under them at the small of her back. As we started up, Longinus began to make small grunting noises with each step. When you are injured, it takes a lot more to go up or down steps than it does to walk a flat surface. Twice he got unsteady and I held him up by his arm.

He nodded in thanks and I took the second to mouth to him to be ready. He gave another nod and continued up the stairs.

At the top, we entered the vestibule of the church where we first came in. I thought I knew the layout and I was right. We had been in the Sunday school department, which was at the bottom of the stairs that led down. I was pretty sure the stairs that led up went to the steeple. The vestibule was the same—covered in spiderwebs and still creepy as hell. The doors to the outside were closed, as were the doors to the sanctuary.

Charlotte led us toward the sanctuary doors and I slowed my steps slightly so that I drifted back, closer to the cowboy vampire. My fingers casually draped over the handle of the knife I had hidden in the laces of my pants. I stopped walking, bracing myself. Western Jim bumped into my back and rocked back on the heels of his boots, making those silver spurs jangle.

I took a deep breath and struck.

The blade of the knife ripped free of the laces in my pants and streaked through the air. Spinning, I drove the knife as hard as I could. The blade lodged in the vampire's neck and scraped on the bone of his spinal cord. Black blood shot out of the wound, splashing me across the face. It was thick, cool, and sticky, like pressurized jelly.

Cursing, I wiped my eyes so I could see.

I let go of the knife in the other hand and grabbed the western-style bolo tie around his neck. His eyes bulged out and his fingers scrabbled at his throat, trying to dislodge the knife. Snatching his Colt from its holster, I shoved him away. The six-gun was a single action and the rough hammer bit my palm as I slapped it back. Four pulls of the trigger and four slaps on the hammer pumped four bullets into Western Jim's chest. Blood burst from his sternum as the silver bullets shredded his undead heart. The impact of the bullets pushed him into Charlotte, who was just turning to see what was happening. Stumbling into her, the vampire knocked her off her feet.

I used the moment of distraction to put the last two bullets into my dead friend's skull. He collapsed into himself, leaving nothing behind but his boots, a pile of clothes, his hat, and his gun belt on a pile of dust.

Via con Dios, my friend.

I shoved the six-gun in my waistband; the barrel hot against my hip. I grabbed Longinus by the arm, dragging him to the outside doors my head spun from all the exertion and my chest had a band of iron around it.

My shoulder slammed into the doors and they did not open.

Dammit!

The back of my head grew hot with rising power. Appollonia was on to my escape attempt. Leaning back, I planted my foot against the door with all my weight. It slammed open, crashing against the wall. Jerking Longinus in front of me, I shoved him out the door.

I took only one step out onto the front landing of the church when two things happened at once that threw me down the stairs ass over teakettle.

Charlotte landed on my back and rode me to the ground, and the doors to the sanctuary behind me exploded with the force of Appollonia's fury. Her vampire rage rolled out of the sanctuary like thunder, a giant fist slamming into me. Thankfully, Charlotte on my back took the brunt of the force. The power hit so hard it flipped me over, tossing her off my back and me down the stairs. The searing tear of flesh being abraded flared across my kidneys as I skidded down the concrete steps. My lower back with no shirt on had the top layer of skin scraped away by the concrete. My ass was fine because of the leather pants, but my lower back took a beating. I stopped tumbling on the ground in front of the church and lay for a second with my face in the mud.

It had begun to rain while we were inside.

Great.

My name being called made me look up to see Longinus standing a few feet away, just on the other side of a giant steel cross with Father Mulcahy. A smile crept on my face in spite of the pain. God bless Father Mulcahy. He had gotten it done.

The plan had been that once Larson came out, Father Mulcahy would load him and his family up with Kat and Tiff, who would drive them back to Polecats. He would then set up around the building a perimeter of blessed steel crosses driven into the ground in front of all exits, which would keep any vampire inside. After that he would wait for me to come out. If I wasn't out by dawn, he was to burn the church to the ground with me inside, then drive the Comet back. We both knew if I was trapped till dawn that I was dead.

Or worse.

I'm good with dying. Don't let me be a fucking bloodsucker.

The rain was cold on my back and arms as it sluiced down my body. It actually felt good on my lower back and washed the mud and blood from my face. I scrambled toward where Longinus and Father Mulcahy stood.

I wanted on the other side of that cross. I could still feel the pulse of Appollonia's power, but it was muffled, muted. As I stood beside the cross, Father Mulcahy made a motion with his shotgun and Longinus yelled at me to get down. There was no time to duck when Charlotte slammed into me again, but I was ready for it.

I let the impact roll us across the wet ground. I wound up on top with my hands around her throat. It was bony underneath the skin and the fur prickled my palms. Charlotte lay still and I kept my hands loose but ready to crush down if I had to.

"I can think." She said, red eyes unblinking up at me.

I had hoped that being on this side of the cross perimeter would free her mind and it seemed to have done the job.

"Can I let you up?"

She nodded and I eased up off of her. I offered my hand to help her to her feet and we both stood in the rain. I motioned to Father Mulcahy that it was all right and he moved his gun from her back to the church.

She lifted her arms up into the rain and it looked as if the gray fur washed from her body. The four spider legs shrank and folded away into her back. Lids developed on all her eyes and they receded into her skin, leaving only the two human ones. It took only a second for her to change from creepy spider lady to normal suburban housewife. Her hair became long and black, all the grey receded away. Wide eyes stared from a strong, noble face. She was still long limbed and thin, but her skin was smooth, her muscles sleek.

After a moment of standing in the rain her hands went behind her back. There was a light tearing sound of cloth ripping and both hands came out holding my guns. Webbing hung on them in wisps where she had them secured on her back. I smiled and gladly took them from her. Instantly, I felt better.

"It has been a long time since I have been able to be fully human." Her normal, three jointed fingers smoothed back her rain-slicked hair. "It feels good."

I lifted my semiautomatic up like a toast.

"This feels good too. Now I'm going to see what I can do about our friend back there."

Vampires crowded the front landing of the church. They stood silently in a formation. The steel crosses throwing pale blue light on the steps in front of them. That was the great thing about having a priest around, you never had a shortage of blessed objects. The vampires weren't reacting to the light from the cross, but it was keeping them corralled on the landing. From the back they began jostling each other, bumping and moving the group apart.

Appollonia strode from their midst and they fell back before her. Red energy pulsed around her slender form, her anger and power made manifest. She held the Spear in front of her. Fury throbbed in her voice and it carried across the distance between us.

"Come back to me, Charlotte. You are mine. I command it."

Shaking her head, Charlotte stepped back and bumped against Longinus's chest. He put an arm around her shoulders protectively. Father Mulcahy slipped a blessed crucifix over her head. He tossed me one to hang around my neck. I could still feel her power, but between the cross I wore and the one we were sheltering behind, it was a dull throb instead of a pounding ocean.

Sighting down the barrel of the pistol, I put a red laser dot on her head and squeezed off a shot. The gun bucked in my hand, but I was close enough that my aim was true.

Appollonia's head jerked back as the bullet entered her forehead and passed through the back of her skull to hit a vampire behind her. The vamp behind her fell, knocking over the others who were crowded near him. Appollonia remained standing. I watched as her ruined head re-formed itself like clay animation. The back of her skull pulled itself together, and the skin on her forehead smoothed like water. As quick as Charlotte had changed form, Appollonia was healed.

Shit.

"You cannot kill her with guns, Deacon," Longinus said, still holding Charlotte. "She is too close to the Curse."

Double shit.

Father Mulcahy whistled to get my attention. He pointed to the cross in the ground before us. A stream of tiny spiders were crawling up it and beginning to weave webs to cover it. They worked fast, already the lower foot of the cross was covered.

Jerking my head toward the Comet, we started moving that way. Father Mulcahy and I kept our eyes, and guns, on Appollonia and her crowd of bloodsuckers. As the tiny spiders covered more of the cross, the vampires began to make their way down the steps of the church.

Longinus and Charlotte fell into the back seat and Father Mulcahy slid into the passenger's side. I was opening the door when Appollonia spoke again. Her voice was seething with wrath and power. It carried across the air to me, rolling like thunder.

"Before dawn breaks, I will kill you all."

I stood one leg in the car, rain falling cold against my skin, and I raised my middle finger to her.

"Right back at you, bitch. Right back at you."

TWENTY

THE ASS END of the Comet slung around as the tires met asphalt. I stomped the accelerator and the car shot forward down the road. Vampires boiled out of the tall grass that hid the road from view. They had caught up with us about halfway down the dirt road from the church and had been hot on our trail ever since. Several times they had almost overtaken the car because I could only drive so fast on the twisted dirt road that had turned to slick mud in the rain. Now that we were on the asphalt, I put the hammer down.

A loud screech of talons on metal ripped through the roar of the engine as one of the vampires tried to claw his way onto the car. Another crazed vampire hit the driver's side door with a thud. Looking over, she was holding on the edge of the windshield, her mouth distended. Fangs clicked on the glass as she tried to chew her way in through the window on my door. Long, tangled hair streamed in the wind flow from the car. Spittle smeared the glass until I couldn't see anything but her shape.

I jerked the steering wheel back and forth, making the car swerve wildly across wet asphalt. Her scream sounded over the roar of the engine as she was slung off the car, ending with a thud into the asphalt behind us.

In the rearview mirror I watched her roll to a stop and then get up, her arms broken and twisted into obscene wings. She still ran after us even though one of her legs was broken and made her lurch to one side as if she were drunk. Her fellow vampires caught up with her but were growing more distant every second. Even the flyers would never be fast enough to catch the Comet on the open road. I turned my eyes back to the road.

"We're leaving them behind. We can outrun them, but they will follow us."

I glanced over to Father Mulcahy, who was lighting a cigarette. He had put his shotgun between his knees in the floorboard.

"Did Kat get Larson and his family back to the club?"

I pointed at the glove compartment and he opened it. Pulling out a bottle of ibuprofen, he popped the cap and poured three of the brown pills into my outstretched hand. My fingers twitched in a "keep 'em coming" motion and he spilled out four more. Bitterness stuck to my tongue as I swallowed them. I hate taking pills dry, but the aches and pains of my injuries through the last two nights were starting to pile up and I had work to do.

"They did, she called just before you came out of the church."

Blue smoke billowed across the roof of the Comet and around his head as he turned to look in the back.

"And who might you two be?"

A thin, elegant hand extended over the seat.

"My name is Charlotte."

Father Mulcahy took her offered hand, blew out a stream of smoke, and lowered his lips to kiss the back.

"Father Dominic Mulcahy." A smile crossed Charlotte's face and the priest matched it with one of his own. "It is a pleasure to meet you."

"My name is Longinus."

The Celt made no move to lean up, just waved his hand. Father Mulcahy did the guy nod of acknowledgment. The one where you just move your head up and down because you recognize the information as important but you have no idea why.

"He's THE Longinus from history, Padre." I kept checking the mirrors for vamps as I drove. "Just so you know."

This should be interesting. Catholic priest meet someone who actually was a partaker in the Crucifixion of Christ. Father Mulcahy turned his body until his back was against the car door. He took a long drag from his cigarette and flicked the ash out the crack in the window behind him.

"St. Longinus? Longinus of the Long Spear? Bearer of the Holy Lance?"

There was a hint of...*something* in his voice. Awe? Yep, a hint of awe in his voice.

I nodded and Longinus frowned in the dim light of the back seat.

"Don't think too highly of him, Padre, he's the reason we have the most powerful vampire I have ever met hot on our trail." I flicked the windshield wipers on high, swooshing the rain from left to right. "Hell, he's the reason we have vampires at all."

"I don't know what that means," Father Mulcahey said.

"Trust Deacon's word. I am no saint to be revered, but rather the worst sinner to be despised."

Deep-sunk eyes cast down to the darkness of the floorboard.

Father Mulcahy's voice was thick with cigarette smoke.

"That is a story I would like to hear. And I will make my own judgment, thank you very much."

"Text Kat first and tell her we are coming and to be ready. Larson's family, Tiff, and Larson himself can go ahead and get the hell out of there. We'll figure out a way to take Appollonia and her vampires out when they show up."

Nodding, he pulled out his cell phone and began sending messages. I turned on some music, low so the others could talk, but enough to let me go off in my head and think. Robert Johnson began to moan about hellhounds on his trail. His voice ghosting out of the Comet's speakers, weary and full of hopelessness. I knew exactly how he felt. I had to figure out what to do. Appollonia was coming, hard and fast on our asses like a rabid hellhound on a bloody steak. We would get to the club first, but we wouldn't have much time, maybe an hour before the Vampocalypse arrived on our heels.

Vampires were fast, not as fast as the Comet, but fast nonetheless. We could run, but then they would probably go on a killing spree. That would put too many humans in harm's way.

Fuck running anyway.

That's not my gig. Not my gig at all.

Dying without stopping the monsters wasn't my style either.

The only thing I could think of would be to hole up, gather as many weapons as possible, and lock the club down except for one entrance. Let them pour in to get me and lock them in. We'd see who made it until morning. It was a crap plan, but it was all I was going to have time for.

Father Mulcahy would insist on staying with me, but, just like the plan for going to Appollonia first, I could maneuver him into getting Kat to safety and making sure the vampires were secured inside with me. That would put him outside and out of danger. Longinus could come in and get his spear once the ashes settled. I would make him join me, but he was so weak he would be useless in a fight.

Yep, it was a crap plan, but it was simple and it could work.

Yeah, right.

I tuned back in to the conversation between Longinus and Father Mulcahy at the end of Longinus's story. That was fine, I had already heard it before. Longinus fell silent when he had finished confessing his sins to the priest. We sat and listened to the rumble of the engine, the swish of the windshield wipers in the rain, and Robert Johnson moving on to the crossroads.

Father Mulcahy was the first to break the silence between us as he looked at Longinus and then turned back around to face forward. Bowing his head slightly, he settled into the leather seat. His fingers moved quickly, touching his head, his hear, and his shoulders making the sign of the cross. The cigarette dangling from his lip did not fall out when he spoke.

"That is one hell of a story, son. One hell of a story indeed."

I looked in the rearview mirror at the back seat. Being on the highway I could look in the back more and still stay on the road. It was a rainy night and just after midnight according to the clock on the stereo, so traffic was light, especially this far north. Longinus looked out of the window at the darkness. Charlotte sat next to Longinus in the back seat, one hand on his arm, touching him for comfort. I didn't know if it was his comfort or hers, but I guess it didn't really matter.

Asking the question that had been bothering me since the confrontation outside the church brought Charlotte's eyes to meet mine in the mirror.

"Longinus, what the hell happened with Appollonia when I shot her? Vampires do not stay standing with a bullet to the brain. Was that the Spear's doing?"

He didn't look up, just kept staring out into the dark.

"I told you she is too close to the Curse for bullets to work on her. The speed of her healing was the Spear's influence, but your bullet would not have killed her."

I've killed some old-ass vampires in my time. Everyone of them went down with a bullet to the brain. Yeah, you had to take the heart to kill them dead, but a headshot will stop them from moving.

"Exactly how old is Appollonia?"

"The best that I could figure when I first hunted her was two generations from the Curse. She was turned a vampire by someone who was a vampire I made myself."

He shifted, now looking ahead over the seat. Sweat poured from his skin even though he was wearing the least amount of clothes of us all.

"She is old, and that gains her power, but even if she were newly dead, her lineage would make her immune to bullets."

"What will kill the bitch?"

Muscles corded on his arms and shoulders as a convulsion of pain wracked his body. When he spoke, it was through clenched teeth.

"When a vampire is close to the Curse, then they are bound more tightly to the conditions of the Curse. The Spear would kill her, but any wooden stake through the heart as a proxy to the Spear would do."

Well, that explained the stake through the heart part of vampires. I had always wondered about that. I knew that a stake through the heart would kill a vampire, but never could figure out why it was something so random. Now I knew. Because Longinus, who started vampirism, was cursed to die only by the Spear of Destiny, then the trickle-down effect must be why a stake through the heart worked on vampires today. Apparently if the vampire was close to Longinus, then it could be killed only by wood through the heart.

That made shit considerably more difficult. Somehow I didn't think Appollonia was going to lie down and let me shove a stick into her chest, no matter how attracted to me she was.

The sound of retching came rolling over the seat. Father Mulcahy turned to look and I glanced in the rearview mirror to see what was happening. Longinus was now leaning over, his head resting on the back of the seat. Arms wrapped tightly around his stomach, he was dry heaving and convulsing. Charlotte's hands fluttered on his back in soothing gestures. She looked up to my eyes in the mirror.

"His injuries are catching up to him. I think he needs blood to heal himself."

"No!"

Longinus threw himself against the corner of the car, as far from her as he could get in the confines of the back seat. The tendons in his neck stood out like steel cables.

"I will heal, it will pass."

"You have not been fed in weeks. I was your captor, I know how weak you are." Her voice was soft, soothing. "You need to take blood so you can fight Appollonia and regain the Spear."

His head lashed side to side, eyes wild and teeth clenched.

"I do not drink from the vein anymore. My sins are great enough without that. I will wait for blood until I can get it somewhere else."

Sweat ran down his face and arms. The hoarseness of his voice did nothing to cut the venom as he spat.

"I will *not* die."

"You are needed tonight to fight Appollonia. You must have your strength."

She pulled her hair to the side, sweeping it off of her neck. Holding up her hand, one thin finger extended and morphed into a razor-sharp needle of talon. Delicately, she pushed the edge of the nail into the vein on her neck.

The blood welled up, bright and crimson on her dark flesh. The rich iron smell of it filled the inside of the car, mixing with the cigarette smoke. Unbuckling her seatbelt, she crawled into his lap. He didn't fight her as she placed her open vein beside his face. Teeth sank into his lower lip and his head shied away from her, pressing deeply into the leather of the seat behind him. Nostrils flaring, he began to tremble.

"Drink from me."

Her finger was normal again as she wiped blood from her neck.

"You talk of sin. I was made to sin against you, let me atone for that now. Lycanthrope blood is powerful to vampires."

Even in the dim light of the Comet's interior, her fingers smeared scarlet across his lips.

"Let my blood heal you."

His tongue darted out, drawing some of the blood from his lips into his mouth. Eyes closed, he savored it for a moment. Tears streamed from down his cheeks as his mouth opened wide. Slowly his canines slid out into fangs. Charlotte's face was calm as she waited for him to drink. Tenderly, his arms wrapped around her, drawing her against him and pressing his mouth to her throat.

Father Mulcahy turned back to face the windshield, pulling another cigarette from the pack.

I turned up the music to cover the wet sounds of thirst from the back seat and drove on into the night.

TWENTY-ONE

THE TABLE before us was laden with weapons and explosives.

Father Mulcahy was off finding clothes for Longinus, who was looking hale and hearty after his meal of Were-spider blood. The spider lady in question was a bit shaky, but she promised that would pass as she drank a steaming cup of coffee from the kitchen. Long fingers held the mug gracefully and her eyes closed with pleasure as she sipped the steaming drink. The fang marks on her throat were surrounded by a black-and-blue bruise that extended from her ear to her shoulder. Kat watched Longinus unwind the webbing around his chest and stomach. The skin underneath was whole and smooth. Larson sat watching Kat and I was so angry I could spit nails.

The reason for my fury sat across the table from me looking adorable in a Sandman comic T-shirt.

"You are NOT staying. I'm throwing you out on your ass. I will NOT be responsible for you dying."

Guns clattered on the table as my fist pounded home my words.

Eyes flashing, Tiff leaned in, pointing her finger at me.

"I AM staying and you are not 'throwing' my ass anywhere."

Standing to her feet, she leaned over the table.

"I am in this and that is the way it is. I didn't ask for it, but I have made my choice and THAT is final."

She was pissed at me, but fuck her, I was pissed at her right back. I liked her, but that did not make me any less angry. This girl was not a warrior. She needed to go away for her own safety and I didn't have time to argue with her about it.

Leaning in, my voice became very quiet. Not a whisper, but low. I don't yell much when I am angry. I yell to make a point because it is very effective. Raising my voice tends to make people listen. When you hear me begin to speak lower and lower, *then* take notice.

That is the sound of the storm gathering.

"Listen to me very carefully, little girl. In about an hour, *hundreds* of vampires are going to come knocking on this door, led by the most powerful hell-vamp on earth. You have no idea the death and destruction that they will bring with them."

Both of us leaned over the table staring eye-to-eye. Even pissed I noticed how blue they were, bright cerulean with ice pale streaks through the irises.

Longinus was done unwrapping himself. Bundling the webbing up into a ball, he tossed it into a trash can.

"Deacon, now is not the time. If the girl wants to fight perhaps—"

I rounded on him.

"Shut up, Longinus."

Anger boiled in my blood, primed to erupt, and Longinus had put himself directly in the line of fire. Three steps brought me face-to-face with him. Heat washed over my neck. I knew I was red as he gave me calm eyes.

My finger pounded into his sternum, hitting the hard breastbone, driving in my point. He backed up a step.

"It's all fine and good for you to talk about letting people fight. You are fucking immortal. Nobody else here has that luxury, least of all her."

He took another step back and I pushed his chest again. Stepping forward, I stayed close to him.

"Everybody else dies. If she stays, not only will she die, but she will get someone else killed protecting her."

My finger swung out to point at Tiff.

"She is NOT a fighter."

Leaning back, I threw my hands in the air.

"Fuck it. I should lock you in here with Appollonia and her brood. This is your damn fight anyway. You started it all; you should finish it instead of any of my people getting hurt or dying."

From the corner of my eye Kat stood up and held her hand out.

"Deacon—"

Her voice was questioning, entreating.

My finger shot out in her direction, cutting off her voice before it could finish.

"Sit down and be quiet, Kat. You were told to get her the hell out of here and you didn't get it done."

A small hand touched my shoulder. The skin was cool against the fever of my anger. Looking over my shoulder, I found Tiff standing there. Big blue eyes glistened with unshed tears. The heat in my face and head drained away at the sight of her. I did not move when her hand slid around me and her cheek pressed into my back.

"I don't want to get anyone killed because of me, Deacon."

Turning, I lifted my arm over her head. Moving in front of me, she looked up at me with her arms still around my chest.

"Just let me help you and I will leave when the time comes."

She pushed her face against my chest, snuggling into me.

"I want to help you if I can. That's all. Even if you can't find something for me to do, then let me stay as long as I can and I will leave before trouble gets here. I promise."

I was beaten and I knew it. My deep breath came out as a sigh. Gently tousling her blue–black hair, I knew I was making a mistake.

"You are a lousy liar, little girl."

She smiled and I felt it against my chest.

"Am not," she said very softly.

Father Mulcahy came into the room holding a pile of clothes. His coffee cup was balanced on them along with his pack of Kool's. Sitting the coffee on the table, he handed the clothes to Longinus and sat in a chair. A fresh cigarette flared to life from the tip of the one in his mouth. Switching them, he snubbed the old one out in the saucer under his cup.

Longinus stepped outside to change. I'm sure he would like a shower, but we didn't have the time. The priest's scarred eyebrow raised sardonically, he stared at me and Tiff. I had untangled our embrace when he entered the room, but we still stood close enough to touch.

"What is the plan, son?"

Cigarette smoke streamed from his nostrils. I stood in front of them all, studying them, weighing them in my mind.

Father Mulcahy smoked his cigarette, impassive. He was in the fight. That knowledge was an absolute certainty. The amount of times he had fought by my side had proven that. Reliable and not afraid to die, the truest thing about Father Mulcahy is that he would play clean up also. If I ask him to stand outside and burn the building to the ground with me in it, he would. He had no sentimentality when it came to fighting evil.

Blond hair hung over Kat's eyes. She was looking at her feet. I know she felt bad for not getting Tiff out like she was told, but she was a good soldier. Maybe not the strongest in direct confrontation, but a good soldier nonetheless. She was loyal as a pit bull and a good shot, but I hoped I could get her out of the line of fire.

Larson was a different man from the one I met just last night. The things he had faced and especially the rescue of his family had burned away some of the softness in him. He still had next to no combat experience, but I could see in the set of his shoulders and the glint in his eyes that he would stand with me. He had made his choice and he would lay down his life if I demanded it.

Too bad for him it looked as if I was going to have to.

Charlotte sat daintily in her chair. The coffee was done and she had a nice color back in her face as she looked at me. Delicate in appearance, like your friend's mom who was nice to you, but she was a powerful lycanthrope. The strongest and fastest in the room, she was the only one who could match a vampire without an equalizer. She would be a hell of an ally as long as we could keep a cross around her neck to stop Appollonia from controlling her.

Longinus stepped back into the room, he was wearing a pair of my black BDU pants. Thinner than I am, but just as tall, they were a good choice because of their adjustable waistband. His shirt was one of Father Mulcahy's without the white tab in the roman collar. It was a tight fit, but he was dressed now. I did not recognize the shoes on his feet, so they were probably the priest's. Now that he was healed, thanks to Charlotte's blood, he would make a good soldier. Being immortal had its advantages.

He was the only one here who had no choice tonight, he was going to fight no matter how he felt about it. I'd paint him in blood and throw him in the middle of the vampires if he tried to refuse.

That left Tiff. She would be nothing but a liability in the fight, and I did not want to see anything happen to her. I would get her out of the way before the vampires got here. Maybe I could convince Kat that she needed to get Tiff well away. I know, I know, call me a caveman all you want, but I feel the need to protect the women. If I didn't know just how powerful Charlotte was, I would've put her on the list to protect too. I can't help it, it is how I was raised.

But looking around the room, I knew we would not escape this unscathed. In fact, the only one who might live would be Longinus, and that was only because he was immortal. Death is not too high a price to pay to stop evil. Possessing the Spear of Destiny made Appollonia a real threat to humanity. Tonight, though, if we were willing to pay the price, we had a chance to put an end to her. If we failed and she gathered even more power and vampires enthralled to her, then there would be no stopping her.

"The plan is that we have to get as many of Appollonia's vampires and herself in the club here. Once they are in the trap, we lock them in and unleash hell on their asses. We hold the line here and kill them as they come."

Larson raised his hand.

"Will she come in here? Wouldn't she see the trap and back out?"

"Even if she sees the trap, she will come."

Charlotte stood and walked her cup over to the sink.

"Her pride has been hurt by Deacon. He resisted her charms and he freed her captives—"

"Don't forget, I flipped her off too. That had to sting."

Charlotte gave me a look for interrupting her; apparently she did not find that funny. I couldn't help myself, though. With a sigh, she continued.

"She feels herself invincible, a goddess to be worshipped, not refused and mocked. Her arrogance will drive her to us, and she will believe that she will kill us no matter what we do to fight."

It was good to have my thoughts confirmed. Father Mulcahy got up to refill his coffee and dump the ashes and butts from his saucer. As he was filling his cup, he asked,

"We are bringing them inside the club?"

"Yes."

"This building will only hold about two hundred, three at the most. They won't all fit."

"Maybe." I had thought of this. "But it is the most secure building we have access to. We can lock them in with us and do what we have to with no worry about the neighbors catching stray bullets."

The lighter in his hand flared against the end of his cigarette; his eyes did the same on the other side of the filter.

"They won't all fit."

His voice was harsh, barking the words out.

"If they do not all come inside and we do manage to kill the one holding their leashes, we will leave our neighbors to deal with a horde of angry vampires who will be uncontrolled."

"She does not feed them enough."

Charlotte looked at me with fear in her eyes.

"If we free them from her control without killing them, they will massacre anyone in the area. They will be crazed with bloodthirst."

I wasn't angry. Really I wasn't, but we did not have time to do anything else. Out of options and almost out of time, I put force behind my words.

"Look, I understand the problem, but we have to do what we have to do. This is our only option, and Appollonia is the priority. We have zero time and no other building."

Everybody went quiet. Father Mulcahy was the only one who looked at me instead of the floor. His eyes were hard as flint.

From behind me a soft voice piped up.

"Um, actually, that isn't true."

I turned to see Tiff with her hand raised slightly and her eyes turned down to the floor. I realized what she was saying.

"You have the keys to Helletog?"

Tiff was really cute when she looked sheepish. Nodding, she fished in her purse. When her hand came out it was holding a set of keys on a skull key ring.

"When you told me to leave I locked up and hung a Closed for Remodeling sign on the main doors. If you killed Gregorios, then the building will be empty and unused."

"It is on that big open parking lot in the industrial part of the city. No one around for a few miles," Larson added.

"How many exits does the place have?" I asked.

Her head tilted to the side, blue–black hair sliding over her neck as she thought.

"There's the main doors, the fire exit in the back of the main room, and the band load-in doors. But I have the key to them all, and they are all made of steel."

Empty building on an asphalt lot, limited access with lockable steel doors, and a large open room to fight in. Plus, it was right off the highway, so if we led them there it would minimize any chance of them spilling into any residential areas.

I glanced at my watch. 3:21 a.m. We had about thirty minutes before the vampires got here, if not less. It was now or never.

"Okay, that's the new plan. We have to hustle. Everybody grab the weapons you want. All silver bullets and tracer rounds. We'll go over the ins and outs of what we are doing on the ride over. Kat, you need to get an incendiary for the gas main. Father Mulcahy, once you are done, grab your holy gear, we are going to need it."

I looked at my watch again.

"Five minutes and we are gone."

Everybody began to move, following orders, the new folks taking the lead of Kat and Father Mulcahy. I walked over to the door leading to the back of the club.

"I'll be right back, I need to get something from the garage."

Scar tissue masquerading as an eyebrow raised in question, Father Mulcahy looked at me.

"Are you going for the flamethrower?"

"Not with us inside the building. We're not that desperate. Not yet." A smile shot out of me in spite of our grim circumstances. "I'm going to get Gertrude."

TWENTY-TWO

LADEN WITH EQUIPMENT, one by one, we all filed into the club. It was a big open room. As a dance club, it was a big floor space with lights hung over it, speakers stacked along the walls, and two bars on each end of the room for patrons to buy alcohol. We hauled the equipment in and began to unpack while Tiff located and turned on the lights.

Kat had found the gas main to the building. In her bundle she had an incendiary designed to blow the building to splinters and use the gas line to feed the fire. It would kill every vampire in the building. The good thing about Atlanta is that even if the building currently used only electricity to heat itself, there was still a gas line from the old system and it would just be capped at the main on the building, which meant that there was a pipeline full of natural gas attached to the building that had a safety blowback valve that would stop an explosion from getting in the system. It would provide more than enough accelerant to destroy the building but still be fairly safe for the surrounding buildings.

At least, that's how I understand it. Planned explosions are Kat and Father Mulcahey's department. I handle the unplanned ones.

The lights came on while I was looking for Tiff. I climbed up the steps to the light and sound booth. Turning from the light board to come join us, she almost bumped into me. I smiled at her little girly exclamation and her blush.

"We need to talk."

Nervousness climbed her features. She leaned back on the sound console and I stepped up to stand next to her. Small white teeth trapped her full lower lip in a pout and her eyes cut to the side, avoiding my gaze.

"I know what you are going to say."

"Doesn't matter. I still need to say it again."

She nodded at this. I reached out and touched her arm.

"Listen, once we are set here, you and Kat are going to the car and going to a safe watching distance. You are to *stay with her*."

She looked at me with a raised eyebrow. "What will stop me from coming back in here to help?"

My beard slid through my hands, bristly and thick. It was shot through with enough silver to make me look menacing. I stroke it sometimes when I am thinking. Or when I am annoyed.

"Kat will. And you will be no help in here. You stick to the plan like you promised."

"But you will be in here fighting for your life!" She grabbed my shirt in her fists. "I can't stay outside while that happens."

"You can and you will."

I cupped her chin and made her look at me. The bones of her face felt fragile and delicate in my rough fingers.

"If you come in here, you will get me killed. The only way I can fight without distraction is if I know you are safe. You. Follow. The plan."

My hand stroked the smooth skin along her face.

"Besides, if we fall here today, I need you and Kat to contact others who do what I do. She'll know what to do, but I need you to help her do it. Others will have to know about Appollonia to stop her."

Her hair was soft on my hand. Silky and light, it flowed over my fingers.

"Can you do that for me?"

Tiff nodded, her eyes glistening. Small hands moved up to my face. Fingers caressed my lips and her palm slid over my cheek. Grabbing my head, she pulled my face to hers. Soft, full lips crushed against mine and parted eagerly. The kiss was fierce and heated. She rose up into it, really putting forth an effort.

The thrill of her touch washed over me and I kissed her back passionately. One arm slid behind her and my other hand moved to cup the back of her neck. Thick hair tangled in my fingers and I pulled it tight, swallowing the moan it brought to her throat. Her hands came up to my chest, breaking the warm line of contact between us. Pushing back, she looked me in the eye through her tears.

"Don't you DARE get killed on me."

Her voice was muffled with swallowed passion, thick with lust but fierce.

"You come back to me."

With that she pushed past me and ran down the stairs. I watched her go join the group who were setting things up.

Damn.

I felt it happen.

I was sunk.

That little girl had me and I barely knew her.

Turning to the soundboard, I flipped the switch to bring the power on. Red and green lights flicked to life and the whole unit emitted a dull hum. Next to the board was tablet that had no password but a list of mp3s. Looking them over, I saw that it was crap on top of crap. Finally at the bottom I found a set of Rob Zombie's *Voodoo Blues*.

Rob Zombie was good fighting music. He never feels the need to have a ballad on his albums, so it is pure aggression from start to finish. *Voodoo Blues* is a great album of old blues songs remixed into Rob Zombie's industrial rock style. He sampled recordings of old bluesmen and digitized all the instruments they played like the slide guitar and the harmonica. Add in Zombie's normal mayhem and you got your self a chunky stream of aggro music.

Head-choppin' music.

Perfect.

Playing the music would also make the club look like it was open if anyone drove by and would help mask the sound of gunfire. And I expected there to be a lot of gunfire tonight.

Pushing Random and then Play gave me the opening notes to "Death Letter Blues" originally sung by Son House. The original was a mournful song about the death of a loved one; Zombie's version was much more sinister. That would work. I didn't know why this particular album was there in amidst all the crap, but I threw up a silent thank you to God that they were.

Nobody should have to die to a crappy soundtrack.

Leaving the sound booth, I walked to the back of the dance floor where the others were gathered. It gave us a wall to our backs and the most distance from the door to pick off as many vampires as possible. Racks of weapons and ammo boxes stood sentry on legs. Father Mulcahy was in the middle of the group wearing his priestly vestments and holding a bottle of anointing oil.

I joined the others kneeling in front of him. Stepping up to me, he touched my forehead with a glistening finger. The oil felt warm and slippery as he traced the sign of the cross against my skin. His voice rumbled gruff in Latin. I couldn't understand what he said, but the power of his faith spilled from every word, flowing into me.

"*Ego to linio oleo salutis in Christo Jesu Domino nostro, ut habeas vitam aeternam.*"

Stepping to the left, he reached out to do the same to Longinus, who knelt beside me. The immortal leaned back out of reach. His hands came up to ward off the priest.

"No, Father, I am cursed. I am unworthy to be anointed with the cross."

Father Mulcahy sighed loudly.

"Are you fighting evil tonight?"

Longinus nodded slowly.

"Then you are doing the Lord's work. Shut the fuck up."

He traced the cross on Longinus's head, spoke the words, and moved down the line, doing the same to each of us. When he was done, he sat the oil down and raised his hands over the group of us.

He took a deep breath and then his voice rolled out of his mouth full of priestly authority. A small shiver ran through me at the power of that voice.

"God of power and mercy, Maker of love and peace, to know You is to live, and to serve You is to reign. Through the intercession of St. Michael, the archangel, be our protection in battle against all evil. Help us to overcome war and violence and to establish your law of love and justice. Grant this through Christ our Lord."

I traced the sign of the cross around my chest and stood. A heavy feeling of purpose settled onto my shoulders, left in the wake of the priest's prayer.

Catching Kat's eye, I jerked my head toward the fire exit. She nodded and grabbed Tiff by the arm. Tiff stared at me for a second, blew a kiss, and then followed Kat around the stage where they would go out the back door, locking it behind them. Once the bloodsuckers were inside, it was their job to lock them in.

I turned to the rest of the group.

Father Mulcahy had a rack of AK-47 rifles near him and he was checking to make sure they were all steady and ready. I knew he would have them all set to semiauto. The Father was a crack shot and dead reliable under pressure. He would not fire randomly, and every shot would count. With the rack of rifles, when one clip was done, instead of changing it he would just pick up a new gun. Next to the guns leaned a double-headed ax, not an ancient one, but a hand-forged modern one. It had a carbon fiber haft and stainless steel blades with silver-filled etchings just behind the bit. Once the vampires got too close for the rifle, he would switch to it and go to swinging.

Charlotte had shifted back to her spider lady form and was also using an AK-47. She only had one rifle, set to full auto, but next to her was a crate full of clips. She had shown that with her extra spider legs she could change clips as fast as she could empty them.

I asked her if she wanted a close-range weapon and she replied, "I am a close-range weapon."

Charlotte had also informed me that her brand of lycanthropy was brown recluse. The venom of a brown recluse spider kills flesh and breaks it down. Normal brown recluse spiders are pretty damn vicious; apparently a Were-brown recluse was like a thermonuclear tiger.

Larson had shed his coat, wearing just his black T-shirt and jeans. The blessed crucifix was back around his neck. He had removed it on the way over so that Appollonia would be able to track our move by the power she had pushed into his brain last night. He had started this thing as bait for me, now he was bait for her.

He'd been given a rack of pump shotguns because he was still an untrained son of a bitch. With the shotguns he wouldn't have to aim, just pump and pull the trigger. He had a large blessed cross made of steel leaning against the rack. It was the size of a Louisville slugger.

Longinus had surprised me by picking a pair of Uzi's. For some reason I didn't think he would go for a firearm. I guess in his 2,000 years walking the earth he learned how to use a gun. Made sense, guns were superior to hand held weapons in almost every scenario, sometimes even close combat.

A pair of katanas were strapped to his waist. The samurai swords rode at his hips, the scabbards curving behind him. Katanas are wicked sharp and these had silver etched into their nearly three-foot blades. The design of a katana with its gently sweeping blade makes it perfect for beheading vampires.

My hand flipped the latch on the long ammo box at the head of our loose semicircle. Inside was a row of flat round drums full of shotgun shells. The shells were alternating high-charge silver shot loads and silver-plated deer slugs. I picked Gertrude up and locked a drum of shells into place.

Gertrude was a small gun, flat black and very sleek. Damn near dainty despite her blocky silhouette. Gertrude's factory designation was AA-12, or to be technical, an Atchisson Assault Twelve-Gauge Shotgun. The world's only fully automatic combat shotgun. She worked on a drum system. Each drum held thirty-two shells, and she could fire those in under six seconds at full auto. I could change a spent drum for a full one in less than two seconds with one hand. She also was designed to be low recoil so I could stay on target. Gertrude was a real heartbreaker. She was absolutely devastating to a large group of enemies and she would cut down on the number of vampires we faced dramatically. In short, she would unleash total fucking destruction on our enemy.

I was still strapped with the CZ-75 and the Taurus, as well as a kukri knife. The kukri is a large knife with a curved blade. It was from Nepal and could remove a head from its shoulders with a single blow.

Wooden stakes were strapped to all our thighs specifically for Appollonia's sake.

I slid goggles down over my eyes and pulled the white painter's mask over my mouth and nose. There would be a lot of dust flying around shortly. Everyone else took my cue and did the same. With the first drum locked and loaded into Gertrude, I turned to my team, looking at them all.

We all stood a very good chance of dying here tonight.

I made peace with the idea we would not all walk away unscathed even if we lived. There were simply too many enemies for us to pull this off without losses, and I was not the only one who knew that. My heart swelled with pride at the heroes standing by my side. They were willing to pay the ultimate price, to sacrifice their lives, if need be, to stop evil.

Appollonia drew near.

I could feel the pressure of her power grow like a coming thunderstorm. It intensified, consolidating into itself and building like someone drawing a last breath. Turning back to the doors at the entrance of the dance floor, I settled Gertrude into the cradle of my right arm. We all stood, shoulder-to-shoulder, waiting for storm. The pressure of vampire magick became a weight in my bones. I knew I was not the only one who could feel it. Longinus's knuckles went white on the handles of his guns. The air trembled like a soap bubble waiting to burst. The anointed oil crosses on our foreheads began to glow with a diffused light.

Behind me, Charlotte whispered, "She's here."

TWENTY-THREE

THE DOORS to the interior of the club burst forward in a shower of dust and a screeching of metal. Appollonia strode into the room dust swirling around her body like fog, simultaneously covering and revealing, the Spear of Destiny still in her left hand and her bloody cat-o'-nine-tails in the other. A brilliant scarlet cloak whipped from her shoulders. Beyond that she wore a diaphanous shift that looked like more spiderwebs.

Behind her surged a mass of heaving vampires. They all wore their predator faces, and the fangs gnashing behind her made a metallic sound, a cacophony of death.

Appollonia flipped her hair over her shoulder and pinned me with a glowing crimson gaze.

"I am here to keep my promise to you, Deacon Chalk."

I didn't answer. I let Gertrude do it for me. She only bucked against my arm a little as she fired. Holding her trigger, I sent silvered death spitting out to Appollonia.

Two things happened with the first shot I fired.

The first thing: everyone else opened fire also.

The air filled with streaks of colored light. They were all using silver-jacketed tracer bullets. Tracer bullets have a bit of phosphorus in the shell that leaves a streak of light for the eye to follow. The military uses them to pinpoint a target for multiple shooters to hit. We use them because phosphorus really does a number on vampires. It lights them up like you doused them with gasoline.

The second thing: the vampires behind Appollonia surged around her to form a wall of undead flesh.

The bullets we sent shredded that wall. Burnt nitroglycerine filled my nostrils through the thin paper mask and burned my sinuses. Vampires exploded into dust or caught fire under the hail of bullets we sent.

The air grew thick with gunpowder, vampire dust, smoke, and the smell of a paper factory from the phosphorus. It took mere seconds for us all to run through our first round of ammunition.

Dropping the first drum, I slid the second home. Larson and the Father had already grabbed new guns. To my left, Charlotte was still firing her AK-47. As one clip finished a spider leg would eject the spent clip as another slammed a replacement into the rifle. It was so quick that an almost uninterrupted stream of bullets flew out into the wall of undead.

We continued to fire, mowing down vampires as they boiled and surged from behind Appollonia. We poured hundreds of bullets into them and still they inched closer. The ones who could fly swooped above us to be picked off by Father Mulcahy. The second they would break from the group he put a tracer round in their skulls and they dropped in a roil of flame and black smoke, consumed before they hit the ground.

The gunfire was thunderous and drowned out the sound system, as well as the screams and wails of dying vampires. Noise rolled off the walls of the club and I felt it thud in my chest. I knew I was screaming as I continued to pour death into my enemy, but I couldn't hear myself.

Adrenaline surged in my bloodstream, pulling everything into hyper-focus. Battle high. I was buzzed on chemicals rushing through my system. The air was thick like fog and nearly impossible to see through. The big open room filled with a haze that was broken only by the occasional flare of a vampire going up in flames. I didn't know how many vampires we had taken out, but the dust on the floor was inches thick.

From the corner of my eye I saw a vampire grab Charlotte's gun, wrenching it from her hands. Too fast to follow, her spider legs clutched and tore his head from his shoulders. Dust peppered us both when he exploded.

A gigantic vampire appeared in front of me, his thick chest ramming into the barrel of Gertrude. I squeezed the trigger as she was knocked from my grip. The vampire fell back, his arm torn from his body by her blast being an inch away from his armpit. He writhed on the ground until three more vampires stepped on him to get to the rest of us.

Appollonia had thrown enough vampires at us to overcome our firepower. The battle was on in close quarters. The CZ filled my hand and I put it to the head of the next vampire. A pull of the trigger and he exploded into dust.

Charlotte leaped past me and into the coming knot of vampires. She was a superhuman blur of motion. Spider legs tore vampires to pieces, sending arms and legs spinning into the air as she grabbed another and sunk her fangs into him. Pushing him away, she grabbed another. I watched her first victim stagger and fall as the undead flesh where she bit him turned black and began to crumble away.

Her venom dissolved him into a puddle of goo.

If we lived, I would remember not to ever piss her off.

Longinus danced into the group from the other side, katanas flashing silver in his hands. Graceful as a lion, he used both swords to weave death among the vampires. He swirled around his enemies, taking limbs and heads in a swath of destruction. Chunks of undead flesh whirled around him like a tornado through a trailer park. Vampires turned to dust or fell back incapacitated as he mowed them down.

Father Mulcahy had his ax in hand now and was using his Shaolin skills to take down vampires. His leg kicked the feet from under one vampire, and as it went down the ax removed its head. He spun gracefully, wrapping a thick arm around the throat of another bloodsucker. Leveraging it backward, he shoved the ax head into its chest. Black blood splashed up, coating his face. Dropping the vampire, a swipe of his arm cleared his eyes to see. Nicotine-stained teeth flashed in a grin at me and he buried the ax in the neck of another vampire.

Larson was now swinging the heavy cross at a circle of vampires. He wasn't killing any of them, but they were staying back out of reach, thanks to the cross. One of them darted in as he swung to drive away another and he spun to intercept it. The arm of the cross sank into the skull of the darting vampire, caving it in with enough force to shoot the vampire's eyeballs out of their sockets. They rolled on the floor, moisture picking up dust and coating them like a snowball rolling downhill.

The swirling smoke was beginning to thin as the dust settled and I could see we had cut Appollonia's horde to almost nothing. A glimmer of hope rose in my chest that we might live to see this through.

I kept fighting, grabbing a vampire by greasy hair and shoving the barrel of the CZ into his neck. His fangs still gnashed and chomped as I pulled the trigger in rapid succession. Four bullets tore through his neck to sever the head. It came away in my hand and crumbled to dust. I put four more bullets in the chest of a vampire who was naked and had sprouted wings from his back when I was slammed into the ground from behind.

The blow took me at the base of the skull and off my feet. My face slammed into the floor hard enough to make my vision go black. The hard plastic of my goggles was driven into the swollen side of my eye from earlier. Air ran wildly from my lungs, pushing vampire dust away from my face. I rolled, blind as a bat, but I moved because I knew there was another attack coming.

I wound up on my back as my vision cleared enough to see.

Appollonia stood over me. Her cloak billowed around her and rage twisted her features. She was pulling the point of the Spear from the floor where I had been knocked down. It was wedged into the floor almost ten inches. She was not interested in seducing me anymore. That had been a killing blow she had tried.

My gun was still in my hand. Sucking air in, I fumbled a new clip out and slammed it home. She wrenched the blade from the floor as I emptied the clip of 9mm bullets from the CZ into her chest. As she staggered back, her skin blossomed into red flowers of blood and she fell to the ground. Shaking my head, I tried to get my eyesight to stop wavering and slammed another full clip home.

A glance around showed the battle had turned. Even though we had decimated the horde of vampires Appollonia had brought, the few left had gotten the better of my people.

Larson lay facedown in the dust with a vampire on his back. With his teeth, the bloodsucker pulled flesh from Larson's lower back in strips, and I saw a gleam of white that meant exposed bone. Larson wasn't moving, just screaming.

Two female vamps had Father Mulcahy pinned, holding him with his own ax handle across his throat. They had him down, but he still fought thrashing and twisting against their strength.

Charlotte was in a crumpled heap, two of her spider legs twitching beside her, blood pumping from their stumps. She was unconscious and covered in cuts that bled black on her gray fur.

Longinus crouched over her holding five vampires at bay with one sword, the other katana was gone. He was coated in grime and blood from a dozen cuts and scrapes. A gash on his forehead ran in a crimson stream over his face, his eyes white rimmed and wild in the mask of blood.

All of the other vampires were dead. I scrambled to my feet and put bullets into the vampire on Larson and the ones holding the Father down. They fell back, scrambling from the pain of the silver, one exploded into dust.

Hissing and snarling, the vampires surrounding Charlotte looked over at what I had done.

Longinus took the opportunity to leap and swing the katana in his hand in a wide arc that removed three of their heads. As they exploded, he continued his swing and the blade flashed upward to split one of them from crotch to jawline. That one crumbled and he shoved the sword into the chest of the last one remaining.

Cranking his arm in a circular motion, he carved the heart from its chest.

As the vampire burst into dust Longinus fell to the ground in exhaustion.

I turned to locate Appollonia and fire wrapped around my right arm, shooting up and lancing pain deep into my chest. Looking down, I saw the lashes of her damned cat-o'-nine-tails were wrapped around my forearm. Bits of steel and glass bit into my flesh like the teeth of a piranha. Appollonia stood a few feet away, the strands of the cat stretched between us like an alien umbilical cord.

With a vicious yank, she dragged the lashes off my arm. Metal and glass tore my flesh, cutting furrows deep into the meat. The CZ dropped to the dust-covered floor and blood burst from my skin. Every inch of my forearm was cut and abraded. Fire burned through the nerves from my armpit to my fingertips and radiated into my chest with a pounding throb. Staggering back, I reached for the kukri knife on my belt. My fingers slipped on the handle because they were covered in my blood and not working right.

The vampires swung the cat-o'-nine-tails behind her, ready to lash me again.

Father Mulcahy rose behind her with his ax over his head.

Even without seeing him, Appollonia crouched and spun, swinging the Spear around. Like magic, the blade parted his pants leg and the skin beneath it, opening a wide mouth of a wound across the muscle of his thigh. The priest fell to the ground, throwing his ax as he went. It spun in a lazy circle, the blade set to bury in her head when she batted it away like a toy. The Spear rose over his fallen form and her arm tensed to drive the blade into his chest for a killing blow.

I fired the Taurus into her back.

All five bullets hit her in the shoulders, knocking her around. She didn't fall, but she did turn away from Father Mulcahy. The skin on her chest was already knitting back together, tendrils of skin closing up from where the bullets had burst through her.

Longinus stepped to her, sword swept back and at the ready. Snarling like a rabid tiger, she jabbed the Spear at him and he danced back out of reach. Even with its length cut down, she had a better reach with the Spear than he did with the sword.

"I should have killed you when I had you at my mercy, Longinus." The Spear darted toward his chest and he jumped back from its point. "I will not make the same mistake twice."

The pain in my arm had subsided slightly from the flash fire of agony into sharp throbs of excruciation. Feeling slowly crept back into my hand, aside from acid-etched torment, and I finally got the kukri knife out of its sheath. It was the only weapon I had left. Moving up next to Longinus, I stayed a step or two to the side to not get in the way of his sword.

"Give it up, Appollonia. You are outnumbered and you are going to die. Now, have the good grace to go quietly."

Long fangs flashed as she snarled at me, stripped of all pretense of humanity now. Her demonic-vampire side rose fully to the surface. Those once-honey eyes were all blood-red and black pupils, the skin of her face pulled thin against the muscles, blue veins standing out like wires. That long black hair whipped around in the frenzy of power that rolled off her.

"Do not speak to me with such contempt," she spat at me. "I have lain your comrades low." The Spear pointed at me to emphasize her point. "You will be next."

"Fuck you," I spat back. "We kicked your ass. Your vampire army is dust under our feet, and you'll be following them to hell soon enough."

I kicked up a pile of dust to emphasize my words.

"I will kill Longinus and take you for my slave." Arrogance painted her features. "I will own you, Deacon Chalk, in ways you did not think were possible. Then, with you under my yoke, I will rebuild my army and conquer humanity and pour their lives out for my pleasure."

Stretching her arms out, she raised the Spear of Destiny over her head. Throwing her head back, she screamed, "All of humanity will bow and worship at my feet!"

Her head snapped down and that shapely arm flashed, launching the Spear faster than the blink of an eye.

Longinus tried to dodge out of the way, but he was too slow for her inhuman speed. The Spear took him in the stomach and exploded out of his back in a shower of blood and gore. Horror filled his face as he fell to his knees with the Spear coming out of both sides of him. As he looked down at the Spear, his mouth moved silently up and down, trauma robbing him of even a scream of agony. His hands locked around the shaft of the Spear. Slowly, he slid to his side, crumpling like an old tissue.

Appollonia let out a war cry of triumph and leaped on me.

Before I could even think, let alone react, she was on me. I only had time to put my arm between us when she slammed into me. Her hands wrapped around my left arm as she rode me to the ground. Talons sank deep into my arm. She wasn't going for blood, she was trying to pull the muscle from bone.

Pain exploded in my shoulder.

Taking the kukri knife, I buried its blade under her ribcage, digging for her heart. It slid in a flow of blood over my hand. It must have hurt her because she drew back with a scream and shoved me away with her forearm.

It was like being hit in the chest with a baseball bat.

I rolled on the ground, bouncing like a skipping stone. Vampire dust stuck to the blood coating both my arms now. My left one was a leaden hunk of agony from the damage she had done, but I managed to hold on to the kukri in my right.

The thought of defeat crept into my mind.

Appollonia was too strong. I was too hurt, and this was it. The voice of doubt in my head told me: *We are all going to die here and she is going to win. Not only win, but triumph and continue on with her evil ways.*

I told that voice to shut the fuck up.

Pushing myself to stand, my grip tightened on the handle of the kukri. Its blade felt like it weighed fifty pounds in my hand. My left arm hung at my side, almost useless. Every bone I had felt like it was bruised. Pain coursed through my body, racing along my bloodstream and nerve endings in a mad sprint with exhaustion. The side of my face had swollen, shutting my vision on that side. Bleary-eyed, I turned to face my enemy.

She stood hunched at the waist. Blood coursed down her hip and thigh from the gash I had put in her stomach. Even as I watched it was knitting closed. It wasn't the liquid magick of earlier when she held the Spear, but she was still healing. As the wound closed, she straightened. Covered in blood and grime from the dust, she looked like hell. Hell with blood-colored eyes that flashed lightning rage just for me.

Appollonia tensed and I saw it in those eyes that she was about to make her move to finish me once and for all. She was faster than me, stronger than me, and almost impossible to kill, but I was ready for her.

Ready for this to be over and done with.

Waiting, I faced her dead-on the kukri held back slightly behind me. I felt the air pressure change as she leaped at me. Twisting to the right, I let her slip past me, her skin brushing mine, sliding on the blood that covered both of us. I threw my nearly useless arm under her outstretched one and wrapped my fingers in that thick hair. My grip jerked her up short, feet skidding out to kick in the air as I lifted her up by her scalp. I used the one second I had to slam the kukri's blade into her throat and draw it across as hard as I could.

Blood shot out in a cold spray that forced me to close my eyes. I felt the edge of the blade catch as it bit into vertebrae and then continue as it separated them.

My left arm went slack and I couldn't hold her up any longer. I let go. Her hair pulled at my fingers, sticky and tangled with viscera. Shaking loose, it slipped away so that she fell to the ground at my feet. Blinking away the blood, I looked down, watching her eyes dart about wildly. The gash in her throat yawned open, white bone sticking out from a red mess. Only the thinnest bits of viscera held the two sides of her neck together.

She made gurgling sounds and clawed at her throat. I waited for her to turn to dust, but she didn't.

I had almost completely severed her head. The bitch should be done; instead, as I watched in horror, the flesh of her neck began to mend and repair itself. Like taffy made of gore, it stretched across the wound, pulling it together, closing it. I screamed in rage and frustration, my voice tearing its way from my throat.

"Remember the Curse." Longinus's voice was barely a rasp as he called to me. "Remember…"

Dropping the kukri, I fumbled the wooden stake from its sheath on my thigh. It was a two-foot length of hawthorn that was straight and true and ground to a fine point on one end. I stepped over her with it in my hand and knelt, sitting on her hips. Weakly, her legs thrashed trying to dislodge me. One hand left her throat, moving to protect her heart.

I knocked her hand aside and put the tip of the stake to the right of her breastbone. Placing the butt of it against my own shoulder I leaned over her.

"Enjoy your time in hell," I growled as I let my weight push on the butt of the stake. "You deserve it."

The stake sank into her chest with all my weight behind it. The thick breastbone slowed it down but didn't stop it. Her ribs cracked as I forced the wood through them. Blood welled up around the stake as I jerked it back and forth to widen the pathway. With a sudden give, the stake tore into her heart like paper and I felt its point thud into the floor beneath her. Her power poured out when I pierced her heart, rushing around me like a cold, dead wind.

One tear of blood trickled from her eye; then she exploded into dust beneath me.

"That's what you get for fucking with me."

Slowly, I stood and walked over to where everyone else was. Every ounce of my body was a knot of pain. My joints felt like they were locked in place. Every inch of my skin felt like it had been scraped off, and my head was pounding from exertion on top of injury from back at the church. But I was alive, the monster was dead, and the day had been saved.

One foot in front of the other, I went to check on my people. The line had been held, but just barely, and it was my duty to count the cost.

I knelt next to Charlotte beside Longinus. She had shifted back to human form and tears streaked through the bloody grime on her face.

Pain-filled eyes looked at me. "Help him."

Longinus's face was chalky with pain and blood loss. His eyes had sunk into dark hollows and sweat poured out of him. The slaughterhouse smell of torn intestine hovered over him. The blood had slowed its rush out of his body and was now pulsating slowly into a puddle around him. It was black. The lethargic pulses meant his heart was slowing down. The Spear jutted from his back, coated in gore from his body.

I put a hand on her arm. Shaking my head, I said, "I think it is too late."

"No!" she cried. "He is immortal, he can't die! I have seen him recover from worse at her hands."

I shook my head. "He said the Spear is his weakness. It alone can kill him."

Tears ran freely down her face now.

"Help me take it out of him to make his last minutes as comfortable as possible."

Charlotte nodded and helped me roll him on his side. A groan of pain escaped from his lips. I steadied his shoulders with my hip because my left arm was a dead weight at my side. Appollonia had done too much damage for it to work. My right hand wasn't in much better shape, but I grasped the Spear behind the blade where it went out of his back.

When my hand closed on the Spear, heat from it poured into my hand and swept up my arm. Strength returned, following the flow of power. Slowly, carefully, I drew the Spear from Longinus's body. It made a wet sucking sound, and blood and gore spilled out behind it.

The longer I held the shaft of the Spear the more I felt the power of it crawl into my body. The sensation was very nearly like when the angel had transfused me with her essence. Fire ran in my veins. As the power passed through me my strength returned and my wounds healed. As I watched, my skin reknit and repaired itself. I felt whole and vital.

I felt like I could conquer the world.

Looking down at Longinus, I saw him with new eyes. My ability to feel supernatural abilities had amped up, supercharged like it was on steroids and crack.

I could *see* the power of immortality that lay in every fiber of his being. It had a scent, like roasted almonds and some bitter burnt herb, that filled my nostrils. I knew without doubt I could call that power to my will. The Spear of Destiny amplified my ability and pushed it to the next level. I not only could feel Longinus's power, I could control it, make it do what I wanted it to.

I could see a possibility.

Holding the Spear, I put my other hand on his forehead, his skin slick with oily sweat and cold under my fingers.

I don't know how to explain what I did next. Bear with me.

My power unfurled inside me and slid down my arm, sinking into his flesh and bone. It called his immortality to awakening. Coaxing the sparks of immortality in his cells, I made them work again and forced them to begin mending the damage done by the Spear. With my new sight I saw the words of God's Curse written on his bones, glaring out at me through a curtain of flesh like radioactive scrimshaw.

His eyes flew open and flared with golden light. That light filled his pupils until they shone like tiny lamps in his skull, the glow from them chasing highlights along his cheekbones. This did not seem weird to me because I knew mine were shining the same. Under my guidance, the power of his immortality re-formed his body and healed the wound.

When it was done, Longinus sat upright, gasping for breath.

There was a tug to my power, drawing my eyes to look at Charlotte. As our gazes met, my power arced between us like electricity. I could feel her animal inside her and I knew I could call that out too. I knew with certainty I could make her change into a spider or even into her half-spider form.

I could strip away her humanity if I wanted.

Her lycanthropy was mine to control.

I couldn't take it from her, no more than I could take Longinus's immortality on myself, but I could push her animal so far inside her that she would never turn again.

My power probed deeper in her, just exploring. It was curious about the flavor of her abilities. Her animal reacted to me. It felt me and tried to hide from my gaze. Charlotte gasped and I knew she felt it scurry inside of her. With my power roiling around in there, I felt it too.

I knew everything about her in that moment.

Strumming the healing part of her animal like a delicate instrument, I used it to repair her also. Her side closed where her spider legs had been torn off, sealing like a ziplock bag. She would be whole the next time she changed, I knew it. With wide eyes she examined her arms and legs. They were now smooth and free from cuts.

Standing, I walked over to where Father Mulcahy cradled Larson. He looked almost as bad as Longinus had. His short red hair was plastered to his skull. Those thin arms clung to the priest, but his legs lay sprawled and still. Father Mulcahy looked up at me.

"I saw what you just did. Can you do the same for him?"

Extending my hand to Larson I also extended my power. It probed Larson, looking to see what flavor of power I could use. Gritting my teeth, I shoved the power into him, forcing it through his limbs, inserting it under his skin.

Searching, seeking, *hunting* for the means to mend his injury.

And came up completely empty.

There was nothing supernatural inside him to draw from. He had no special ability I could use to heal him. Larson was completely human. I shook my head, remembering what I had seen the vampire do to him.

"No, I can't. Let's load him up and get the two of you to the hospital. Then we will blow this Popsicle stand."

TWENTY-FOUR

I *HATE* HOSPITALS. Everyone does. People who work in hospitals hate them. They smell all wrong, disinfectant and sickness roiling around to make an atmosphere of suffering. You have to be quieter than you do anywhere else when everything in you wants to scream and fight and cling to life. Here I was, though, in a hospital room.

It was a double room. Father Mulcahy lay on the bed closest to the door, his leg swathed in bandages from hip to calf. He sat up, Bible open on his lap.

Longinus nodded to me from beside him.

Charlotte and Tiff both gave me small smiles.

The other bed held Larson.

Father Mulcahy had called in some favors from the Bishop to get them roomed together. It was St. Joseph's hospital, after all.

Larson was pale, hair greasy from being unwashed, and skin still waxy looking. Tubes ran from his arm into an IV and a morphine pump. Kat sat in a chair next to him, holding his hand. She looked like she hadn't slept in the three days since Larson had been checked in. I knew for a fact she had been here all of them.

Neither of them were looking my way, their focus on the white-coated doctor at the foot of the bed.

"...damage to the ligaments surrounding the spine, and the spinal column itself has been compromised. Surgery to close the wound was successful and you show no sign of infection, so that is promising."

The doctor read off the chart in his hand, not looking at anyone.

Larson cleared his throat loudly.

"Are you done dicking around now?" he said, his voice soft but strong.

The doctor adjusted his glasses and straightened up.

"Excuse me, Mr. Larson?"

Red flush rose up Larson's neck and into his cheeks. The look in his eye said it was anger and not embarrassment, like it once would have been.

"I asked if you were done dicking around with the diagnosis. Tell me in plain English the only thing I give a shit about."

"What is that?"

"Will I walk again?"

The doctor's chest puffed out. "Now, we can't say anything for sure, there is swelling in the area, nothing is certain—"

"Bullshit." Larson pointed his finger at the doctor. "You have spent three days doing three different surgeries. Now, cut to the chase and tell me if I will ever walk again."

The doctor's face mottled purple and his jaw clenched, bulging in rage. He drew in a breath to lay into Larson for his tone.

The priest threw his blankets back.

The Immortal, the lycanthrope, and I all took a step in his direction.

Kat stood to her feet, fire boiling in her eyes.

The doctor's eyes flashed wildly around him, subconsciously realizing he was a jackal in a den of lions. Visibly, he gathered himself together and his voice was tentative when he spoke.

"No, you will most likely never take another step."

Larson's head settled back into the pillow behind him. Exhaustion swirled in his eyes.

"Thank you, Doc. I appreciate your honesty."

His eyes closed slowly, the lids purple to match the hollows around his eyes.

"Now piss off and leave me to be with my friends."

The doctor put the chart down and brushed past me. My gun stuck out of my open jacket and he eyed it nervously as he went by. The door to the room shushed open and then closed, and we were alone together with just the hum of the morphine pump.

Nobody said anything.

The near-silence grew heavy, so I spoke up.

"Well, that was a different Larson than the one I first met."

The man in question gave me a pained smile.

"I guess I am just too tired to listen to bullshit."

Kat smoothed her hand down his arm. It was covered in bandages. Larson was pretty busted up. Aside from the injury to his spine, he was covered in cuts and scrapes. So, he was bandaged up like a high-school play's version of the Mummy. We had told the ER that he had been in a motorcycle accident and then been attacked by a wild animal as he lay until we found him.

Yeah, I know, but we couldn't very well tell them the truth.

Father Mulcahy would be fine. He had a deep cut through his quadriceps from the Spear, and that required some surgery, but he would heal.

I was glad he had gotten them in the same room. Larson would need help adjusting to his condition, and there was nobody better for that than the priest.

Walking over to Larson's bed, I touched his shoulder. His eyes opened to look at me. Reaching over, I took his hand from Kat and put it in mine. I shook it gently.

"Thank you," was all I said.

Nodding once, he closed his eyes again.

I mouthed good-bye to Kat, who smiled at me, and walked around to the priest. He pointed to his eye and then pointed to Larson. I nodded and moved to leave the room. Longinus and Charlotte fell in step behind me.

Once the door had closed I turned to them both.

Longinus wore a long, dark trench coat that hung on him like a cape. I knew the Spear of Destiny lay hidden under its folds, close at hand for him. He had purchased new clothes, including the coat. He stood wearing charcoal slacks over a pale pink button-front shirt. I'm a jeans and T-shirt guy, but I could see that his clothes were very expensive.

Charlotte stood next to him, her arm touching his in a line. Her hair was pushed back and held in place with a beautiful matching set of ivory combs. A sleek ivory colored dress hugged her like a lover, displaying her body without sacrificing her dignity. She looked as if she were headed for a date.

Longinus extended his hand to me and shook mine in a tight grasp.

"Thank you once again for the rescue, Deacon."

"No problem. Are you heading off to the airport now?"

He nodded.

"Charlotte is willing to give me a ride there."

The Were-spider in question blushed a bit as I looked her way. It was hard to see, but the hospital had bright lights.

"How are the others getting settled in?"

The Were-spiders under Appollonia's control had been left behind after her demise. Lycanthropes are amazing creatures, but they would have never been able to make the speed and distance the vampires had managed. When we killed her, it left them at loose ends. Most of them had no one to return to because the vampire bitch had slaughtered their families when she took them under her spell. Charlotte had taken it on herself to find them homes and jobs here in the Metro-Atlanta area.

Normally, Were-spiders formed clusters according to subspecies and didn't intermingle, but with the trauma of their shared experience, it seemed we would have the world's first commingled group.

"It's going well. They are all finding places. There is a lot of pain and anger left still, but I have found therapists who are aware of exactly what they are dealing with to help." She smiled. "I almost have my house back to myself."

"Good." I turned my attention back to the Immortal. "If you are flying, what are you doing with the Spear? Surely TSA will frown on it since it is a blade over 3 inches in length."

He smiled widely.

"Long ago I discovered one of the benefits of being a legendary holy relic is that it doesn't register with any technological device. As long as I keep it covered under my coat, I can pass through metal detectors and X-ray machines."

That explained the long coat.

"Well, that's handy."

He grinned.

"Almost as if something bigger than technology had created it."

His face grew serious. Leaning in, he dropped his voice so that only the three of us could hear it.

"Deacon, do you remember the first time we spoke?"

I nodded that I did.

"When you told me your name I said something in another language."

Another nod.

"It was Hebrew and what I said was *Dam Mala-chaim*."

I waited for it. I didn't know what he was about to say, but I knew something was coming.

"It translates mostly to 'Blood of Angels.' That is the name I have heard for you before." His eyes burned fiercely as he leaned closer. "Be careful. There are people and things of this world talking about you. The same people who talk about me and seek my immortality and the Spear's power."

Understanding made my chest tight.

The kind of power and magick you could manage if you fueled it with an Immortal who had been cursed by God would be incredible.

Damn near devastating.

And after Appollonia I was well aware of what the Spear of Destiny in the wrong hands could accomplish. Even from my short time holding it, I had been affected. If those same people were talking about me, then I would have to watch my back. Nodding to Longinus again, I put my hand on his shoulder.

"Thanks for the warning. If you need anything, give us a ring."

"You do the same, and if I hear anything else about you, I will call."

We stood for a moment, the tension building between us from the weight of what he had said. It was broken by Charlotte reaching out to hug me. Her arms circled around my chest and mine went around her shoulders.

After the connection through the Spear of Destiny, and almost being killed by the same vampire, I felt a kinship to her.

We broke apart and she took Longinus's offered arm. With a final wave and a nod they walked away, heading down the hallway to the elevators.

I stood, thinking about what the immortal had said. All I needed was a mysterious set of enemies I knew nothing about.

Ah well, to hell with it. I would burn that bridge when I came to it.

The soft click of the hospital room door made me turn.

Tiff stepped out into the hallway. She gave me a smile and walked toward me. Reaching out, her hand slid down my jacket sleeve until it reached my own. I took note that she reached for my left hand, leaving my right free to get to my gun.

"I'm glad I caught you."

My eyebrow went up and a smile crossed my face.

"Oh really? Why is that?"

"I know it will be a little while until Father Mulcahy is ready to leave the hospital, and Kat seems to want to stay with Larson, so I wanted to offer you my help. I have club experience. If you wanted, I could help you with Polecats until they get back."

I looked down at her. Her hand still touched mine, her skin warm and soft.

I remembered that kiss she had laid on me before the big fight.

Those big blue eyes stared up at me, wanting to know where the two of us stood after everything that had happened. I wasn't sure myself, but I wanted to find out.

Smiling, I took a cue from the priest and raised her hand up. Pressing my lips softly to the skin, I kissed it.

"I would really like that. Thank you."

Her smile exploded across her face. Quickly she rose up and kissed me on my cheek, lips warm and soft on my skin. Her arm slid into mine and we began to walk to the elevators.

I would be glad for her help. There, I admitted it. Yes, we had stopped Appollonia and saved humanity, and that had seemed to quiet things down for the last few days. But monsters are like buses. Wait long enough and there would be another asshole coming around the corner, trying to enslave humanity or destroy the world, or whatever evil plot was cool at the time.

There always was.

That's what keeps me in business.

A WORD FROM THE AUTHOR

Loyals and True Believers,

Thank you!

Truly and deeply, from the bottom of my heart, thank you for buying *Blood and Bullets*. I hope that you enjoyed reading it as much as I enjoyed writing it. I worked my ass off to give you one helluva thrill ride.

Now, if you did enjoy this book, I need you to do your part. What's your part, you ask? It's simple really.

Go out and tell someone about this book and this series. Tweet it, post it on your status, blog it, write a review. In short, tell all your book-reading friends about it.

Spread the word.

We are in this thing together, me and you. I write the books, I entertain. You read the books, you spread the word. You are my Loyals and True Believers, fans of the Deaconverse and all that is still to come. I love you one and all, and I cannot wait to meet you in real life.

Until then, check out my Web site for extras, news, and places you can meet me in person, and keep reading!

www.jamesrtuck.com

Take care,

James R. Tuck

ACKNOWLEDGMENTS

Thank you to all of you Deacon Fanatics. Y'all have made this magick happen. Your faithfulness to the main man and his crew have kept this train rolling. You are all magnificent.

Thank you to Kensington Books for publishing this the first time around and to John Hartness and the crew at Falstaff Books for doing it the second time around.

ALSO BY JAMES R. TUCK

THE DEACON CHALK SERIES

That Thing at the Zoo

Blood and Bullets

Spiders Lullaby

Blood and Silver

Circus of Blood

Blood and Magick

STANDALONE NOVELS AND NOVELLAS

Venom Lethal Protector

Arrow: Fatal Legacies

This Way Lies Madness

The Cold and the Dark

Theok the Indomitable

Hired Gun

Love and Vengeance

Kill the Children, Save the Food

FRIENDS OF FALSTAFF

Thank You to All our Falstaff Books Patrons, who get extra digital content each month! To be featured here and see what other great rewards we offer, go to www.patreon.com/falstaffbooks.

PATRONS

Dino Hicks
John Hooks
John Kilgallon
Larissa Lichty
Travis & Casey Schilling
Staci-Leigh Santore
Sheryl R. Hayes
Scott Norris
Samuel Montgomery-Blinn
Junkle

CPSIA information can be obtained
at www.ICGtesting.com
Printed in the USA
LVHW041620071222
734760LV00020B/647/J